Much Ado in Meryton

Pride and Prejudice meets Shakespeare

RIANA EVERLY

MUCH ADO IN MERYTON

Cover design by Mae Phillips at coverfreshdesigns.com.

Front cover image: Gouache Painting "Tea at Englefield Green" by Paul Sandby (1731-1809) By Permission of Nottingham City Museums & Galleries

ISBN-13: 978-1-7771504-7-1

Dedication

To my family, whose support is unwavering

Contents

RIANA EVERLY

Acknowledgements

No book is a solo effort. There is always a team somewhere inspiring, supporting, and feeding the author. In the case of *Much Ado in Meryton*, this team includes two people who had no idea they would ever be involved in such a novel: Jane Austen and William Shakespeare. For where would we be without the brilliant inspiration of Pride and Prejudice and *Much Ado About Nothing*? So while I cannot thank them personally, I would like to acknowledge their genius and set down my admiration and appreciation for everyone to read.

I have more personal acknowledgments to make as well. As always, Mikael Swayze, editor and proof-reader extraordinaire, deserves accolades. I also would like to thank Liz Martinson, Shanti M, and Nikita S for their excellent editorial comments and critiques, without whom this book would not be nearly the creation it is now. Likewise, my heartfelt thanks to Juliane Weber and Jennifer Joy for their eagle eyes.

Thanks also, as always, to Mae Phillips for her beautiful cover art. The image on the front cover is *Tea at Englefield Green* by English landscape artist Paul Sandby (1831-1809). Used by permission of Nottingham City Museums & Galleries.

Cover design by Mae Phillips at coverfreshdesigns.com

Thou and I are too wise to woo peaceably

Benedick, 5.2

William Shakespeare, *Much Ado About Nothing*

Chapter One

Only you excepted

(Benedick, 1.1)

Fitzwilliam Darcy shifted in place as the carriage bounced over another rut in the lane. It was quite black outside and the curtains were drawn, allowing nothing of their surroundings to be seen. Surely they must soon be at their destination. Beside him on the squab, his friend drew his own curtain aside enough to peer through. He gazed into the void for a moment, then turned back to the occupants of the carriage with a broad grin.

"Surely you cannot see anything, Charles. There is no moon and we are facing backwards. The lamps will show you nothing." Darcy shifted again, trying to stretch out his long legs without disturbing the women sitting across from him. He had spent a great deal too much time in a carriage today. Perhaps if he had insisted upon using his own for this short ride, he might be more comfortable, for his coach was both longer and wider than Charles Bingley's. But his men and horses had made the drive up from London that very morning and they deserved a rest. His friend's carriage was adequate. Just.

His young friend widened his grin. "I own it is full dark, but we shall be there very soon. Look! There is the first house." He drew the curtain open to reveal a small cottage with lights flickering behind two windows. "I do believe I shall like this town very much indeed." He smiled indulgently. Then, turning a worried frown to his tall friend, asked, "Darcy, you will be polite, will you not?"

A very pretty young woman on the forward-facing bench gave a delicate sniff. "Mr. Darcy is unfailingly polite. When it is merited."

The other woman beside her tittered. Her carefully contrived ringlets bounced against the hat that marked her as a married woman. "I doubt he shall have to exercise those skills tonight, Caroline. I cannot imagine a single creature here who is deserving of Mr. Darcy's charm. Really, Charles," she turned to the beaming young gentleman, "why have you brought us here? London is far preferable at this time of year. Could you not have found a more..." she turned to the closed window and sniffed, "civilised place to let an estate?"

Caroline nodded. Her face, lovely though it might be, was not made lovelier by the disdain that crept across it. "Surely, Mr. Darcy, London is your preferred place. Why, you stayed an extra three days after the rest of us came up to this sad part of Hertfordshire." She batted her eyelashes at him.

The rumbling of the carriage wheels turned to a jostling bounce that suggested cobblestones rather than a packed dirt lane. They must be well within the village now. It was not so large a place, this market town called Meryton, but prosperous enough if they had stone streets, and Charles had spoken of a rather grand set of assembly rooms.

"My personal business kept me in town," was all Darcy replied.

Bingley added, "And Darcy was most gracious in cutting that business short so he could attend the assembly with us." His smile became more serious. "I do thank you for this, Darcy. I have met many of the gentlemen of the area, but this shall be my first introduction to the local society as a whole and I am pleased to have you at my side. Not that I am nervous, but I wish to make a good impression." Then he turned back to the two women who sat across from him. "And I shall assume the same excellent behaviour from you as you expect from my friend. This is my home now, and for all that you are my sisters, I shall be quite put out if you turn the people against me with your high and mighty ways."

Caroline sniffed again. "You are so easily led, Charles. One man tells you of a grand estate to be let, and you are ready to sign the lease before setting an eye on it. Another tells you Meryton is as fine a town as any in England, and you accept his very word as truth without question. You are always so determined to like a thing that

3

you never consider it for yourself. I shall see for myself whether these people are worthy of my consideration."

Her sister, Louisa Hurst, said not a word, but beside her, her husband gave a snort. "Good wine and food, you say? Cards and good hunting? Jolly good. Then we shall get along very well."

By now the carriage had pulled to a stop and the party of five alit from the vehicle to get their first sight of the assembly rooms. The edifice that faced them was grander than anything Darcy had expected and looked really rather fine from the square. Finer than he had expected, to be honest. The building was large and rectangular, with two short wings on either end and a Grecian portico over the large double doors. The style was of the last fifty years, and it looked, in the light of the burning lamps about the square, newly painted and in excellent repair. Darcy suspected the building functioned more often as a space for town meetings and local business than for assembly balls. Tonight, however, it was the centre of local society, to judge from the number of carriages lining the square and the sounds of revelry from the tavern across the way where any number of drivers and footmen must be whiling away the hours until they were needed again.

Bingley and his party promenaded inside the building and divested themselves of their outerwear, then proceeded to the main doors that led to the grand hall. Darcy could hear the noise from inside abate even before the doors were fully open. Of course. Their arrival must have been long anticipated, and speculation as to their names, numbers, and bank accounts must have filled the air since the building saw its first guests that evening.

True to his expectations, no sooner had the party of newcomers set foot into the grand hall than the whispers started. "Five thousand..." came one voice. "No, ten! And an estate in Derbyshire!" came another. He even heard someone suggest, "Related to the king!" This last was quite ludicrous, but it was not the strangest thing Darcy had heard. He was well used to being the subject of such whispers and rumour. In fact, whilst he despised it, he rather expected it. This *sotto voce* rush of words provided the carpet upon which he walked into a room, and likewise provided the insulation he so often relied upon to protect him from an onslaught of false admirers. It was easy to avoid conversation when one was seen to be so much above one's company. He straightened his spine and raised his chin a bit, so as to peer down his nose upon those around him. This was the armour he donned to protect himself from the rabble, and the armour was all but impenetrable.

A man came rushing up to the group as they moved into the assembly hall. He would have been elfin had he been smaller; his gestures and physiognomy seemed more suited to a little creature than this large man. But he bowed prettily and spoke with cultivated tones as he offered his greetings.

"Mr. Bingley!" he gushed as his fingers danced in the air. Was the man trying to cast a spell? Darcy clenched his jaw and exhaled slowly as the man prattled on. "Delighted that you have come. Delighted! The whole town is anxious to meet you. And what charming guests you have brought. Capital, just capital! Please, if you will?"

Bingley made the introductions. The man was Sir William Lucas, former mayor of the town of Meryton and self-appointed master of local society. He was, Darcy grudgingly admitted, a pleasant enough person, if a bit overblown in his own self-importance. Darcy pulled himself to his full height once more and returned the older man's bow.

"And my sisters," Bingley continued the introductions, "Miss Bingley and Mrs. Hurst, and my brother Mr. Hurst." Bows and curtseys were exchanged in a most formal manner before Sir William grabbed at Bingley's arm like a schoolboy to pull him into the room.

"You must allow me to introduce you to…" His words were lost in the growing din of the gathered company. For lack of any alternative, Darcy followed.

The next half hour seemed interminable. Every face looked the same, every coat and gown interchangeable. There was too little of fashion and taste, and too much of vulgarity. The ladies' gowns were dated enough that even he knew they were last year's styles, and not a single gentleman, other than Sir William himself, wore the latest cut of waistcoat and collar points. Furthermore, everybody talked too freely, too loudly, like farmers at a harvest festival. These—*these*—were the haute ton of local society? What had Bingley got himself into?

"…my daughter, Charlotte."

Darcy blinked and brought himself back to the present. Sir William was still speaking, introducing the new arrivals in the neighbourhood to everybody in the space. Darcy turned to take in the woman now before them. She looked sensible enough, and about his own age of twenty-seven, but she had no particular charm or beauty. Was she married? No, it seemed not. Bingley greeted her, saying, "A pleasure to see you again, Miss Lucas." To be unmarried still at her age did not bode well for her future felicity in life. He must take care to find a good husband for his sister Georgiana to save her from this same fate; although his sister, at least, had the sort of fortune that made spinsterhood a choice rather than a sad fate.

But he had no time to worry about ageing spinsters. Sir William and Bingley were weaving their way through the throng once more and Darcy must follow them. Sir William was still talking. "You have, I believe, previously met Mr. Bennet of Longbourn, Mr. Bingley. He is not here this evening, but do not fear! Pray, allow me to introduce to you his lovely daughters. This way, I see them together by the fern."

He traipsed behind Bingley and Sir William as they waded through the crowd, which parted before them like the waters of the Red Sea before Moses. Everywhere he glanced, he met an ocean of fascinated eyes. The whispers were quieter, but they had not stopped. One ruddy country face after another looked upon him with variations of awe, reverence, and other intimations of being in the presence of a superior creature. He held his head high, not deigning to meet any one person's eye, certainly not daring to smile. He was not one to crow about his place in the first circles in London, nor to bask in the glow of his noble relations, but neither would he lower himself to befriend these rustic imitators of society. For Bingley's sake he would be coolly polite, and even civil should he find himself in suitable company, but these people were not of his class, and they must know it.

He glided across to where Sir William was now introducing Bingley to a matron and a gaggle of young women, all similar enough in feature that they must be sisters. One or two were rather pretty. But not of his class. From their giggling and gestures, they seemed quite countrified. There was no suggestion of elegance, no lingering benefit of a dancing master's tutelage in the finer points of deportment and carriage. Except for that one. One of the sisters had caught his eye. He stood still whilst Sir William introduced them all, allowing his eye to linger on the elegant one for a moment.

The matron was Mrs. Bennet. She was a handsome woman, old enough to have five grown daughters, but still striking enough that Darcy could see she must have been quite beautiful in her youth.

"A pleasure, Madam!" Bingley's smile lit the room. "I had the pleasure of meeting Mr. Bennet when I first came to the neighbourhood two weeks ago. I am delighted to meet you."

The lady fluttered and cooed, and Darcy stood as rigid as a statue as he received her exaggerated curtsey. Her motions were fussy, like an overly decorated doily, with a great deal of flounce and frill, but no taste and less elegance. Then came the sisters. "Miss Bennet," Sir William began with the eldest. She was the one who had caught Darcy's eye. She was rather pretty. No, he corrected himself, she was particularly lovely. Tall and slim, she had the sort of figure for which the fashions of the day were created, and she moved with an innate grace that a good dancing master would turn into a sort of art. Likewise, her face was a model of classical beauty, symmetrical and regular, her skin perfect alabaster tinged with rose, her expression everything pleasant. Neither by feature nor by appearance would she be out of place in any fine soirée in London.

As Darcy glanced over to his friend Bingley, he noticed his friend all but gaping at this lovely creature. It seemed, by the look on Bingley's face, that Miss Bennet would equally be welcome in his salon. If not elsewhere in his home.

There were three other sisters gathered about their mother, whose names Darcy only half-heard. Mary, Catherine, and Lillia... no, Lydia. He was tired from his long day of travels, and his interest in these silly looking creatures was minimal. He blinked his eyes and nodded his head in greeting and then excused himself to stalk towards the wall where he might stand and watch the proceedings. The band had reassembled on the dais and a dance was forming in the centre of the room. He closed his eyes for a moment and stifled a yawn. As he took a deep breath to return himself to the good regulation that was his pride, he scanned the crowd again. Was that Bingley, leading the eldest Miss Bennet to the line? So it was. And Sir William was gesturing them to the head of the dance; they were to lead, it seemed.

"Had you asked me, I should now be calling the dance." A voice sounded at Darcy's shoulder.

"Miss Bingley." She was beautiful to gaze upon until she began to speak. "But I did not ask you, and therefore that honour belongs to your brother and Miss Bennet."

She tilted her head in the manner she had, whereby she seemed to look down her nose at him despite his superior height. "When you ask me to dance later, we shall show these... people... what excellent dancing is." She tapped his arm with her fan and drifted off, leaving Darcy gazing once more into the crowds.

The people avoided him, afraid to come too close. Most had not been introduced, after all, and his stern demeanour (so he had been told) deterred any who might dare break the conventions of polite society. Their eyes still landed upon him with their expressions of reverence. He abhorred the attention, but quite depended on the acknowledgement of his superiority... but what was that? There was one face in the crowd that seemed to look upon him with blatant disapproval! It moved behind one head and in front of another, and all he could tell was that it belonged to a young woman. A young country woman, scarcely more than a girl. Curling her lip at him! The impudence!

He squared his shoulders and stood taller, making himself all the more formidable, and thus he stood alone and unmolested all through the long country dance until at last Charles Bingley delivered his lovely partner to her mother and sisters and came to find him once more.

Bingley's forehead was aglow with the tinges of healthy perspiration and his smile was as wide as ever Darcy had seen it. The young man's eyes flickered constantly to where Miss Bennet was now in a tight group with her mother and one or two young ladies her age from the town.

"She is pretty," Darcy opined. There. That was his attempt at friendly civility this evening. He wished nothing more than to be back at Bingley's newly leased estate with a warm fire before him, a good book on his lap, and a brandy at his side. But he knew his duty to his friend and he would make some effort.

"Pretty? She is more than merely pretty. Look at her, man! She is everything lovely. And charming too. I have already requested a second dance later this evening. See how she smiles at me!"

Darcy deigned to cast his eye in Miss Bennet's direction. She was, indeed, smiling. She smiled at Bingley, she smiled at her mother, at her friends. "Yes, indeed. But she seems rather indiscriminate with the bestowal of her smiles."

"Really, Darcy, you are a bore! I like her, and you cannot tell me not to wish to further my acquaintance with her. But have you not danced? Not at all?"

Darcy stifled a yawn. The day had been long, far longer than he had hoped. "I was up very early to conclude my business with my agent before departing London."

"Yes?"

"I wish only to stand here."

"And disappoint all these charming ladies hoping to meet you? No, indeed! Come, Darcy, this is quite wrong. I must have you dance. I hate to see you standing about by yourself in this stupid manner. You had much better dance."

His eyelid twitched. He had hoped to avoid such a discussion, but there was nothing for it. He was weary and not well pleased by his circumstance, and that look he had seen on that one girl's face, that look of derision, had set him quite in a foul temper.

"I certainly shall not." Somewhere, a twinge ran up his calf from sitting too long in the carriage. "You know how I detest it, unless I am particularly acquainted with my partner. At such an assembly as this," he narrowed his eyes as he peered around the room, "it would be quite insupportable. There is not a woman in the room whom it would not be a punishment to stand up with."

Bingley rolled his eyes, a habit Darcy had not been able to rid him of. "You are a bore indeed! I would not be as fastidious as you are for a kingdom. I have never met with so many pleasant girls in my life, and there are several of them who are uncommonly pretty."

Perhaps there was something in Bingley's statement, but Darcy was now set against the very idea. It was bad enough that he would have to dance with Miss Bingley later. "You," he said at last, "were dancing with the only handsome girl in the room."

"Oh, she is the most beautiful creature I ever beheld!" Bingley cried. *Indeed*, thought Darcy, *not since the last ball we attended in London.* Bingley was somewhat lacking in constancy. But he said nothing, and Bingley continued. "But there is one of her sisters sitting down just behind you, who is very pretty, and, I dare say, very agreeable. Her name, I believe, is Elizabeth. Do let me ask Miss Bennet to introduce you."

Heavens! Not another Bennet sister. Was there no end to them? "Which do you mean?" he asked. He turned around and saw none other than that country girl who had turned up her nose at him earlier. A wave of anger rippled through him. That impertinent chit must learn her place. He looked again. She was sitting with a friend—Miss Lucas, if he recalled—but it was most assuredly her. Her! One of the Bennet girls. This was most unpleasant. His jaw grew tight again.

He looked at her for so long that he caught her eye, and in that moment that she returned his frank gaze, he sensed her sneer once more. He withdrew his eye and said with all the ice he could muster,

"She is tolerable, but not handsome enough to tempt me." Had she heard him? He certainly hoped so. "I am in no humour at present to give consequence to young ladies who are slighted by other men. You are wasting your time with me."

Bingley gave another great roll of his eyes and stalked off to return to Miss Bennet and her friends, and Darcy shifted his weight, the better to withstand another tedious country dance. Then, to his side, he caught a flash of motion as the annoying Bennet sister rose from her chair and walked towards him.

She stopped in her path and pivoted to glare at him directly. Her dark eyes flashed and her chin thrust forward as she scrutinised him in the manner of a distasteful piece of meat left out in the sun for too long. Then she stated in clipped syllables, "How fortunate it is that I have no interest in dancing with you. Any lady of quality must have her standards, and I only dance with gentlemen. And you, sir, despite your airs and wealth, are no gentleman." With which, she turned her back on him and melted into the crowd, her friend scurrying behind her.

Miss Elizabeth Bennet, so it seemed, had just declared war.

Chapter Two

A kind of a merry war

(Leonato, 1.1)

"Really, Lizzy!" Charlotte hurried after her. "That was rather unnecessary. He shall never like you now."

Elizabeth Bennet wrinkled her nose. "No, perhaps not. But he hardly seemed disposed to like me before, and so I venture that very little has been lost."

"You spoke rashly, Lizzy. You and he will likely be in company a great deal over the next while. Such a display cannot make that at all pleasant."

"Then I shall attempt to be my most charming self to all and sundry other than he. They shall all adore me, and if that unpleasant person offers me more insults, they shall find all the unpleasantness on his side." She tossed her head.

"It was rather an unfortunate thing to overhear..." Charlotte began.

"He spoke deliberately so I could hear him, my friend. This was no accident. He is very rich, by all accounts, and likely feels he may give offence wherever he goes, and be praised for it too. But not by me. I shall never give consequence to a man who expects to make his way in society solely by means of his income and not by his character. Look, there is Jane, talking to Mr. Bingley. He does not seem too quick to leave her company to seek a partner for the next dance. Could it be that he has taken a liking to her?"

Charlotte clucked her tongue. "Tsk, Lizzy, they have only met. You are like your mother, ready to marry Jane off to every handsome man with some sort of fortune who comes her way."

"And why not? *She* is beautiful and sweet, and *he* seems handsome and charming. They would make an admirable couple."

She followed Charlotte's eyes to where Mr. Bingley was now handing Jane a glass of negus. He seemed oblivious to the existence of anybody else in the rooms, his attention solely upon the lovely young woman smiling at him. Charlotte sighed.

"So I see. They do look well together. But do not be precipitous. A happy first encounter is merely one event. One must be practical."

Elizabeth flicked her head. Her artfully arranged ringlets bounced on the back of her neck with the gesture. "Always sensible,

Charlotte! Yes, I shall be chastened by your words and shall not tease Jane about her conquest. But allow me to hope." She cast a grin at her friend. "Look, there is James Tuff. He might only be the miller's son, but he is invariably pleasant company and speaks nothing but good of people. *His* good character supersedes his supposed importance in the world. He is my idea of a gentleman, no matter his rank or status. Perhaps he shall ask me to dance."

And she turned her feet to greet her friend, with Charlotte in her wake.

The rest of the assembly ball was more agreeable, with no further encounters with the stern and rude Mr. Darcy. She danced once with Jimmy Tuff, once with Mr. Bingley—whom she admitted was a most personable young man—and once with Mr. Hurst, whose rather elegant steps belied his portly appearance. By the time the family's carriage returned to their home at Longbourn and the mother and five exhausted sisters tumbled out, Elizabeth had almost forgotten her unpleasant interlude with that miserable person from Derbyshire.

Elizabeth had no further cause to think about Mr. Darcy for several days. She presumed—although based on what supposed information she never could say—that he had come to see his friend Bingley established at Netherfield Park and would then soon return to London, never to pollute the shades of happy Meryton again. His insult was a singular event not to be repeated, and she was of a happy enough disposition that she never thought to cast her eyes or thoughts upon him again.

In this, she was wrong.

The ladies of Longbourn soon paid a call upon Miss Bingley and Mrs. Hurst at Netherfield, where Elizabeth learned that Mr. Darcy—who was thankfully out at present—was to be a more permanent presence at Netherfield than she had expected.

"Oh, dear Mr. Darcy!" cried Caroline Bingley. "He is so very kind to those he deems worthy of his attention. So charming. He is very superior, of course, being the grandson of an earl and master of his own great estate in Derbyshire, but he considers us deserving of his company. As he should." She wrinkled her nose for a moment as if she had smelled something bad. "He is helping my brother learn about estate management. Charles could not wish for a better friend. I believe Mr. Darcy has no immediate plans to return to Town, nor to Pemberley. He has told Charles that he will remain for as long as he is needed at Netherfield. But I believe it is really because of the company that he stays." She cast her glance downward. Was she trying to be coy, to pretend that the attraction was all on the part of the gentleman? If so, her efforts were laughable, and Elizabeth believed she would have contrived a blush if it were at all possible. Nothing more needed to be said. Fortunately for Miss Bingley, the lady would find no rival in her!

But this was not good news. It was now almost assured that their paths would cross often. Mr. Bingley was a most sociable sort of gentleman and would wish to be out in company a great deal. And if he were to visit, it would be almost unthinkable for his friend not to accompany him. Elizabeth's jaw tightened. She would have to be prepared, then, for any further ill-mannered behaviour on the part of this rude man.

And so it proved to be. The Bennets dined with no fewer than four-and-twenty families—now five-and-twenty!—and the family were often at one soirée or another. When the gatherings were small and intimate, limited to old friends, there Elizabeth had respite from the new arrivals in the neighbourhood. But all too often their hosts wished to befriend the new residents of Netherfield Park, and consequently, along with the familiar faces from the area, were Mr. and Miss Bingley and their houseguests.

At first, it was an easy matter to avoid the odious Mr. Darcy, even at these gatherings. His very pride and arrogance, which soon set the entire town against him, were the means by which Elizabeth was able to stay out of his company. He stalked the edges of rooms, never engaging in conversation unless it were unavoidable, never deigning to smile or offer a kind word. There seemed always to be a disdainful look upon his face as if he disapproved of the wallpaper, and his eye was always critical.

Elizabeth saw how he sniffed in derision at the fine table linens that Mrs. Long displayed for her guests, brought over from France in the last century and adorned with the finest lace and embroidery. Did she really hear him whisper to Miss Bingley that these were nothing to the simplest of linens at Pemberley? Perhaps that conversation happened only in her imagination, but it could well have been real, she was certain! And he turned up his patrician nose at the platter of very fine beef that graced the table at Mrs. King's house. "What sort of sauce is this?" Miss Bingley asked in too loud a voice, and Mr. Darcy glanced at her and inclined his head. Later on, Charlotte insisted that he was merely trying to stop Miss

Bingley's complaints, but Lizzy was certain he was in agreement with the sentiment. Proud, unpleasant man!

Furthermore, he made a point of dressing in the finest garb that ever had been seen in Meryton. Did the man not know how to be comfortable? Had he ever owned a pair of buckskins, or heaven forbid, corduroy riding breeches and a comfortable coat? Or were all of his garments silk and superfine wool, all perfectly cut to his body, all immaculately clean and pressed with nary a spot of lint or dust even after a long ride, more suited to the court of St. James than a country market town?

He spoke little of Pemberley, but it was soon known how large and gracious the estate was; how prosperous and well managed; how great his income. Hertfordshire could hold nothing to compare with it. Likewise, his fine house in town, his splendid carriage, and his noble relations. For—and this was whispered about town everywhere he went—his grandfather had been an earl; his uncle now an earl. His custom was the finest of society. This neighbourhood could only disappoint him with its poor sort of company.

And his manners! What seemed so superior was, in truth, abominably rude. For what use were manners other than to make others feel comfortable? This is what she had always learned at her mother's side. But Mr. Darcy's stiff city ways only made those around him feel little and rough, which Elizabeth was certain was his aim.

No truly fine man would elevate himself at the expense of those around him. That was the lowest sort of pride. That she could not forgive.

"These are just his ways, Lizzy," Jane insisted after one night at cards. "He is not a great talker, to be sure, but we have seen just these manners in London while visiting our aunt and uncle. They are all openness, but recall our Aunt Gardiner's friend Mrs. Dyson. She seems quite cold and superior at first, but is in truth the most warm-hearted person I know, save our aunt herself."

Elizabeth peered at her sister. "There is something in what you say. But in the case of Mr. Darcy, I am convinced his manner merely reflects his character." And nothing Jane could say would change her mind.

Neither was there anything in Mr. Darcy that engendered affection, or even the first glimmers of amity. He was aloof and silent, condescending only to join the company when they were seated for tea or for cards. He attempted no conversation and was engaged in none in return. In one instance, he sat very close to Mrs. Long for a full half hour without venturing to say a single word to that good lady. Elizabeth later assured Mrs. Long that this was definitely to her benefit, for no word of value could ever pass so proud and unpleasant a man's lips!

She had only just uttered these words when a motion behind her drew her attention. There stood the man himself, his eyes boring into her. His jaw was clenched and his brows almost met in the centre of his forehead, and Elizabeth was certain that if looks could harm, she would be grievously injured. She thrust her chin forward and gave an impertinent shake of her head, feeling her ear drops swing as she did so. He scowled even more and stalked off, his hands balled into fists at his side. For a moment, she prayed that even he was too civilised to hit a woman. But thankfully, he did nothing so untoward, and she smiled at his retreating back. This skirmish, at least, she had won.

At almost every engagement Elizabeth was thrown into company with Mr. Darcy, and at each her dislike for the man grew, although she made every possible effort to keep away from his unwelcome gaze. At every encounter she managed some quip against him, and at each she felt his scorn and enmity grow.

But as the frequency of these undesired meetings increased, so did the necessity of exchanging some words. These were not always pleasant.

On one particular evening towards the end of October, they were all gathered in Mrs. Robinson's parlour for an evening's amusement at cards and games. The Robinsons were a family of comfortable if not excessive means, their lands bordering upon those of Netherfield. Mr. Robinson had offered his assistance in any matters which Bingley required, and hoped to be a good neighbour to the newcomer. It was therefore to Mr. Bingley's advantage, as well as personal satisfaction, to befriend the man and his family, and he was present at every event held in that house.

Elizabeth and Charlotte were sitting on the settee with Miss Margaret Robinson, talking about some diverting, if quite inconsequential matter, when Mr. Bingley and his party arrived. All rose and a series of bows and curtseys ensued, with one remarkable exception. Mr. Darcy most definitely did not offer any manner of salutation to Elizabeth. He bowed to Charlotte and muttered appropriate words to Miss Margaret, and quite ignored her very existence. It was the Cut Direct if ever she had seen one. She gaped after him as he walked on.

"I was correct, it seems," she observed for any ears that happened to be near, "when I presumed Mr. Darcy to be no gentleman."

To which, Mr. Darcy surprised her by turning to speak directly to her for the first time since the night of the assembly. "How fortunate then, Miss Bennet, that you are no lady to care." He turned his back and began to move into the room.

What? The nerve of that man! How dare he insult her in such a way? She had, a small voice in her head insisted, started this particular skirmish, and ought to ignore his taunts and show herself to be the superior creature. But her pride would not listen to this quiet voice of reason and her mouth began moving almost before her brain agreed with it.

"How happy that his purse is full then, for the man himself is an empty pocket." There. That should put him in his place. She ignored Charlotte's gasp of horror at her side, as well as the tinge of guilt that nagged at her conscience.

He turned once more and glared at her, eyes narrow and jaw tight. "How happy that we are so distant from Egypt, lady, for your tongue is more venomous than all the asps in the Nile."

"Darcy!" Mr. Bingley was at his side in a trice. "What are you doing? This is most unlike you. I know you have a hot temper at times, but I have never heard you speak to a lady like this. You were the one who told me always to take the higher path. What is this? Come away at once."

Darcy sniffed and stuck his nose up into the air and walked away without another word, Bingley hissing into his ear. That man's back was his best side, to be sure! If only his face weren't so handsome.

"Lizzy?" Charlotte's voice was concerned. She waited until the two men had passed beyond hearing. "Is it wise to make an enemy of such a man as this? I have long known you to be impertinent, but never cutting. You were quite cruel. Has he injured you so gravely?"

Elizabeth sighed. What was it about Mr. Darcy that set her so on edge? He irritated her to the essence of her being for some reason. Perhaps she was not accustomed to having anybody engage her in a game of wits. But the man was a terror. She needed to put him in his place.

She turned her attention back to Charlotte. "There is something about him that turns me into a termagant. His every word is like a cat clawing at my legs, calculated to annoy and cause grief. And I am not the only one in Meryton who seems to dislike him. I do not believe he has uttered two friendly words to anybody in the neighbourhood since he arrived, save Mr. Bingley and his sisters. And Mr. Bingley is so open and friendly a man. I wonder that they should be friends at all, they are so very different."

Charlotte clucked her tongue. "That they are! Two more different men it is hard to imagine. Mr. Bingley is so determined to like everybody that he, in turn, is sure of being liked wherever he appears. Whereas Mr. Darcy is so determined to be dissatisfied with everything and everyone that he continually gives offence. They are a strange pair indeed."

"Just as we are, Charlotte," Elizabeth laughed. This was more her natural manner; she was at once more at ease, for she was made to laugh and not to fret. "You are prudent and practical, and I am all impertinence and frivolity. Come, let us forget vexatious men from the north and see instead what Miss Robinson has to play for us on the pianoforte. Perhaps she might try a Scotch dance later; I am certain Mr. Bingley would be pleased for any excuse to ask Jane to dance."

"Really, Lizzy, you really are just as bad as your mother!"

"Am I wrong? See how he gazes at her, how his eye cannot leave her for more than a moment before returning. He brings her tea and fusses over her comfort. You cannot have missed it."

Her friend shrugged. "Yes, perhaps. It has been hard to ignore, as much as one ought not to remark upon it. They have only been acquainted for two weeks."

"And look how he swans about her. He surely likes her."

"Then she ought to act to fix him!"

"Fix him, Charlotte? What can you mean?" The words came out in a bubble of laughter, but they were born of surprise.

"Do not be missish, Lizzy! She must act to assure him of her growing affection. Very few of us have heart enough to be really in love without encouragement. In nine cases out of ten, a woman had better show more affection than she feels."

"You must be jesting! Jane's affection shows clearly upon her face. I have never seen her smile so much."

"Ah, but he does not know her disposition as you and I do. For someone who has only now met her, she must seem quite unaffected. Her manner is so uniformly pleasing that genuine affection can easily go unremarked. Listen: Mr. Bingley likes your sister undoubtedly, but he may never do more than like her if she does not help him out."

"I can hardly hear this, Charlotte," Elizabeth tittered. "What is she to do? For if a woman is partial to a man and does not endeavour to conceal it, he must find it out."

Charlotte remained silent for a moment, her brows drawn in thought. "Perhaps he must," she said at last, "but only if he sees enough of her. But consider this: though Jane and Bingley meet tolerably often, it is only for a short time, and as they always see each other in large mixed parties, they have not so much time for conversing together. Jane should," she spoke slowly, enunciating each word, "make the most of every half hour."

"And this will fix him? This will let him fall in love with her?" Charlotte nodded. "And even when he has been encouraged to fall in love with her, she still ought to show more affection than she feels? Is this your meaning?"

"Assuredly so. For when she is secure of him, there will be leisure for falling in love as much as she chooses."

Elizabeth laughed again and wrinkled her nose. "Would you act this way?"

Charlotte thought for a moment. "I believe I would. In the interests of a secure future, I would go a great distance to convince a man of my regard. Would you not, Lizzy?"

"No! Heavens no. I could not think of marrying where there is no real love."

"Love can develop after marriage. I have more need for a home and security than a great passion."

"That is where we are different. Only the deepest love could tempt me into matrimony. I should much rather remain an old maid than commit myself to a man I liked only passingly."

"Surely not! If a good enough offer came your way, you would consider it most carefully, I warrant!"

"You are quite too sensible for words, Charlotte, and quite preposterous. I cannot imagine what, other than genuine affection, would lead me to accept a man, no matter his other assets." She let out a chuckle. "It is fortunate that Mr. Darcy has no affection for me, for his worldly assets are great. I should be hard pressed to refuse such riches, and yet, assuredly, I would do so." She grinned at her friend. "But be assured, if Jane falls in love with Mr. Bingley, she will let him discover it and I dare say he will come to love her in return."

Charlotte sighed again. "I do hope you are correct."

Their next encounter came about a week later, when Sir William Lucas hosted a large party of guests. As was usual, the Bennets were the first family to arrive, the better for Mrs. Bennet to have a *tête-à-tête* with her intimate friend Lady Lucas. Elizabeth did not object, for she too was pleased for some time for private conversation with Charlotte. Soon enough, the appointed hour arrived, and the visitors began to arrive. Mrs. Long and her niece came first, then the Robinsons, and then Colonel Forster. This gentleman was newly arrived in town, there to be the commander of a militia regiment who would be training over the winter. He was a jovial man in his early forties with a great laugh and a manner suited to please. But Elizabeth could see his stiff resolve beneath the friendly surface, and imagined he would be a most effective commanding officer. Even his most offhand comments were uttered in such a way that it was clear he expected complete compliance. His underlings would have no easy time of it, and Elizabeth wondered what sort of men these would be, to serve as officers under Colonel Forster's command. Perhaps she would meet some of them in time, for her papa had suggested that officers often dined with local gentlemen. After his appearance, the rest of the invited guests arrived, until the room was quite buzzing with activity.

Elizabeth was sitting with the colonel and Charlotte when Bingley and his party entered the room some time later. They always seemed to be the last to arrive; in her uncharitable moments, Elizabeth was certain that Miss Bingley contrived matters thus, thereby to make a grand and memorable entrance and to be supplanted by none. So large was the gathering and so distant were Elizabeth and the colonel from the door that they paid little attention to the party's arrival and continued their conversation undisturbed.

"And how long do you presume to remain in our small part of Hertfordshire?" Elizabeth asked of her companion. The idea of having the militia in such close proximity to the town was exciting, for there would surely be men to frequent the shops, thereby encouraging the proprietors to bring in exciting new goods. And, of course, there was the prospect of handsome young officers, resplendent in their red coats, brightening the streets and salons of the town.

"I cannot say for certain," Colonel Forster replied, "but I would be surprised if we are to remove long before the summer. We shall go for further training at Brighton in May, but I believe we will be your neighbours until such a time arrives."

"How wonderful!" Elizabeth exclaimed. "And will there be a great number of officers?" Any answer the colonel might have offered was forestalled by a tittering voice behind her.

"Officers? How many? Oh, I do love a man in a red coat!" Elizabeth turned around to see her youngest sister Lydia standing with Maria Lucas by the windows right behind them.

Colonel Forster puffed his chest. "Indeed, Miss Lydia, a great many officers. Some have already arrived to establish our camp, and others will be here within the week. I cannot promise that they will all be young and handsome, but I shall do my best to oblige you." He gave her a wink and she tittered again.

Elizabeth sighed. At only fifteen, Lydia was far too young to be in society, no matter what her mama insisted. She looked very much a lady, almost as tall as Jane, well grown and with an elegant carriage, but her behaviour was still that of a girl. She was, to put it simply, very silly indeed. Worse, she encouraged Kitty, older by two years, to that same childish behaviour which did credit to neither young woman.

Alas, it was too late to return either sister to the schoolroom. Luckily, they were well known within Meryton society and there was little damage they could do before they grew mature enough to be considered truly elegant company.

Lydia now placed all her attention upon the colonel, asking every manner of question about the incoming members of the militia, and at last seemed satisfied in the number and quality of the officers. She giggled one last time and skipped off in search of others her age.

"She is a delightful young lady," Colonel Forster smiled. "Her spirits are high. I believe she will suit my betrothed well; they must meet when we return here after our wedding."

The conversation then turned to the colonel's imminent nuptials, which were to take place in London in two weeks' time. Once again Elizabeth sensed a presence behind her, and expecting it to be Lydia once more, paid it little attention.

But when that person cleared his throat, it was a man's voice and not Lydia's that she heard, and turning, noticed Mr. Darcy—of all people!—standing close by to listen to their conversation. He caught her eye and turned red and hurried away in the direction of the card tables.

"Loo? Is that where the men are all heading? I do believe that is a fine idea! Pray, excuse me, ladies." The colonel rose to find the other men, leaving Elizabeth and Charlotte alone.

Elizabeth glowered after both men. "Whatever does Mr. Darcy mean by listening to our conversation? It is quite annoying."

In her usual calm manner, Charlotte shrugged. "That is a question which Mr. Darcy only can answer. He did not seem angry, nor prone to offer more insults. He might not find you quite that objectionable, Lizzy. He was merely standing nearby."

"I do wish he would cease. How he pesters me. The more he loiters about, the more I must let him know that I see what he is about." Elizabeth let out a snort through her nose. "He has a very satirical eye, and if I do not begin by being impertinent myself, I might even grow afraid of him. And that never shall do! I shall counter his satirical eye with my satirical tongue!"

"Do not vex him, Lizzy! You do not know what he might do, or what his aim is."

"Fear not, Charlotte. I know well enough. He looks at me only to find fault, and in doing so gives me a great deal of fault to find in him."

"Hush, Lizzy! People can hear you. It can do no good to encourage his disapprobation. He shall never like you now."

"Let them hear me. It is no secret that we are not friends. Indeed, he is such a disagreeable man that it would be a great misfortune to be liked by him! There. I dare anyone to contradict me." What a pity that the man was undeniably handsome, and with a quick, if unpleasant, wit.

Charlotte sighed and looked heavenwards. "You will regret your words, Lizzy. Pray, let us have no more of this. Come with me to open the instrument, and then you can play and sing for us. Let Mr. Darcy save his breath to cool his porridge, whilst you save yours to swell your song. It is a far better use for it than this merry war you seem to have on."

"Very well, my friend. My fingers await your command. Let us find some music."

Chapter Three

A plain-dealing villain

(Don John, 1.3)

Not for the first time did Will Darcy regret his offer of assistance to Charles Bingley. The estate his friend had leased was fine enough, a respectable manor set in the middle of some good land with productive farms and hardworking tenants. The younger man had much to learn about managing that estate, but there were no impediments that Darcy could see other than lack of experience. No, that was not the problem.

Neither was the town of Meryton itself a source of trouble. It was larger than Lambton, the village closest to Darcy's estate in Derbyshire, and closer to London. A man on a fast horse could ride to and from Town in a day. Furthermore, the town boasted a fine selection of shops, a pleasant teahouse, a good tavern serving strong ale with a clean inn above, and all the provisions a local squire could want to supply his home.

Even the society was not quite as savage as Darcy had expected. Despite his initial predispositions against the denizens of the neighbourhood, it was not as dreadful as he had feared. Of course, it was nothing compared to the circles in which he was accustomed to moving in London. Even in Derbyshire, his own estate bordered those of a baron and another untitled gentleman of great fortune and breeding, with his uncle's earldom a mere half-day's ride away in even the slowest carriage. No, Meryton was not Lambton. He was used to the finest of society, but these people here in Hertfordshire were not unacceptable in their own way. If one were to overlook their country manners and occasional rustic crassness. They were... tolerable.

No. It was she. That harridan, that shrew in a frock, that harpy in angel's garb. Miss Elizabeth Bennet. To be true, she was not hard to look upon. She did not, perhaps, have the classical beauty of her older sister Jane, but few women did. Bingley had an eye for beauty and he had found it in Miss Bennet. But Miss Elizabeth was—he grudgingly admitted—rather pretty, and her own form of loveliness increased in his eyes every time he saw her, no matter that her tongue spewed vile acid with every word she uttered.

But there were lovely ladies aplenty in London, and in London he would far rather be, if only to escape her caustic wit. What had she called him last night? A popinjay! A lackey! How dare she? And then she had likened his face to foulest February, all full of frost and storms and cloud! He was not a vain man—heaven forbid—but he had often been called handsome and not only by his aunts. What was that virago on about, anyway? And why did he always find himself in her vicinity, to be victim to her assaults?

He huffed into the wind, letting it blow about his face.

"Are you still in the doldrums, Darcy? I have never seen you like this. Surely one slip of a woman cannot be the cause of all this distress." Bingley's cheerful voice dragged him from his stew. "If you stand outside in this weather without a coat or hat, you shall take ill and Caroline will never forgive me. Come, let us ride into the town, for I would like to know the shopkeepers better. I might see about having gloves made; I have heard good things of the glover and I shall need something sturdy for winter. It will give you something cheerful to ponder, rather than Miss Elizabeth.

"Although," Bingley added after a moment, "I must say I find her quite charming. Her manner is, perhaps, a bit impertinent, but she is witty and bright, and so kind to her sister. There is not one person I have met in all of Hertfordshire who has a single bad word to say against her."

"How fortunate I am, then," Darcy grumbled, "that all of her defects should fall about my ears."

"No, no, my friend, you quite misunderstand her. She is a bit brazen, to be sure, but it is all in good humour. She loves a laugh, and all who know her love to laugh with her. Why, only the other day, when I visited Longbourn whilst you and Hurst were hunting, I was telling her of a man I knew in Scarborough. For every word I had to say, she replied with ten and all in good humour and great jest. She means no harm by it, if you will allow her the joy."

"Her jests are jabs, Bingley. She would be kinder with a javelin."

"Really, Darcy! It is merely her way. She means no ill by it at all. She is welcome company in these parts because of her smart words."

Darcy huffed. "Those smart words become sharp swords when turned against me, I am afraid. Very well, let me call for my coat and hat. Ready the horses and we shall meet your glove maker."

He watched Bingley disappear back through the large doors into the drawing room, then turned and followed. It was well after breakfast; surely Caroline would be cloistered somewhere with the housekeeper now. He had taken to hiding in his rooms or pacing the gardens in the morning to avoid her. Hers was another pretty face marred by a less charming character. Were she less mercenary in her pursuit of wealth and less obvious about her infatuation with his estate, he might find more to admire in her. But she was too calculating by far and he had no wish to bind himself in any way to a toady, no matter how pretty the wrapping. His shoulders slumped as he slid through the doors and found a servant to get his riding coat.

Soon enough, the two men were on the lane into town. It was a short ride, little more than two miles, and the day was sunny, if a bit cool. The trees were resplendent in their autumn garb and most of the leaves had not yet fallen, making the trip a welcome outing more than a mere necessity. Past the bank of trees edging the lane,

Darcy could see teams of farmers pulling in the final crops from the fields, or wagons dragging hay towards unseen barns to be stored through the coming winter. It was a picturesque scene, worthy of a landscape painting, something his sister might undertake.

"Do you approve?" Bingley asked as they turned onto the road by the old stone cottage. "I rather find I like the place myself. Here, slowly over the bridge, Jasper," he urged his horse. "That plank is loose. There is Mrs. Raleigh; she's the baker's wife." He waved and was greeted in like fashion by the woman. "And there is the road to where the widow Hawkes takes in laundry. Shall I see if her daughter wants a position at Netherfield? Cook says she needs another hand on market days. Look, Farmer Nuttal is bringing grain into the mill... or is he heading to the brew house? The brewer makes a fine beer. I could stand an ale, and maybe a bowl of hot stew. What say you, Darcy?"

He kept up this string of words for another few moments, flitting from subject to subject like a butterfly in a field of flowers, until at last they slowed their horses on the bustling main street of the village. Townsfolk and men from the militia wandered from building to building and horses trotted up and down the street, some with single riders, others pulling some sort of cart or wagon. Here a group of children gathered at a puddle with a muddy dog and a large stick, and there, further along the busy road, a small knot of ladies stood by a shopfront, talking with a red-coated officer and two other men.

"I say!" Bingley exclaimed, "Is that Miss Bennet? It seems very like her. I should know her looks anywhere. Let us ride over." He turned his horse before Darcy could open his mouth to respond.

Yes, it did look like her from this angle. That profile and her tall figure certainly seemed like hers. From this distance, he thought he recognised two of her sisters and Miss Maria Lucas. Of the men's faces, he could see little since they were turned away from him. But the harridan seemed not to be amongst their number, and so he guided his own horse after Bingley's.

"Miss Bennet!" He heard Bingley cry as he leapt from his mount. "Oh, I beg your pardon, Miss Lydia! I quite thought you were your sister Jane."

The girl tittered. Could she make no other sound? "Mama always tells me that next to Jane I am the prettiest, and therefore we must look alike! Is that not the funniest thing? But look, we have just been talking to my friend here. He is an officer in Colonel Forster's regiment, just arrived from Bedfordshire! Is it not exciting? Is he not smart in his scarlet coat? Oh, coo, Denny, have you not met Mr. Bingley yet? I must introduce you! Wait... There is Mr. Bingley's friend. We shall all be introduced. What fun! Mr. Darcy, Denny was just introducing us to another new officer. Mr. Wickham will be a lieutenant..." She stopped. "Mr. Darcy? Are you well?"

Darcy had ridden over to the gathering, expecting nothing worse than a few minutes of meaningless babble before continuing with Bingley to his business. But this... this was worse than encountering a regiment of Elizabeth Bennets in the gaggle of girls! This was a disaster. He felt his face drain of all blood and a dagger of ice attacked his spine.

"Wickham." He spat out the name. What in heaven's name was he doing here? Every sin he had ever committed was now crashing down about his shoulders, and his every waking moment was his penance. Wickham! In Meryton. First Elizabeth, now Wickham. The gods surely must hate him.

A man of hot blood by nature, Darcy prided himself on controlling his temper. This skill had been learned slowly over a difficult youth, but he had learned to master himself. Regulation was everything to him; a gentleman never acted out of pure, raw passion. But the sight of George Wickham before him made all his resolutions dissolve into a mess of bottomless fury, and for a moment the world swam. He envisioned himself stripping off his coat and pounding a fist into that handsome face until it swelled white like a turnip and ran red with blood. *No! You are a Darcy! You are better than this.* He pulled himself together and grit his teeth to regain control of his faculties.

Such was the intensity of this internal struggle, that he scarcely observed that man's face go quite red at the encounter. Was Wickham as disturbed by the meeting as he? Darcy hardly cared. He only needed to be away from the blackguard at once, lest his self-control fail him. Without another word, he pressed his calves into the horse's flanks and urged the beast forward, hurrying away from the square where the ladies and the officers stood.

"Darcy..." Bingley called after him, but he had no time for civility. If he stayed another moment in the presence of that cur, he would say or do something he might regret. No, he corrected himself, there was very little that he would regret were he to speak his mind to Wickham. Besides which, his war of words with Elizabeth Bennet was well enough known that scant few in the neighbourhood had a good opinion of him already. Some choice words to this scoundrel, or a well aimed fist, would hardly blacken his name further. Still, the best way to deal with George Wickham was to be as far away as possible from him, and so he spurred his beast onward. Bingley would catch up with him in time. He would rather fume in peace.

The clatter of galloping hooves slowed him in his ride.

"Darcy!" He heard Bingley's voice from somewhere behind him. In a moment, his friend caught up and the two walked on at a more moderate pace. "Is there some poison in the water here that affects only you? What was that about? First Miss Elizabeth and now Mr. Wickham, who seems a most gentlemanly sort of person. Whatever is eating at you?"

What ought he to say? The tale was not entirely his to tell. He steamed for a moment as he chose his words. "George Wickham and I have... we have met before. We were friends of a sort in our youth. Our friendship did not survive coming into adulthood, and I would not wish him to be too close to those I loved or protected. He has caused great harm to one I care for. Let that suffice."

"Really, Darcy. I do not understand you at all sometimes. We have been friends these many years and I have not heard a word of Mr. Wickham until today. And, I must tell you, he seemed none too pleased to see your face again. He looked to have some tales of his own to tell."

Darcy slowed his mount to an amble and Bingley came up beside him, to talk rather than shout across the distance. "Ah, and just as you left, Miss Elizabeth came out from the shop with Jane... Miss Bennet. They were inquiring after some sweets at the confectioner's. I left them all talking, although I had much rather have stayed to talk with Ja... with the ladies. They are all so very charming."

"Hmmphhh." It was not the pinnacle of his eloquence. "Return to your friends, Bingley. I am in no mind to make idle chatter with that sort right now. We shall all be happier if I am left alone. Perhaps I should return to London. You seem to have an idea of how to manage the estate, and I can be reached by post."

Beside him, he saw the younger man's face fall. "If you must, I suppose... But I had hoped... Oh, dash it all, Darcy! Go if you must, but I had really hoped you would see me through these first months here. I have yet to deal with the rents and the harvest is only in now, and the tenants are starting to come with lists of the repairs they need, and there was a letter from the butcher only yesterday about some irregularities in the accounts. If I had a steward..." He let that fall. "Will you stay just a few more weeks? Please?"

That last desperate plea was his undoing. He was not a heartless man, despite what Miss Elizabeth might think, and Bingley had been a good friend to him in the past. There was really nothing for him in London. His sister was away with his aunt and her companion, and those few men he considered worthy of his friendship were all at their estates, there to rusticate over the winter before the recall of Parliament. He would have a great deal of time to sit in solitary comfort in his study, but he would indeed be alone. Even a fastidious man such as himself needed companionship some of the time. And Bingley was good company, despite his unfortunate relations.

"Very well. Let me think. For now, return to Miss Bennet and her smiles, and I shall see you when you return to Netherfield. Perhaps

Caroline will not find me in the billiards room." He held back a snort at the thought. He would rather spend an age in the irritating company of Miss Elizabeth than an hour with cloying Caroline Bingley.

"You are a gem, Darcy!" Bingley pulled up on the reins to urge his horse back to the street in Meryton where the cluster of girls hopefully still stood gabbing with that blackguard Wickham.

By now, Darcy had ridden a fair distance back along the road to Netherfield. The most sensible thing would be to continue to the house and make his way to the library or his rooms. But if Caroline discovered him, he would have to explain himself and that he had no wish to do. His affairs with Wickham were his alone to fume over, and if she caught even a glimmer of what had most recently transpired, well... another much more innocent person would be the one to suffer. That he could never allow to happen. Perhaps a longer ride, then.

He had been around the neighbourhood with Bingley in the two weeks since his arrival in Hertfordshire, but he had not taken the time to explore on his own. Rather, they had surveyed the park, taken account of the fences and lanes, made the acquaintance of the tenant farmers, and looked over the fields. Today, Darcy decided he would just ride and learn more of the area. That way, in the far distance past the wooded area, the land seemed to rise. He thought he saw a small hill past the trees. There might be a fair prospect from the top of that hillock. He felt in his pocket for an apple for his horse and guided the beast in the desired direction.

They sped over the fields, ignoring the tracery of lanes, and leaping hedgerows and rivulets as they came to them. This was the freest Darcy had felt in weeks. In months. He had forgotten how to breathe. First, that awful affair this past summer, and its time-consuming aftermath, then the rush up to Netherfield to see the place with Bingley and now this leap into the position of mentor and nursemaid in one with Bingley. He had not realised how stifled he had been. In a normal year, he would have ridden up to Pemberley before the heat of the summer abated and overseen the harvest, but that had not been possible. He thanked Providence for his excellent steward, who had ensured that matters proceeded smoothly. He would have to thank the man with an extra bottle of fine brandy and perhaps a few hundred pounds toward his daughter's dowry.

He took another deep breath, letting the cool, fresh air fill his lungs. It was cleansing and invigorating, and he spurred his horse to even greater speeds. What was that over there? Another manor house nestled in the woods? Ah, he had approached Longbourn from the back. At least he knew Elizabeth was not here, for she was in the village with Wickham. How they deserved each other! He found another path and rode in the opposite direction for a while.

After some length of time—perhaps an hour—he began to tire and he found a sunny spot near a stream to sit and rest. His horse drank greedily, and he found in his pocket another apple for the beast and a roll that he had taken from the breakfast table for himself. He sat for a long time against a tree, staring in the distance and thinking of precisely nothing.

Eventually, he knew he had to return. He thought he knew his way back, but the cleared fields held few landmarks he knew and the river kept diverting his path. He rode this way and that before spying Longbourn in the distance once more. He knew the path from there and hoped to come across it without having to ride within direct sight of the house. If somebody saw him, he might be obliged to pay respects to the family.

He had visited Mr. Bennet with Bingley but once, always finding some excuse to avoid the family. Bennet was a pleasant enough gentleman in his vague way, more concerned with his books than with the proper raising of his daughters or the good management of his land. He could be counted on for a half an hour of mildly interesting conversation, but the older man had too little passion for anything to become truly desired company. Mrs. Bennet was no better than the rest of her kind, always ready to pass on the next piece of gossip, constantly looking for some suitable man to whom to marry her daughters. That she had fixed on Bingley for Jane was no secret; Darcy only wished she would be less voluble on the subject.

That left the daughters. Only Jane seemed acceptable company. She was uniformly charming, with a kind word and a sweet smile that never varied. Despite Mrs. Bennet's whispers, Darcy could see no particular attachment on her part to his friend. They had been acquainted only a short time, it was true, but had there been any growing affection, surely he would see some signs of it. As for the rest of the girls, the younger two were very silly creatures with hardly a worthwhile thought in their heads. It seemed all but impossible that Lydia was about the same age as his sister Georgiana. Georgie was quiet and elegant with the tastes of a young lady of great discernment. Lydia was, well, a hoyden. Very pretty, but a hoyden. There was no other word for it. He sighed in relief that the two should never meet.

Mary, the middle daughter, was scarcely worth noticing. She was quick to offer words of judgement or to offer to exhibit at the pianoforte, but her desire to be noticed was too great to bring any true joy or feeling to her performances.

And then there was Elizabeth. She always intruded upon his thoughts for some reason. Perhaps she wished to vex him even in her absence. Now he did not hold back his snort. Pestilence in a frock. No, it was imperative that he avoid visiting Longbourn. He skirted the park around the house and saw the hillock once more. On impulse, he decided to ride in that direction, to see what he had originally set out to discover. There seemed to be a path that wound about the rise that his horse would take easily, and he climbed the small hill as his thoughts whirled around that unfortunate lady like an eddy in muddy waters.

She was vivid, alive, unmistakable. Even as she spewed her barbs of poison, her dark eyes sparkled. They were remarkable eyes too, beguiling in shape, dark-lashed, more eloquent than most people's words. Paired with a happier disposition, they would be a fine asset to her, almost enough to atone for the dreadful lack of dowry he had learned was her lot.

Her figure was fine too, being light and pleasing, and round where a woman ought to be round. He spared no charitable thought for her, but he could not find ugly what was not so. In his mind's eye, he saw her hair glistening in the sunshine, loose from its confining bonnet, her arms twirling at her sides as she spun about surveying the scenery from the top of the hill.

He pulled his horse to a halt. It was no imagining. It was she, mere yards before him, and she had seen his approach. He could not avoid the greeting now. Not even he was that rude, not even to her.

"Miss Elizabeth." He barely bobbed his head and his voice was cold.

"Mr. Darcy." Her knees bent a touch in curtsey. Her eyes narrowed as they traced him, and she fussed with the hat in her hands. There was something in her glance that suggested he would emerge from any confrontation more bruised than bruising. And he had been bruised enough by his unwelcome encounter with Wickham. Perhaps it would not hurt to be friendly. Or, at least, civil.

"A fine day." He nodded at the horizon.

She blinked in surprise. "So it is." A scowl. "You have not come to castigate me on some matter of my manner or appearance?"

He forced a smile. "No, indeed, madam. I had hoped instead to enjoy the scenery for a time." He strove to fill the silence with something unobjectionable. "Do you come by this way often?"

Her stance softened. "It is one of my favourite places. I like to walk here when I wish to think. And," her eyes levelled on him, "when I wish to be alone." Then she blinked again. "That is not to say, however, that I am unhappy with company."

This was her olive branch. He remained on his horse, still some distance away from her, and gazed out over the surrounding countryside, afraid to speak lest he say something that would spark her ire. He was as guilty as she in this merry war between them, but he suspected her tongue was the sharper of the two.

The silence grew heavy. He must speak more. "Is such pleasant weather common at this time of year?" The weather was a safe subject, was it not?

"Only when the sun shines, Mr. Darcy." From his seat in the saddle, he could see her eyes light up. Yes, she enjoyed a bit of mischief. Very well.

"And does it choose to do so often?"

"As often as it pleases." Another arch look. "But in truth, we can have as much rain as sunshine. It is not unusual to have several days in succession of heavy rain. I fear that even now there are clouds gathering where we cannot quite see them."

Was she alluding to the weather? Or to this temporary entente between them.

"Ah. So I see." Another ocean of silence loomed. He must say something else. "But for the moment, it is one of the pleasantest places I have seen. It is," he joked, "almost as lovely as the darkest parts of Derbyshire."

Her shoulders stiffened and he saw her jaw tense. He had said something badly amiss.

"The darkest parts. Indeed." Now ice ran through her voice. "Then perhaps, sir, you would be best enjoying it from within the warmth of Netherfield. I am certain you would not wish to block out some of the only sun I am to see for some time. Pray tell, what of our delightful neighbourhood displeases you? For your every glance seeks only to criticise. Are the leaves not crisp enough for your pleasure? Is the smell of the earth too dark? Has the landscape offended your discerning eye?"

Heaven help him, was there no way to find peace with this lady?

"Must your every word hide a dagger, Miss Elizabeth? I do believe you delight in trying to vex me. Do you find joy in being as unpleasant as possible in my presence?"

She raised her chin to address him. All thoughts of conversation were at an end. "One is only as pleasant as one's company, sir. I beg you, one of us must leave, and since you are mounted and may move faster, I suggest that it be you."

This was as handy a dismissal as ever he had heard. "Very well, Miss Elizabeth. Perhaps, in future, if we may find such fortune, we may be better strangers."

And spurred his horse down the hill and back across the fields to Netherfield, cursing the day that first he met Elizabeth Bennet.

Chapter Four

Can the world buy such a jewel?

(Claudio, 1.1)

I t was not long afterwards, on a grey Monday morning, that breakfast at Longbourn was interrupted by the appearance of a footman with a note for Jane. "From Netherfield, Miss," the man stated before returning to his duties.

Elizabeth raised her brows in a smirk as Jane blushed a delicate pink. "Netherfield? I do wonder who could have written it!"

Her mother's interest was greater still. "Well, Jane, who is it from? What is it about? It must be from Mr. Bingley! Writing to you, and still not engaged! Young people these days! What does he say? Make haste and tell us, my love!"

Jane cast a bashful glance at Elizabeth and broke the seal.

"It is from Miss Bingley."

Her mother huffed and fell back into her chair in a cloud of lace and ruffles. "Well, read it anyway."

"Here, let me read. Miss Bingley says:"

My dear Friend,

If you are not so compassionate as to dine today with Louisa and me, we shall be in danger of hating each other for the rest of our lives, for a whole day's tête-à-tête between two women can never end without a quarrel.

"So you are to be the entertainment. How fortunate, dear sister."

"Hush, Lizzy!" Jane admonished with a small smile. "Let me finish."

Come as soon as you can on receipt of this. My brother and the gentlemen are to dine with the officers. Yours ever, Caroline Bingley.

"Oh, that is a pity," Mama wailed. "Dining with the officers! Then he shall not see you at all. Still, you had better go. Perhaps you will meet him before they depart. He might change his mind and remain to dine at home after all."

"Will you go?" Elizabeth looked out through the window. "It is quite overcast and will surely rain soon."

"They are very thoughtful to invite me. I know you do not find them altogether pleasing, but they have always been kind to me and I am honoured by the invitation. Papa, may I have the carriage?"

"Oh no, my dear!" Mama interrupted. "That will not do at all. You had better go on horseback, for if it does indeed rain, you must stay all night."

"Mama!" Elizabeth gasped. But it was soon settled. Jane was to ride to Netherfield in the hopes of the weather stranding her there until morning. And, indeed, the weather seemed eager to cooperate, for only minutes after Jane departed the threat of rain was realised and torrents of water fell from leaden skies. This rain continued through the day and into the evening; there was a certainty that Jane would stay the night at Netherfield. Mrs. Bennet was quite pleased with her scheme.

But when morning came, instead of Jane arriving in a carriage from Netherfield, a servant appeared instead with a note for Elizabeth.

My dearest Lizzy,

I am writing to you because I do not wish to alarm our parents. My horse slipped during our ride yesterday, and I have injured my ankle. I was not so long outside in the rain that I am ill, but I cannot stand or walk without pain. I do not think it anything serious, but my kind friends will not hear of my returning home while I am so injured, and insist upon my seeing Mr. Jones. I cannot think anything gravely the matter. Please relate to our mother and father that I am well, merely indisposed for a short while.

Your loving sister,

Jane.

"Injured her ankle?" Papa peered up from behind his newspaper. "There, Mrs. Bennet, your plan was most successful indeed. Our dear Jane shall never walk again, but you may rest happy in the knowledge that it was in pursuit of Mr. Bingley."

"Oh, pish, Mr. Bennet! One does not become lame from a turned ankle. No, better, she shall sit prettily upon a chair by the fire, and Mr. Bingley will sit at her side and read poetry to her. There is nothing like poetry to bring two people together. They will be engaged in a fortnight, you may count upon it."

Elizabeth shook her head. "Whatever Mr. Bingley does or does not read to her, she surely needs me to look after her."

"Is that my cue to summon the carriage?" Papa asked.

"No indeed! The rains have stopped and I am in want of exercise. I shall walk."

"You will be in no fit state to see Mr. Bingley!" Mama was aghast.

"No, perhaps not, but I shall be fit to see Jane, and she cares little for the state of my hair."

Within the half hour, Elizabeth set out on her way to Netherfield at a fast pace. The fields were muddy, and the streams ran high, but she welcomed the sunshine after yesterday's dreary rain. She leapt over stiles and bounded over puddles and arrived at last at the great house with mud about her ankles and a glow of her face from the warmth of the exercise. She really was in no condition to greet the Bingleys, but the maid who let her in insisted upon presenting her to the master of the house. She followed that woman down the long hallway, cringing at the thought of the trail of mud she must be leaving behind her.

All were assembled in the breakfast room when she was shown in. Mr. Bingley sprang to his feet to greet her.

"Miss Elizabeth! What a surprise, and a pleasant one at that! I had not expected to see you so early, although we had thought you might come to see your sister. We are still at breakfast, as you see. Mr. Jones is tending to Ja... Miss Bennet at this very moment, and I hope to have a good report from him. Here, please do sit. Caroline, perhaps Miss Elizabeth wishes for a cup of tea or a muffin."

The others about the table also rose in greeting, and the two Bingley sisters said everything proper and polite, although their voices held no warmth and their eyes remained hard. Mr. Hurst, Louisa's husband, said nothing, but Mr. Darcy atoned for that man's silence.

"Perhaps Miss Elizabeth would be more comfortable waiting in the scullery until the mud on her petticoats dries. Like a country rustic, she has been walking some great distance through muck and mire."

"Darcy!" Bingley hissed. "Enough, man."

"Please, Miss Eliza, do sit." Caroline pulled out a chair for her. "Ignore my brother's friend. He is often a bear before drinking his morning coffee."

"Thank you, Miss Bingley. I shall sit only until I can see my sister. As for Mr. Darcy, I have learned to ignore much of what he says. There is only so much wit a man can offer, and Mr. Darcy's store is rather bare."

Elizabeth saw his lips tighten into a grim line as he contemplated his retort and she sat back, ready to accept his volley. But at that moment, the door opened anew and Mr. Jones entered.

Meryton had no doctor, and the apothecary tended to all minor complaints in the neighbourhood, and he served his town well. Now he peered at the assembled party at the table with an inscrutable look on his face.

"Dear sir, how is Miss Bennet? Do tell us she is well!" Mr. Bingley's concern was palpable.

The apothecary gave a small grimace. "She will suffer no lasting injury, sir, but I am afraid her injury is worse than we thought. It is not a sprain that troubles her ankle, but a break, although thankfully, not a bad one. She must not walk or attempt to use that foot, for several weeks. I have bound it with splints, and she is in little pain."

"Oh, poor Jane!" All thoughts of tea and Mr. Darcy's barbs were forgotten. "I must go to her. Can I see her, Mr. Jones?"

"Of course, of course, Miss Elizabeth. She is in the back parlour with Mrs. Nicholls. I have left her some draughts if her ankle gives her too much trouble."

He stayed to confer with Mr. Bingley, but Elizabeth had no wish to talk further. She excused herself at once and dashed through the house, as fast as decorum allowed, to find the parlour where her sister sat with her broken ankle.

"Lizzy dear!" Jane called from the chaise where she half-reclined. Her leg rested on the long seat and Elizabeth could see the white bindings of the bandage about Jane's delicate ankle. "I had not thought that you would take the trouble to come so soon."

Elizabeth nodded her greeting to Mrs. Nicholls, who bobbed a curtsey and slipped from the room, and then hurried to sit at Jane's side. "Oh, my sweet, how could I not? I cannot leave you to the

Bingley sisters' ministrations. I see they have quite forgotten you already in favour of their toast and chocolate."

"They have been very kind to me. I can only be pleased by their concern. And even before hearing this news, they have insisted that I must stay until I am well enough to walk."

"*Mister* Bingley insisted, you mean," Lizzy teased, "and his sisters merely had to agree with him, for it is, after all, his house. But a sprained ankle will heal in days; a broken one will take weeks."

"Then weeks she shall stay. Or until Mr. Jones declares her strong enough for the carriage ride back to Longbourn." Mr. Bingley stood at the doorway. "May I come in?"

Jane nodded, and he entered, taking a chair and placing it beside the one where Elizabeth sat. His usual wide grin was gone and he spoke with all care and attention.

"Mr. Jones has left. He feels strongly that you should not travel, even so short a distance as to Longbourn, until your ankle has begun to heal. The rattle of the carriage might cause further injury to your leg. And I would not hear of it! You shall most certainly stay as long as is needed. Caroline is talking to the housekeeper to set up a suite for you on this very storey as we speak, and if Miss Elizabeth wishes, she may have the adjoining room. It shall be a merry party..." He paused and his eyes widened. "By gum, yes! That is the very thing! A party it shall be." His accustomed grin began to make itself known once more upon his face. "As long as Miss Bennet is laid up and cannot move through Meryton, then Meryton shall come to her! We shall invite your sisters and friends and the officers to come and keep your spirits up whilst your ankle heals. It is the very thing!"

Elizabeth had to speak up. "You are most kind, sir, but we cannot importune your sister in this way. Let me call for the carriage, to see what kind of support we may contrive for Jane's foot. She can rest well enough at her own home, and with less trouble by far for you."

"You do hurt me, Miss Elizabeth!" She thought he was jesting. "I had hoped to arrange a party soon enough to regale my new neighbours, and this is the perfect thing for it. Indeed, by remaining here as my guests, you shall be helping me! I beg of you, for your sister's sake, to stay."

She looked at Jane, whose face was white. Her ankle must grieve her more than she had admitted to the apothecary. "I do not feel that a carriage ride would be quite the wisest thing at the moment."

With two such faces around her, one so eager and one clearly fighting pain, she had little choice but to smile and accept the invitation. She asked for some paper and in short order she had written a note to her mother, explaining the sad situation and requesting a trunk for her and for Jane. That being sent off, she sat with her sister until Mr. Bingley returned to announce their rooms were prepared, whereupon she accompanied Jane to their newly created suite.

Mr. Bingley was as good as his word. He—or rather Caroline and the indomitable housekeeper Mrs. Nicholls—had turned two of the smaller interconnected salons into a set of rooms, one allotted to Jane and the other to Elizabeth. Furthermore, some industrious servant had discovered a Bath chair in one of the attic storage rooms, and had it cleaned and prepared for Jane's use. No more would she need to be carried about the house by some strong footman. Once she was seated in the chair, Elizabeth or anybody larger than a child could push her to wherever she desired to go.

"Oh, it is rather splendid, is it not, Lizzy?" Jane asked as she sat in her new chamber. "This room is so bright, and so well situated. I believe I shall want for nothing. I shall be quite happy here until I am healed."

"You are so good, Jane! Anybody else would be complaining about the lumps in the mattress and how much your ankle hurts. It does hurt, does it not? I can see your face is pale."

Jane's eyes dropped to her hands. "Well, perhaps a little..."

"Then I shall call for Mrs. Nicholls to prepare one of Mr. Jones' draughts and you can have a rest."

"Yes! I shall feel much more the thing later. There is the bell-pull to call her."

This was accomplished. Within a few minutes, a short and cheerful maid bustled into the room; she was gentle with Jane and efficient, and before long Jane was settled drowsily in the bed that had been brought down, her glass of laudanum empty on the table at her side. She would sleep for a while.

Elizabeth walked through the connecting doorway to explore her own room. As in Jane's, some strong servants had brought down a bed and wardrobe for her use, and a table with a washstand had been set up in the corner. The sofas and chairs that usually sat in this space must be upstairs in the room where the bed usually stood. There was a large window that allowed in all the sunlight a bright November day could supply, a small selection of books on a low table against one wall, and a comfortable-looking armchair that matched the yellow curtains. A second door led directly into the passageway, allowing her to enter her rooms without disturbing Jane. It was, she had to admit, most convenient and well set out.

With Jane asleep, she had the luxury of solitude. She selected a book and curled up in the chair to read, but her stomach soon reminded her that she had eaten only a little breakfast at Longbourn several hours before, and nothing at all since arriving at Netherfield. Perhaps there would be something left in the breakfast room—a roll or a spot of tea. She found a thread to mark her place in the book and wended her way down the hallways.

The breakfast room was empty, and the sideboard had been cleared, but a footman discovered her plight and said he would request a tray. "If I may suggest the back parlour, Miss. It is presently unoccupied and is a pleasant place to sit and read." Of course! She still held the book in her hand.

She smiled her agreement and made her way once more through the hallways of Netherfield. It seemed that the parlour had been untouched since she sat with Jane there some time ago. A scrap of muslin bandage was still sitting in a messy bundle on a side table, and a half-empty glass of water sat abandoned on the low table beside the sofa. Sunlight streamed in through the window, and Elizabeth settled herself upon that same chaise where Jane had reclined earlier, there to read her book and await her tray.

She was at the point in the story where a half-seen shape drifted across the empty graveyard when a sound caught her attention from beyond the large window. She looked up to see none other than Mr. Darcy on the terrace outside. He was partly turned away and his face looked red. When he caught her eye, he spun his great head about and stalked quickly away. Had he been watching her? For what possible reason would he wish to do that? He found nothing of merit in either her appearance or her character—that was a certainty! He was quick enough to tell her at every opportunity, after all, and constantly sought to uncover every flaw he could find.

Her eyes lingered on his retreating back until he disappeared from sight. He cut a good figure in his well-tailored clothing. He must have a valet whose entire purpose was to dress the master to his best advantage. Today he wore a coat in the most fashionable shade of green, altogether too smart for a country estate, if not, perhaps, quite elaborate enough for the finer parts of Town. His pantaloons, too, were of the ideal fabric and cut to stroll down village lanes in the best of style (not that a lady ever thinks about a gentleman's garments below the waist), and he wore them with the comfort and elegance of a man who feels out of place nowhere. His boots were tall and spotless, and he walked with a rare elegance of motion. Were he in possession of a better character, he would be a fine example of a man.

Even that arrogant face, so proud and aloof, was admirable to look upon. His features were strong without being rough, and what few imperfections might have been left to him by nature were well smoothed away by a valet with a good eye to fashion and grooming. What a pity that so uncharming a man should be so handsome. It seemed quite a cruel jest on the part of Mother Nature. Elizabeth gazed out the window in the strange hope that he might reappear.

"Is everything to your satisfaction, Miss Eliza?" A voice drew her attention back from Mr. Darcy's not unappealing physique.

She turned to the door. "Thank you, Miss Bingley. I am most pleased. You have been exceedingly gracious."

"And dear Jane? How does she do?" Oh, so they had moved to the intimacy of first names!

"She is well enough. She does not complain, but I saw her ankle was troubling her still. She took a draught and is asleep." She paused. Caroline did not enter the room, but neither did she move from the doorway. "I am afraid this is not what you hoped for when you sent your kind invitation yesterday. You wished for one guest for an evening, and now you have two for much longer."

"So it would seem." The words were cold, but then Caroline gave a smile. "Do not fret, Miss Eliza. The house is quite large enough for any number of guests, expected or not, and we shall not be in each other's way any more than we wish to be. I hope you will be happy here, you and your sister. My brother has, I believe, told you of his plans to entertain." Again, the smile was there, but the lady did not seem pleased.

"Indeed he has. I tried to disabuse him of them but..."

"But he has an idea in his head and will not be swayed. He has always been that way. He decides upon one course of action and nothing can deter him until another idea comes upon him, and then at once he runs in that other direction. And so, if it is a house party that Charles wants, a house party he shall have."

Her eyes flickered to Elizabeth's book. "I see I have interrupted your reading. Pray, do not let me disturb you. Ah... here is Annie with some tea. Until later, Eliza." And she was gone.

Chapter Five

A skirmish of wit

(Leonato, 1.1)

arcy stalked the gardens. He had gone out to walk through the park immediately after breakfast and had stopped to sit on the terrace before returning to his rooms when he noticed somebody in the back parlour. He peered inside to see who it might be. Caroline was most often busy with the housekeeper in the mornings, and Louisa seldom reappeared until well after noon. It must, therefore, be Miss Jane Bennet, for the harridan Elizabeth would surely remove herself from Netherfield as quickly as ever she could. She could well have departed in the carriage whilst he was out on his walk. It was evident that she wished to be in his company as little as he wished to be in hers.

That thought sat ill with him somehow, although he knew not why.

And so he glanced inside, thinking to see Jane. But it was not her at all upon the chaise longue, but rather, Elizabeth herself. She was half-leaning against the side with her knees tucked up on the long, cushioned seat, one foot showing from beneath her skirts, now thankfully dusted clean of this morning's mud. Her eyes were fixed upon the book in her lap, and one hand toyed with the deep maroon tassel that decorated the pillow beside her. The room was dark when compared to the bright sunshine outside, but she was close enough to the large window that the sunbeams crept through the glass to catch the highlights in her hair.

She looked so innocent. Lovely, even. Something deep inside him thrilled at the sight, and he quashed it as soon as he was aware of it.

Attracted to Elizabeth Bennet? Never! But how appearances could deceive. There was a serpent's heart hidden beneath that lovely face.

He gave a snort, and she looked up at once and shook her head, sending tendrils of hair springing around her face. Damnation! He had been caught.

He had turned his back and strode away, and had been pacing the gardens since.

"Darcy!" He heard his name called from the terrace. Bingley came trotting down from the house to join him. "Dash it, man, I have been searching high and low for you. Are you not cold? No?

Then let us walk. Fine day. What grand weather. This country has the brightest sunshine, do you not think? Ah, I have news. You left before we decided upon our plans, but I am most prodigiously pleased. It was almost as if it were planned... but no, I should never wish ill upon Miss Bennet."

Bingley fretted and walked on ahead, hands stuffed deep into the pockets of his coat.

"What plan, Bingley? Is this something of which I should know?" Darcy hurried to catch up with his friend.

The younger man's smile reappeared. "Oh, of course! I have not told you. The party. The house party, that is! When I heard that Miss Bennet could not travel home, I invited her to remain here until she is well enough for the carriage home, and to keep her spirits high, I have decided to host a sort of house party. We shall invite all the local society and the officers to come and keep her company so she shall not become downcast, and we shall have a merry time of it. Is it not a fine scheme?"

Darcy went cold. "It is... a scheme, indeed."

"And the best part," Bingley continued blithely, "is that her sister Elizabeth is to stay as well to help care for her. What a sweet heart that girl has. I cannot imagine Caroline walking through fields to care for me, nor to offer to tend me in my illness."

He stopped in his tracks. "Elizabeth? Elizabeth Bennet staying here for some time?" Oh Good Lord! This was not good news at all. He stifled a groan.

"You will try to be polite, will you not?"

The majestic head shook in offence. "I? Not be polite? I am a gentleman, the grandson of an earl. I am always polite."

Bingley cocked his head and raised his eyebrows.

"Well, almost always. Bingley, that woman tears at me as if her words had claws. I cannot look upon her but feel the barbs in my skin. I often check my arms to ensure they are not bleeding when I leave her presence. She scolds like a fishwife."

"Come, the wind is colder than I like. Let us return to the house. I do not understand you at all, my friend. I find her absolutely charming."

"Charming? Hah! I would as soon call her a wit!"

The words were out before he could stop them, but that same shiver that had bothered him earlier thrilled through him now. She had a great deal of wit, that annoying creature. It was barbed and aimed at his pride, but she was clever and quick. And too pleasant to look upon for his comfort. He snorted again.

They had reached the terrace, and only now did Darcy notice that the window to the parlour was open. Was she still inside at her book? His answer came at once as her voice penetrated the air.

"Indeed, Mr. Darcy knows all about wit. He has a plentiful lack of it by the quality of his slander." Bother. She had heard him, and he had insulted her again. Now she would, of course, let fly all her arrows straight towards him. Would there be no end of trouble with this annoying woman?

There was movement inside and in a moment she stood at the window, the better to hear and be heard.

"Please, Miss Bennet, do not vex my friend. He is not always at his finest in new company." Poor Bingley sounded rather desperate and had Darcy not been so irritated at Elizabeth, he might have laughed.

"I shall stand down, Mr. Bingley. I have little desire to spar with Mr. Darcy, for his conversation has little of merit to it. I have better ways to pass my time."

Darcy began to see red. He fought to keep his temper under regulation. "Really, lady, I must protest this constant harassment! Have you nothing better to do than throw your crude insults my way?"

"Perhaps, sir, you would do better to find better places to be than where you may hear what I have to say. Others enjoy my company; if you find it objectionable, I suggest the fault lies with you and not with me."

"Perhaps I merely have greater discernment than the crude type you are accustomed to consorting with."

"Darcy! Miss Bennet!" Darcy had never heard Bingley raise his voice thus. The man sounded almost angry. He startled at the sound. "I must protest! You are my guests, and I am delighted to have you both under my roof, but this bickering must end. You need not like each other, but at least make some attempt at civility. Dash it, I sound like my own mother talking to my sisters. Can you not try to be, if not friendly, then polite?"

Through the window, Darcy saw Elizabeth frown. "I shall attempt it, if this... Earl of Insults does not harangue me with his slander."

"As shall I, should Lady Disdain keep her ill-founded opinions to herself."

Bingley rolled his eyes heavenward. "Then let us find our way to some refreshments, Darcy. Perhaps a tankard of ale will blunt your sword."

As they walked away, Darcy thought he heard his nemesis murmur, "It cannot do any more damage to the sharpness of his wits."

The brewery at Meryton produced a good sort of ale, and Netherfield had a healthy supply of it. After a tankard, served with a plate of salty cheese, Darcy felt in better regulation of his temper. Wishing to think no further about Elizabeth than he must, he turned the conversation to other matters. They talked of the fine autumn weather, the society to be found with the recent arrival of officers for the militia regiment, and the neighbourhood in general.

Little to Darcy's surprise, Bingley was delighted with everybody he had met. "You really ought to have taken the time to converse with Mrs. Long," he said between sips of beer. "She seems a simple old lady, but she was in Paris when the troubles began and the tales she tells are beyond anything to be found in one of Louisa's horrid novels. Her recollection is exemplary—"

"Or she is excellent at fabricating detail."

"—and she escaped from the city as much by luck as by design." He took a bite of cheese. "And then there is Mr. Robinson, who, as a young man, studied art in Italy. He is most knowledgeable and has some very interesting opinions on new farming techniques."

"You have decided to stay in Hertfordshire, then? It seems the neighbourhood pleases you."

"As it would you if you gave it more of a chance."

"Bingley, you wound me. I have come to help you establish yourself, not convince you to leave. It is not quite to my tastes, but if you are satisfied, then I am happy for you."

"She is wonderful, is she not?" His eyes were round, his smile lopsided.

Darcy swallowed some of the strong ale. "Ah. I thought this might be the true root of your opinions. Miss Jane Bennet. Yes, she is very beautiful."

"She is an angel! And so sweet, so amiable. Her every thought accords with mine exactly. Never have I met anyone like her." He drifted off, his eyes staring into some space Darcy could not see.

"Must I remind you, Charles, you said almost these exact words about Miss Mardson only last summer in London."

"You must have mistaken me, Darcy. She was nothing to Jane. A pleasant, pretty girl, perhaps, but nothing more." He turned to face his friend directly. "Do you think she likes me?" Those dreamy eyes were now pleading.

Darcy took a deep breath. He had not been paying as much heed to Miss Bennet's intentions as his friend might have wished. "It is not my place to say, Charles. You have been in company with her a great deal more than have I."

"But you must have some impressions..."

Another sigh. "She is charming, I own it. But recall, she is charming to everybody. Her smiles are liberally bestowed. I do not know the lady well enough to detect any particular affection one way or another, but I would advise you to guard your heart until you know hers better."

"Then you believe she cares little for me?" How quickly Bingley's moods changed, one minute elated, and the next dejected. The beer had weighed heavily upon his spirits.

"No, no, my friend. I did not say that. But I urge prudence. Watch her, listen to her, and be guided by her actions."

Bingley nodded and drained his tankard. "Very well. I shall do so. But... Do you think it wise that I consider marriage? In general, that is."

"Miss Bennet has you pondering matrimony? It is a laudable state, to be sure. A man should marry if he meets the person who can make him happy."

"You have never talked of marriage. Do you not approve of the institution?" Bingley cradled his tankard in both hands.

"I am hardly an old man. Seven-and-twenty is not past the age when most men take a wife."

"But will you marry?"

Darcy closed his eyes and let out a slow breath. He had no wish for this conversation.

"It is not something I have considered for myself, never having met the woman who would suit my requirements. I suppose I should at some point, for Pemberley needs an heir, but even that is not necessary. The estate is not entailed. I may leave it to whomever I wish. To Georgiana's sons, should she have such, or to my cousin Richard, or to the housekeeper if I am of that turn of mind.

"No, right now, I have no thoughts of marriage at all. It shall be a long while before anybody calls me Will Darcy, the married man. I am satisfied in my single state."

They did not meet again until the party gathered before dinner. Darcy had gone to his rooms to read whilst Bingley met with the stable master, and he had not ventured beyond his doors until he was washed and dressed and ready to face society. He descended the stairs a bit later than was his habit—why had his valet been unable to tie a suitable cravat this evening?—and the drawing room was abuzz as he approached the doorway. He slowed his steps to peer through before setting foot into the room.

Miss Jane Bennet, it seemed, was well enough to dine with the family. She was pale, but her face looked untroubled as she sat in her Bath chair near the fire. Beside her on the sofa, Caroline Bingley was showing her a series of scenic cards from Italy, and on her other side on a wooden chair, Elizabeth laughed at something amusing that one of the other ladies had said. The carriage with the ladies' trunks must have arrived from Longbourn earlier in the day, for both Bennet sisters were perfectly attired for dinner, with not a speck of mud on Miss Elizabeth's skirts. It was a charming picture.

Elsewhere in the room, Bingley stood arguing some point with Hurst near the side table, and in the far corner Louisa played some pleasant lilt on a delicate spinet. Was this the calm before the storm?

Darcy slipped inside, not wishing to disturb these arrangements, and walked over to the men to join their conversation. He did not quite know what they were debating—was it the merits of raising tariffs on wool? Or were they discussing using old horses for meat in the manner of the French? It mattered little. Nobody would recall a word after dinner.

"You spent a profitable afternoon, Bingley?" he asked at last.

His friend smiled and recounted the decision to purchase such-and-such a quantity of fodder. Hurst's eyes glazed over with boredom. "And you, Darcy? Did you read that account of the wars you brought with you? Good, good. I have no head for that myself;

I never can bring myself to read. I have no patience for it; I would rather be active. Perhaps later Louisa might play a dance, but, oh, dash it! Miss Bennet will not be gracing the floor for some weeks. Still, some bright melody will suit us all well."

Bingley lowered his voice. "You will be polite to Miss Elizabeth, will you not? Caroline gets quite put out to have unpleasantness at a meal."

"I have given my word that I shall try." There was little point in making promises that he might be unable to keep. But he could make the attempt.

"That's very fine then. We can make a merry party indeed if you will allow it. Oh, Miss Bennet is looking my way. Excuse me, gentlemen." He spun about on his heels and hurried over to where the ladies were sitting.

At his approach, Elizabeth rose from her seat to allow him to sit close to Jane, and she walked across the room towards the tea table. Darcy watched her and, unaccountably, found himself walking to the same destination. Perhaps this would be a new start.

"Miss Elizabeth, you look very well this evening."

She eyed him with suspicion, but curtseyed nonetheless. Her movements were graceful.

"Thank you." She looked him up and down. "That coat is a becoming colour on you. The pin in your cravat is handsome."

He fingered the sapphire within its filigree setting. "My sister selected it for me. I am partial to it as much for the giver as for the gift." What on earth had convinced him to talk about his sister? He awaited the onslaught. But instead, Elizabeth's eyes softened.

"She has fine taste. Is she younger than you?"

He allowed himself a slight smile. "She is indeed younger by several years, but her tastes are sophisticated for one of her youth." He paused. What could he say that would not provoke more venom? "She is more of an age with your own sisters than with me."

To his surprise, Elizabeth laughed, and not at him. "No one would consider my younger sisters sophisticated, for all that they pretend to be older than their years. Pray, I would hear more of Miss Darcy."

This was a surprise indeed! But it was a pleasant one, and the smile that teased his lips expanded. There was a great deal he could not tell, but there was enough that he could. "Her name is Georgiana. She is, at present, residing with my aunt and uncle at their estate in the north. They have a fine music master for their young grandchildren, and Georgiana studies with him as well. She is a gifted musician, quite excels at the pianoforte."

Silence. She was not baiting him, nor provoking him, and so he dared another question. "Do you play, Miss Elizabeth?"

She laughed again, a sweet sound from such a cruel lady. "Aye, sir, but only a little, and not very well. Shall you scorn me for that?"

"No, not at all! I—"

At that moment, Louisa started to play a Scotch air he knew well on the spinet. An idea struck him. He had promised to be civil to Miss Elizabeth Bennet. Well, what was more civil than asking her to dance?

"I say, this is a sprightly tune. Do you not feel a great inclination to seize such an opportunity of dancing a reel?"

She gaped at him and then began to laugh. This was not the sweet amusement of a moment ago, but something angrier.

"What have I said that amuses you so?"

She considered him through narrow eyes. "I confess I could not immediately determine what to say! You wanted me to say yes, that you might have the pleasure of despising my taste in music and dance, for we have already determined that I have no particular talent at music. Furthermore, I am certain that in the haute society in which you most often move, such dances are far below you. But I delight in overthrowing those kind of schemes and cheating a person of their desired contempt. I have therefore made up my mind to tell you that I do not wish to dance a reel at all. Now despise me if you dare!"

The affront! Nobody refused Fitzwilliam Darcy when he offered a dance. And there was nothing that aroused his ire as much as when his pride came under assault. His temper started to boil, and rational thought dissolved as he made his reply.

"You had dared me to despise you long before this, I must say. With your very first words to me, you flung down the gauntlet."

She pulled herself to her full height, backbone as rigid as any of his cousin Richard's bayonets, and the flush of emotion that made her cheeks rosy now suffused her soft neck and creamy decolletage. Darcy fought to keep his eyes above her shoulders. The heat that ran through him was not only born of indignation.

"My first words to you, sir, were spawned only by your first words to me. You sought to catch my attention and then flung cruel slander at me. If I responded badly, it was only in kind." She thrust out her chin, a veritable challenge.

His jaw clenched. Being true to his word was more difficult than ever he had imagined; but he had only promised Bingley that he would try. No sane man could stand firm against this manner of provocation.

"I did not offer those words to you. If your pride was wounded, it was because you listened where your ears were not intended to be."

"A gentleman would never have uttered such words at all, to be heard or not by their intended victim or by anybody else. And I repeat, Mr. Darcy, you are no gentleman."

"I say, Elizabeth, you are a virago!"

"Men were scarce and more than one lady was in want of a partner. But we were too far below you and you cared little about pleasing your company."

"There is little choice among rotting apples, Miss Bennet! There was not a person in that hall with whom I would have wished to dance." How untrue this sounded now, in retrospect. But at the time, he had thought it so.

"And yet," she countered, "you only now asked me for a reel. And so you lie, sir. You lied then or you lie now. But if we are to talk of apples, I would put a word in your ear; if you find such a one that will take you, bind her quickly, for you yourself are not an apple for all markets. Now, if you will excuse me, I shall turn pages for Mrs. Hurst."

She turned on her heel and left him without another word.

From her chair by the fireplace, Jane stared at her sister in dismay. "How unlike Lizzy that is. Why can those two not stop fighting? I grow quite weary of it." Her face was serene, but she wrung her hands in her lap. "If I could walk, I should go over now and urge her to soften her words."

Her companion shook his head. "I have spoken to Darcy, or rather, I tried. I have never known him to be so sharp. He can be aloof and arrogant, to be sure, but not bitter. And I have never seen him be so rude."

"Mr. Darcy is a hard man to know. He seems so cold and superior, and yet you are intimate friends with him. He must have a great many good qualities. I wish Lizzy would learn to seek them rather than to constantly enumerate his shortcomings. Which," she hastened to add, "I am certain are few."

"He is a most diligent friend, loyal and trusting, and when he has one's interests at heart, nothing can stop him. He is proud, perhaps, but he has reason to be so, and for all his pride I do not believe him to be vain. Rather, he feels the weight and responsibility of his position, and strives to live up to what is expected of him. He is a fine person to have as an ally, but I would not wish him as a foe." He followed Jane's gaze to observe the two opponents deliberately ignoring each other across the room. "I do not quite know what Miss Elizabeth has done to earn his enmity. I shall ask him again tomorrow and beg him to leave her in peace."

"As shall I of my sister." Jane gave a small shiver and Bingley hurried over to fuss about her, summoning one maid to build the fire and another to find Miss Bennet's shawl, and thus they were occupied until the bell rang to summon them in to dinner.

Chapter Six

We shall have revelling

(Don Pedro, 1.1)

E lizabeth spent a restless night. Jane had assured her that she was in no discomfort from her broken ankle, but Elizabeth knew her sister too well to believe her. Jane's pale face had only grown whiter as the evening progressed, and by the time the company retired for the night, she looked positively drawn. She protested that she was well, and it took a great deal of persuasion, but eventually Elizabeth was able to convince her to take another dose of Mr. Jones' draught. But even whilst her sister slept, Elizabeth could not rest from concern. And, perhaps, from consternation at being under the same roof as Mr. Darcy.

He was perplexing and confounding and thoroughly annoying, and for some reason, she found herself anticipating their next confrontation. Never before had she engaged in so bitter a battle of wits, but at the same time, never had she had so worthy an adversary. She wrestled with her covers all night, despite the bed being comfortable and warm, and finally fell into a fitful sleep only as she heard the first rustles of the servants starting their morning routines.

It was, therefore, far later than was her habit when at last she awoke. Sounds from the adjoining room suggested that Jane, too, had risen, and she hurried through the door to see to her sister's welfare.

Jane was indeed awake and dressed, and Annie, the cheerful maid, was ready to help Elizabeth dress for the day. "Shall I bring a tray, Miss? Mr. Bingley says he expects the first guests to arrive by noon."

Of course! The house party. Caroline had spoken at length last night about the various activities she had been planning with Mrs. Nicholls, and since the aim of the party was to entertain Jane, Jane must appear.

The sisters conferred silently. Years of practice allowed the tweak of a brow here and the twitch of a shoulder there to communicate everything they needed to say to each other without their mother—or servants—being wise to their intent. "A tray here will do very nicely. Let me dress and then we can take our breakfast."

And thus it was that Elizabeth did not see Mr. Darcy all morning, which matter greatly helped her digestion. Jane was feeling much improved and insisted that she was quite happy to sit in her chair and be entertained. The ladies moved to that same back parlour that was so full of light, and with a tray of tea at one hand and a basket of embroidery and books at the other, assured Caroline Bingley that they would be quite content. The sun was not quite as bright as the day before, but it still shone merrily through the window, bathing the room in its warm glow as the morning passed and guests began to trickle into the house.

Charlotte Lucas was the first to arrive. As a particular friend to both sisters, she had arranged with Mr. Bingley to arrive early, before the other guests were expected. She cooed over Jane and expressed all due concern about her health and comfort and then settled in for a cosy chat with the Bennet sisters. Mrs. Bennet and her three younger daughters came next.

"Are you well, Jane? How clever of you to break your ankle, so you have to stay for so long! You must be certain to make the most of this, my dear. If you are not engaged by the time your foot heals, I shall be most distressed. Most distressed indeed!"

"Really, Mama!" Elizabeth chided, but her mother would not be stopped.

"She merely cares about me," Jane soothed later on when her mother had departed, "and wishes me to be well settled."

Mary had little to say other than the customary words of comfort, and she took a seat where she remained all morning. Kitty and Lydia made some noises of concern for their older sister as their mama had surely demanded they do, but soon began to roam about the room, commenting on this or that piece of the decor until a sound from the back garden caught their attention.

"Mama! La! An entire regiment of officers!" Lydia ran to the window as a small parade of smartly uniformed men wandered up from the path towards the house. "They are so handsome in their scarlet coats. Look, there is Denny, and Captain Carter, and look, that handsome man we met, Mr. Wickham!"

"Tut, Lydia," Kitty sounded superior. "I have it from Miss King that Mr. Wickham is now a lieutenant! How well that sounds."

"He is most agreeable, is he not? So well favoured and charming."

"I admired many a man in a red coat when I was a girl." Mrs. Bennet joined her younger daughters at the window, and all thoughts of Jane were soon forgotten, for there were officers to admire.

"Lizzy?" Jane whispered as her mother and sisters compared one officer to another. "Mr. Wickham seemed to like you when we met in Meryton. He certainly seemed eager to talk to you."

"So he did. He is very charming, is he not? Very much the gentleman, quite unlike a certain other man we have recently met."

"Are you certain you have taken the correct measure of Mr. Darcy? He cannot be altogether as bad as you imagine him to be. Mr. Bingley says he is a most estimable man."

Elizabeth's eyes flickered up to ensure Mama and her younger sisters were not attending this quiet discussion. "I have taken all the measure of Mr. Darcy I need take to assure myself that I do not like him. But I confess, I do not quite know what to make of him. I have such different accounts of him. Miss Bingley lauds his every breath, although her motives are clear. Mr. Bingley considers him a friend, and Mr. Bingley is so pleasing a person I cannot imagine him needing to seek companions however they come. And yet, to me, Mr. Darcy is quite the opposite of everything I would expect Mr. Bingley to seek in a friend. His worst fault, I believe," Elizabeth laughed, "is that he finds nothing to admire in me! If he liked me at all, I might find him more admirable myself."

"What are you laughing about, Lizzy? Have you heard news of some of the officers?" Mama turned her attention from her giggling younger daughters. "Oh, look! Here they come now. Stand up, stand up. Not you, Jane."

A group of six officers filed into the room with their dashing red coats and friendly smiles. There were Captains Denny and Carter, Colonel Forster, two others whom Elizabeth had not yet met, and Lieutenant Wickham. If he had cut a fine figure before in his civilian clothing, how much smarter he looked today in officer's red! Mr. Bingley came in last to see to his guests' comfort; of Mr. Darcy there was not a sign. Elizabeth sighed in relief. But what was that glimmer of disappointment that lurked beneath her satisfaction? Surely she was not anticipating matching wits with that... unpleasant person again.

Greetings were exchanged and more tea ordered, and the officers soon found seats about the room. As Captain Denny flirted with Lydia and Kitty, and as Captain Carter and Mr. Bingley sat by Jane to ascertain her thoughts on charades, Lieutenant Wickham took the seat next to Elizabeth.

He spoke easily and without conceit and praised the house, the countryside, and all its inhabitants. "And of all the beauty I have discovered in these parts," he purred, "none surpasses what I see in this room before me. But come, Miss Bennet, what does a charming lady such as yourself do for entertainment during the colder months? I shall be mostly busy at my duties with the regiment, but there must be some allowance for diversion."

"Oh, that there is, and aplenty. I know not what Miss Bingley intends for the cold winter months, but Sir William often surrounds himself with company, and my own mother enjoys nothing more than to entertain of an evening at Longbourn, my father's estate."

"Is it in the vicinity? I have seen so little of the area."

"A mere three miles from here across the fields," she gestured vaguely in the appropriate direction, "and a little more by the lanes. We are only a mile from Meryton, where we met the other day."

"Yes, yes." He seemed distracted. "I am afraid I was not quite at my best on that day, for I had just then seen someone I never thought to see again. I must ask..." he started. Then he paused and looked about to ensure they were not overheard before blurting out, "I must ask how long Mr. Darcy has been staying here."

"It is, by now, about a month. He has an extensive property in Derbyshire, I believe. I wonder that he is not there instead."

"Yes," replied Wickham. "His estate there is a noble one; you could not have met with a person more capable of giving information on that head than myself, for I have been connected with the family since my infancy." He took a piece of the cake on his plate. "You look surprised, Miss Bennet. Do you know Mr. Darcy well?"

"As well as ever I wish to be!" Elizabeth felt her cheeks grow warm. What was it about Mr. Darcy that set her every nerve afire? Even the mention of his name left her shifting about in discomfort.

"I find him a very disagreeable man." She clenched her jaw and fought for composure. "Do my thoughts not align with your own?"

"I have no right to give my opinion as to his character, for I have known him too long and too well to be a fair judge. Is he well liked in Hertfordshire?"

"Other than in this very house, I can assure you that he is not. Everybody is disgusted with his pride, and few will speak favourably about him."

"I cannot imagine he is much troubled by that, or if he even knows of it," Wickham sighed and took another piece of cake. "Wherever he goes, the world is either blinded by his fortune or is frightened by his imposing manners. How wise the people of Hertfordshire are to see him as he truly is. And does he stay long?"

Elizabeth huffed. "Longer than I should wish! How I will survive being in this house with him whilst my sister heals, I cannot say. There is a sort of merry war between us, and neither of us will come out the victor, for we are both torn to shreds at each battle's end."

Wickham put down his tea and leaned forward. "Then I must tell you something." He looked around the room, his eyes settling on one person at a time before moving to the next. "It is a fine day outside. Would you care to walk in the gardens?"

Elizabeth agreed and found her hat and coat and met Wickham at the door to the garden. A gentle breeze blew, sending dry leaves scurrying and whirling about their feet as they strolled near the house, but Elizabeth saw almost nothing of these, so enrapt was she in the tale that Mr. Wickham told.

He was, he explained, the son of old Mr. Darcy's steward, and had been brought up in the great house alongside Will—the present Mr. Darcy. "His father was one of the best men that ever breathed, but the son... alas, his behaviour to me has been scandalous."

He had, Mr. Wickham went on, intended not to enter the militia but rather the Church, for he had been promised a valuable living attached to the Darcys' estate of Pemberley. But instead of it going to him, as the late Mr. Darcy had offered, when the living came empty under the son's tenure, it was given elsewhere.

"Good heavens!" Elizabeth's ire grew. How very like the man she had come to dislike so much. Or was it? He was haughty and rude to everybody in the neighbourhood save Bingley's party, but she had never seen him be spiteful, and never seen him be dishonest. What had Bingley said? That he was most loyal? How could he be loyal to his father's memory if he had done this? She must know more!

"How could he do this? Was the bequest not in the late Mr. Darcy's will? Why did you not seek legal redress?"

Now Mr. Wickham shuffled his feet. "It was... that is... It was not quite so simple." He seemed to be thinking of what to say. "That is, there was just enough informality in the terms of the bequest as to give me no hope from the law. It was a matter of honour... which Mr. Darcy chose to put aside, or to consider it a conditional recommendation. He asserted—can you believe this?—that I had forfeited all claim to it. I feel the point sorely."

"But did you not study for the Church? Would he have disregarded his father's wishes so baldly?"

"I did attend university but did not directly pursue orders. But I should have, had I known the living would come vacant so soon.

No, I am afraid the crux of the matter is that Mr. Darcy and I are very different sorts of men, and that he hates me."

Something of this matter sat ill with Elizabeth, but she still inquired, "Can he not be disgraced publicly for his actions? If others knew of his father's wishes..."

But Wickham shook his handsome head and stared ahead with stoic fortitude. Elizabeth was reminded of nothing so much as an actor upon a stage. "At some point he will be, but not by me. Until I can forget his father, I can neither defy nor expose him." And he had nothing more to say on the matter, turning the topic instead to the colour of the leaves and the prospect of rain over the next several days.

"What did you make of his confession?" Jane asked later. The guests had all departed before dinner, and the sisters had foregone cards and music afterwards in preference of some quiet time to talk and an early retirement. She sat in her bed as Elizabeth fussed about the room, making certain Jane had everything she might need during the night.

"There is a cup of water, Jane, and some of Mr. Jones' draught if your ankle pains you, and here is some lotion for your hands. Shall I rub your leg above the bandages?"

"Lizzy, you are avoiding my question."

Elizabeth stopped her aimless flutterings. She put down the folded shawl she had been carrying about the room and sat down on the edge of Jane's bed.

"Oh, Jane, I do not know what to make of it. It both accords exactly with my impressions of Mr. Darcy and counters them completely. I was so happy to hear another, who has known him for so long, confirm my dislike of, well, everything about the man. And yet, Mr. Wickham's account does not sit well with me. I had never considered Mr. Darcy to be faithless. He is arrogant and rude and looks down upon everyone and everything he sees. I can hate him perfectly well whilst considering him still to be an honourable man."

"Does Mr. Wickham lie, then?" Jane stretched her leg out before her and winced.

"Sit back, dearest. Let me tend to you. Here, Mr. Jones left some arnica balm. Is that too tender? Is your foot too painful for this?" She placed all her focus on her sister's foot for a moment before answering the question.

"Mr. Wickham is very handsome and most charming of manner. It is hard to believe that a man with such an appearance of goodness can have anything of bad about him. I cannot imagine him to be telling such blunt mistruths, but perhaps…"

"Perhaps he misunderstood old Mr. Darcy's intent?" Jane asked.

"Indeed. If the matter was too unclear for a legal resolution, it may have been a thought rather than a deed, or a lapse of comprehension. And yet I still wish to dislike Mr. Darcy so very much!" Elizabeth pounded her hand against the mattress, causing Jane to take a sharp intake of breath.

"They might both have their ends of the truth. Consider, we all see matters only through our own eyes. Perhaps both are honourable in their way."

"Jane, you are so good. If only I could be as sweet as you, I might not be so disliked by—and disliking of—Mr. Darcy!"

Chapter Seven

All disquiet, horror, and perturbation

(Benedick, 2.1)

D arcy's luck ran out the next morning. He had spent the entire first day of Bingley's house party without seeing a soul not of his choosing. He had risen early and ridden back to London to take care of some matters related to his estate. For a single man on horseback, the journey was completed in only two hours, leaving him much of the day to attend to his business. After meeting with his agents, he had spent a pleasant hour visiting his aunt and sister, whom he had not seen since... since that unfortunate incident last summer. As luck would have it, his cousin Richard was also at his family's London house, being on leave for some weeks from his position in the regulars. After so long amongst the rustics in Hertfordshire, he took pleasure in his noble relations' company. What elegance there was in their fine manners, what good taste in their deportment and clothing, what understanding in their cultivated minds. And yet... he missed something of Meryton and its easy country ways.

Instead of riding back to Hertfordshire on his own, therefore, a scheme was quickly devised and executed wherein Colonel Richard Fitzwilliam accompanied him back to Netherfield, his trunks to follow the following day. They arrived in Meryton as the sun was setting, but instead of joining the gathered company at Netherfield for dinner, the cousins requested trays to be sent to Darcy's room, where they might take their meal in casual comfort.

If Caroline Bingley had any complaints about her new houseguest, Darcy did not hear them, for Bingley himself was quite delighted. He and Richard had met just once, and he crowed that he was delighted to further the acquaintance. Thus, by the time the two men had emptied the tray and a good portion of a bottle of brandy, Richard's room was ready. After the long ride to and from Town and the brandy, Darcy slept well and long, not thinking of what morning might bring.

What it brought was Elizabeth Bennet.

She was sitting in the breakfast room when he arrived, sipping her tea and talking quietly to somebody he could not see from where he stood. He thought to hasten back to his rooms and request a tray, but before he could turn, she looked up and her eyes met his.

"Good morning, Mr. Darcy." There was no avoiding the confrontation now. "Do come in. I have just made the acquaintance of your most estimable cousin, Colonel Fitzwilliam." Her voice was as sweet as treacle. And he was a fly caught in that sugary trap.

"Do come in, Will. There is coffee aplenty, and eggs the way you like them." Richard's voice came from the section of the table he could not see. Darcy stepped inside the room. There was his cousin, sitting as comfortably as in his own home, a cup and plate of food before him and a great smile upon his face. "I have had the great pleasure of conversing this last half hour with Miss Bennet. You did not tell me how charming she is. And most pleasant on the eye as well. You were quite remiss!"

Traitor!

"Yes, well... You see... Miss Bennet and I do not always agree on matters."

"One need not agree to find pleasure in a conversation," Richard returned. "Why, we have been arguing about the relative merits of French and English cuisine for this last half hour and I have never been so diverted in my life. I might even ask my mother's cook to make some changes. Come now, do not stand there like an oaf. Sit down. There are plenty of chairs."

With a sigh, Darcy did as he was bid. One must obey a colonel after all, even when he is a relation. Any hopes of the day progressing without an argument vanished like the steam wafting up from the cup of hot coffee his cousin was pouring for him.

There must be conversation. He would make the great effort. "How does your sister, Miss Bennet?"

She regarded him with suspicion in her eyes as he took his chair. "She is improving, I thank you. She slept well, and I believe her ankle no longer gives her much pain."

"I am pleased." What else could he say? He must say something. He sought for some words that would not provoke. Too much. "Did she have a great deal of company yesterday?"

Elizabeth swirled her tea in its delicate cup. "Aye, indeed she did. Our friend Charlotte—Miss Lucas—came for much of the day, and Colonel Forster arrived with a pleasant party of officers from his regiment. Do you know him, Colonel Fitzwilliam? He commands the local militia."

Richard shook his head. "Forster, eh? I have heard his name, but have not had the pleasure of meeting the man."

"There was another of his men whom you might have met." There was a glint in Elizabeth's eye that made Darcy rather uneasy. "He claims some considerable intimacy with your family. His name is Wickham."

"What?" Darcy bellowed. He slammed his cup down on the table, missing the saucer and sending waves of coffee splashing out onto the table. A footman appeared out of nowhere to clean the mess.

"Mr. Wickham spoke to me at length about his connection with you. I am afraid his tale was not entirely complimentary." Every glimmer of any imagined camaraderie between them vanished in a moment. There was, if not spite in her expression, then a definite antipathy, as if she dared him to justify himself.

"Damn him, that blackguard!" More coffee spilled.

"Darcy! There is a lady present," Richard hissed. But Darcy's dander was up and he spoke back before thinking.

"I rather doubt that, cousin. As Miss Bennet constantly reminds me that I am no gentleman, I likewise assert that she is no lady."

"Darcy!"

"Your cousin is correct, Colonel Fitzwilliam. We are neither of us pleased with the other's comportment."

"What lies did he tell you, Miss Bennet? Or did you look at his pretty face and decide to believe every word he uttered?"

"He does have a handsome face, I will readily admit. But I do not judge by appearance, but rather by character, and Mr. Wickham's seems most open and honest."

"Honest?" This came from Richard. "I would beg you to reconsider, Miss Bennet..."

Darcy struggled through the haze of fury that enveloped him to add to his cousin's assertion. "The man has not told a truth since he learned to speak! And if you believed his slander, I would think you quite a dullard indeed!"

"I, a dullard? Is that the best you can do, Mr. Darcy? Not just 'tolerable,' but scarce of wit as well? You under-do yourself."

"Are we to battle again, Miss Bennet? If a war of wits is what you desire, I shall see you on the field and draw first blood. I suggest you stand down and let your betters take the prize."

"My betters, sir? Should I see them, I shall consider it. But here I believe it is you who are outmatched. My wit is sharp, honed and wielded with skill."

"If wit is what we are to talk of, Madam, you are better supplied with earwax than brains."

"Dear Colonel," she turned to Richard. How could her voice sound so calm? "Your poor cousin is sadly mistaken about me. We talk of wit indeed, but I am afraid he is the one lacking. Indeed, most of his wits seem to have gone halting off into the countryside on one of Mr. Bingley's horses, leaving him with not one, but only a half, with which to recommend himself."

"If my wits are scarce, lady, yours are thick! As thick as the clotted cream in this dish, I dare say!"

"Miss Bennet! Darcy!" Richard began, but he was interrupted by Bingley's voice from the doorway.

"Oh dear, are they at it again? Darcy, not another word! Colonel Fitzwilliam, I do apologise. I do not know what to do about these two." He stood there looking rather like a sad puppy dog, unable for whatever reason to please its master.

"I believe I shall inquire after my sister." Elizabeth rose and dropped a curtsey to Bingley and Richard.

"And I shall be in my rooms. Do be so kind as to send a tray." Darcy glared at Elizabeth's departing back. "But, upon second thought, I believe I have lost my appetite, so no need." And when she had been gone long enough to avoid her, he went stalking off to spend the rest of the morning in righteous indignation.

"Oh dear." Bingley sat down in the seat Darcy had just abandoned. "Is this wet? Never mind. I had hoped they would find some way to rub along by now."

"Has this been going on for a while?" Richard asked. He rose to fill another plate of eggs and toast for himself.

"Since the very first time they laid eyes on each other." Bingley fell back in his chair, quite defeated. "If only I knew how to solve this problem. They will both be under this roof for some time, and they must find a way to get along." He wilted in his seat. Only a sound at the door brought him back some of his natural exuberance. "Ah, now we may be cheerful again, for here is Miss Bennet!"

Jane arrived for breakfast now, wheeled in by Annie, and looking quite lovely despite her injury. Introductions were made and pleasantries—long since lacking from the room—were exchanged.

"I saw Lizzy return to her room, full of fire and brimstone," she sighed. "I cannot understand her at all, for this is nothing like I have ever known from her."

"Nor have I seen this from Darcy," Richard replied. "It seems he has taken offence once, and will not be placated, but seeks to find more offence everywhere he looks."

"Then we need to find some way to soothe the savage beast where not even music will do."

They sat mulling over the problem for a few moments, each staring into the distance, until at last Richard sat up and slapped a hand upon the table. More coffee spilled, this time from his own cup.

"Aha! I believe I have it. As the matter stands, our friends are each convinced that the other despises him—or her—and responds accordingly. But what if we somehow contrive to turn this hatred into affection? If we can convince them that the other secretly holds some great affection, perhaps this little war will end in truce rather than bloodshed."

"Lizzy did tell me that Mr. Darcy's greatest fault is that he dislikes her." Jane batted her long lashes. Bingley was lost in the sight of it.

"And my cousin," Richard added, "is affronted by the lack of deference to his position, I am certain of it. He is very proud and greatly dislikes being belittled. Oh, he has said little enough to me, but I know him well, better even than my own brother, and I would swear upon it. If she can be led to think that he likes her—"

"And if he can be led to think she esteems him—" Bingley all but shouted.

"Then we might," concluded Jane, "bring about peace under Netherfield's roof."

"What shall we do?" asked Bingley.

Richard barely suppressed a smirk. "I have the beginnings of an idea. Allow me a day to think, and tomorrow we shall talk further." And he sat back in his chair looking like a cat well satisfied with its dish of cream and would not say another word.

"A dance! We must have a dance!" Bingley whirled about the large salon, taking in its size and proportions. "This will be the very space. We can move the sofas and put a small band in that corner, and set up tables for refreshments there. Perhaps this very night!

Caroline will curse me to her dying breath, but I know it can be done. And not merely a dance, but a masquerade! We shall all be masked, except for Miss Bennet here, who shall reign as queen and command the revellers."

Jane and Richard argued with him for a moment, but the decision was made and the planning began. Caroline and Louisa were summoned and informed about Bingley's idea, and despite their reluctance, the company were soon busy with a hundred activities. Caroline rushed off to confer with Cook about preparing suitable food, Bingley went to discuss matters with Mrs. Nicholls, and Jane, Louisa, and Richard set about writing invitations. These were not to be long, and as only twelve families were to be invited, within an hour, the task was done.

Then a small platoon of servants dispersed throughout the neighbourhood, delivering those invitations, whilst Bingley raced into Meryton to see to some supplies and to hire three or four musicians to form a band. There was a great deal of work to be done, but since no one would expect an event of London's fine standards, it was completed with a sense of enjoyment rather than panic.

All the visitors who appeared during the day to keep Jane amused were tasked with some errand or another, and then sent home to find costumes and dress, and when, at last, the impromptu ball began, it was with a great deal of mirth and good will.

Bingley had procured the local pianoforte master and a contrabass player from the village, and one of his servants proved to be proficient at the fiddle, thereby forming the band. If the musicians kept to a small number of popular dance tunes, there would be no concern about lack of rehearsal, or so the pianoforte master asserted. Cook had brought in three young girls from the village to help in the kitchens, and by evening had produced a bewildering supply of cakes, biscuits, sweetmeats and other treats for hungry dancers, as well as tureens of lemonade, negus, and punch to slake the revellers' thirst.

The floor was not chalked, but the carpets were rolled up and all the seating arranged about the edges of the large room, allowing plenty of space for a country dance or set of quadrilles, and the hurried race into the town resulted in the delivery of enough tapers to light the hall well into the early hours of the morning.

In that same spirit of informal amusement, the guests had contrived a great variety of costumes. Some had outfits at the ready from previous masked festivities, and there were shepherdesses and dominoes aplenty. A black-garbed clergyman stalked the perimeter of the room, only later to be revealed as Mrs. Childe, and Mr. Bennet surprised the company by appearing as a rather drunken-looking pirate. There was a lady's maid, a sailor, an Indian Maharajah, and a Roman empress, and several other creatures whose exact disguises were so rudimentary that none could determine what they were meant to be. But masked they were, and all were welcomed.

A tall domino in a black cloak and a full mask swept into the room and set his eyes upon an angel-like creature in piles of pale silk and a veil that concealed her features. As the band played their introductory chords, he moved towards her. He had been commanded to dance, and he knew he had been enough of a thorn in his host's side that he must obey. This vision before him made his resolution not nearly as painful as it might have been.

"My lady." He bowed before the white-swathed young woman. At least, he thought she was young. Her movements were light and spry, and there was something about how she moved her head that brought to mind an image of someone not much older than his sister. Almost like...

No! He corrected himself. Elizabeth Bennet would never laugh and float around the room like this, casting light before her and bringing smiles to every face she passed. The real Elizabeth would be heralded by a dark fog and the smell of brimstone. Surely.

The not-Elizabeth angel dipped into an elegant curtsey. "Sir." That surely was not Elizabeth's voice.

"May I request this dance? The music promises to be enthusiastic, if not polished, and my toes would be pleased for a turn on the floor." He modulated his voice and accent so as not to be identifiable by his words.

"I would be honoured. I, too, am more pleased by an imperfect performance executed with real feeling than with cold perfection." He could not see her face, but from the lilt in her voice, it seemed that she was smiling.

"Then we are quite of one mind, my lady." He led her to the dance floor and they found a place in the set. The line was short and the music quick and there was little opportunity to talk between their figures, but she moved well, with a natural grace that had clearly been trained into real elegance. He knew he was an accomplished dancer—for so he had often been told—and he imagined the two of them must look fine together on the dance floor.

He was, for the first time in longer than he could recollect, disappointed when the music came to an end and the set concluded. He walked the white angel to a chair near the window and went to procure her a glass of lemonade. Perhaps if she raised her veils he would see her face.

She accepted the drink but sipped it beneath the swath of lace that covered her face. He should bid her a good evening and seek another partner, but he was loath to leave her. His dilemma was solved when the lady herself spoke.

"You are a very fine dancer. I do not believe we have paired together before. You must not be from the village. Are you..." There was a strange note to her voice. "...a visitor to our part of the country?" she concluded after a short silence. "You surely are not from Meryton."

"You are perceptive, my lady. I cannot claim this charming town as my home. Although, with such delightful company, I might be persuaded to remain."

"And where," she countered, "does a militia officer learn to move so well on his feet?"

What? She thought him a mere militia officer, like Denny or that cur Wickham, devil take him? But he stifled his ire at once. She had meant no offence, and many a younger son of some baron or viscount made his way in the militia. It was no insult, after all, and he found a smile, although he knew she could not see his face.

"I cannot divulge that, my lady, for risk of betraying my name. But you are likewise well skilled."

"Should I not be, sir? My mother insists that every lady must know how to dance. For dancing is a sure step towards falling in love, and marriage is first upon her mind for me and... and those my age."

Ah, so she was young, as he had suspected. It would hardly do to be flirting with Lady Lucas or that boring Mrs. Long.

"Have you other accomplishments with which to recommend yourself? For surely such a charming lady as yourself must possess a great many skills and talents." Wait? Was he flirting? Will Darcy never flirted. But something in this lady brought out a playful side that he hardly knew existed.

The vision in white laughed and the sound warmed his soul. "I have few accomplishments that are beyond the ordinary. I dance, I walk, and I play a little. And I read when I can, for there is such joy to be found in a good novel. Do you read, sir? Tell me of your favourite books."

When the music began again, neither of the two noticed at all, so enrapt were they in their conversation. And if others noticed this strange pairing of the black domino and the white angel, they commented not at all, for both were in disguise and there would be no knowing whom to chastise the next morning.

From her chair on the small dais that had been set up for her, Queen Jane smiled benevolently at the dancers and whispered a word here or there to her attendants who had been present at the first schemes that morning. And Richard, seeing what Jane saw, was more and more convinced that his plan would be successful. When at last the dance ended, and the guests departed for the evening, he retired to his bed with a great smile upon his face.

Chapter Eight

One of Hercules' labours

(Don Pedro, 2.1)

"Y ou seemed to enjoy yourself at the dance last night, Lizzy." Jane was awake and sitting in her Bath chair when Elizabeth walked into her room. Elizabeth regarded her sister through sleep-heavy eyes and gave a wistful smile. No matter that Jane had retired just as late as she, and despite her broken ankle, she looked as fresh and well rested as any maiden of leisure had ever looked. Her complexion was fresh and dewy, her hair in perfect order, and not a shadow darkened her cheeks below her bright eyes.

Annie was tidying up and bobbed her greeting to Elizabeth before slipping from the room to leave the sisters to talk in privacy.

"It was a most enjoyable evening indeed! I had not thought that Mr. Bingley and Miss Bingley could bring it off, and yet they did, and most admirably too!" She came to sit close to Jane's side and lowered her voice. "I confess to no great liking for Miss Bingley, and yet her skills at preparing for such grand events cannot be disputed."

She yawned. It was not early in the morning, but the previous night's festivities had gone late and the number of hours of sleep attained were too few. She bent over to rub her one foot. "And I spent too much time in those dancing slippers. How my feet are unhappy with me this morning!"

Jane's usually serene smile took on an impertinent tinge. "You did not give your feet much rest! I saw you dance with that tall domino not twice, but three times! Do you know who he was? Surely you recognised his voice."

Elizabeth's cheeks grew warm. "I cannot say. He spoke in a sort of disguised voice with a strange accent, and whilst there was something familiar about him, I knew him not." Or, a contrary part of her mind objected, she had a rather strong suspicion of who it might have been. But this gentleman had been clever and full of wit, and rather than scorning everything and everyone, he had nothing but compliments for the music, the ball, the town, and—of greatest personal import—for her. She ignored that voice and turned her attention back to Jane.

"But he was tall and seemed well favoured. There are not so many men of our acquaintance with such attributes." Jane's voice was teasing, a subtle lilt that only Lizzy really understood.

"There are the officers, do not forget. I thought perhaps it might be one of them..."

"Mr. Wickham is tall."

"And well favoured!" Elizabeth laughed. "I could not, of course, ask his true name, and he could not tell me if I had done so, but he danced well. I should be pleased to stand up with him again, should he ever ask me. And," she added with a chuckle, "should I ever learn who he was!"

"Well, he seemed to like you well enough. He found you three times, after all! Does he know who you are?"

Elizabeth shrugged. "I disguised my voice, but I cannot say I kept the illusion very well. Still, it is sometimes hard to be heard well over the sound of the band and the other dancers. I liked him a good deal. I hope I shall learn his name soon."

Annie now returned to help wheel Jane to the breakfast room and the conversation of necessity came to an end. But Elizabeth did not cease thinking of the tall man in the domino costume who danced and talked with her so much last night.

Darcy had risen early, the better to avoid Elizabeth and her haranguing tongue. The house seemed all but abandoned as he stalked the hallways in search of his coffee and eggs, and he imagined all the others still asleep. The hastily arranged ball had been much more a success than ever he would have imagined, and the guests had departed late. But he was never a late sleeper, and despite a short night filled with dreams of the angel in white, he was awake and ready for the day.

He took his breakfast in peaceful solitude, enjoying the newspaper at leisure, and then planned his morning. The unseasonably pleasant weather had come to an end, and November's rains now threatened to dampen Hertfordshire's empty fields at any time. He was warm and comfortable and happily fed and had no wish to be soaked by some downpour whilst out in the fields, and so decided upon the library as his refuge for the morning.

The room, like the rest of the house, was empty, if a bit chilly. The temperatures had dropped overnight and there was a draught coming through one large casement window. He made note of this; Bingley would need to have that repair made before the icy winds of winter descended upon the land.

A short and cheerful maid scuttled in behind him. "Come to light the fire, sir, if you will be in here."

"Yes, I shall be here all morning."

The maid dropped her head and set about her work, and soon a bright fire crackled in the grate, filling the room with warmth and dispelling the creeping dampness. Yes, Bingley must indeed see to that window. No matter the sad state of his library, the few books he had would not do well in the damp.

He perused the shelves and at last found something to keep him occupied for several hours. It was an account of the Battle of Trafalgar that he had not yet read, and was written by a sailor who had been on Nelson's own ship. He skimmed the first two pages, and satisfied with what he saw, sought a chair in which to read the rest.

There, just past the fireplace, was a small alcove. It was large enough for a comfortable chair and footstool, and was close to the side window—not the draughty one, thank heavens—which allowed in plentiful light. Of more importance, it was hidden from the door. A person who glanced inside would not see him at all and would not bother him. Here he could read in peace.

He made himself comfortable and opened his book. But he found himself unable to concentrate on the words. His mind, instead, kept drifting to the lady with whom he had danced the night before.

Bingley had urged him to ask her for the first dance, and at first he had baulked. But memories of that unpleasant assembly intervened and he relented. He had eschewed a similar invocation at that time, and it had not ended well. He had insulted a lady—no matter that she deserved every word of it—and had been castigated in turn. Rather than feeling superior for his efforts, he had only rendered himself miserable for the remainder of the evening and had provoked Bingley's wrath, a species very seldom seen!

Thus, when his friend urged him towards the woman in white, he had nodded his acquiescence at once. And he had not been sorry for it. She had been a delightful partner, enough so that he had requested her hand twice more that evening.

It was really quite unlike him to behave thus. The scion of Pemberley must be more circumspect about inviting rumour. But here, at this masquerade ball, in his borrowed cloak and mask, he was not the scion of Pemberley. He was an anonymous figure, a man able to move about with the freedom never afforded one of his habitual status. He was, for this cherished moment, able to cast off his armour and, whilst disguised, be permitted the freedom to act as he wished to.

And he had wished to dance with the white-swathed angel. Who had she been? Once again, he reflected on how familiar she seemed in her stance and her movements, but as had he, she spoke with an affected voice, which in turn was muffled by her heavy veils. He pushed away the notion that it might have been Elizabeth Bennet, for that lady would never offer such pleasant conversation to a stranger! No, it must have been somebody else, one of her sisters, perhaps. The youngest, Lydia, was a bit of a beauty despite her tender years. And even Mary, so plain in comparison to her older sisters, might be a graceful and pleasing dance partner. Yes, that was it. It was one of the other sisters. That would explain the sense of familiarity.

So he pondered until at last his eyes drifted closed and he slipped into that timeless state between sleep and wakefulness.

How long he dozed, he could not say—an hour, or perhaps more?—when his attention was caught by a sound from the door. He sat absolutely still, hoping that whoever it was would leave quickly. But instead of his wish being granted, he heard footsteps inside the library. His jaw tightened. How unfortunate. Perhaps the person would still depart.

Then he heard a voice. Richard! And the words spoken left him quite astonished.

"So you heard it from Miss Bennet herself?" his cousin asked some other person.

"So I did. But wait: I would not have another know this." This was Bingley. There was a moment's pause, and Darcy fought an internal battle over whether or not to speak. Before he could make up his mind, Bingley continued, "There is nobody in the hallway. But we cannot be too cautious, lest we be overheard." Darcy heard the door close. Then, in a low voice, Bingley went on. "Do not repeat this, and certainly not to your cousin."

Cousin? Darcy's eyes snapped open. That could only be him! What did they have to say that involved him, and in so clandestine a manner?

"Miss Bennet told me," Bingley went on, "that her sister is quite in awe of him."

Darcy gasped, then stifled himself. It would never do to let the others know they were being overheard! He pressed himself into the back of the chair and pulled in his long legs.

"In awe? That seems rather... cold," Richard replied.

"Jane... that is, Miss Bennet, was loath to speak too freely. She is so good, she would never wish to bring harm upon her sister, even by a slipped word or mistaken meaning. But I was quite certain what she meant. Miss Elizabeth is so taken by Darcy's eminence and character that she can only respond to him with feigned animosity. She uses her words as a sort of armour to assure herself that he has no power over her, and to try to hide her esteem and admiration from him. It has," his voice dropped to little more than a whisper, "become a point of pride with her."

"She seems a lady who feels strongly. But why is she so afraid to let him know of her esteem? He is the sort of man, after all, who needs to know just how high he is held by others."

I am not! Darcy was about to shout. But he stilled himself and suffered in silence and indignation.

"Miss Bennet suggested that Miss Elizabeth could not abide Darcy's knowledge of this. She is afraid he would tease her and make sport of it, and that would be worse torment than this unrequited affection she feels."

Unrequited affection?

"But how does Miss Bennet know? Has Miss Elizabeth told her? She said not a word to me yesterday that made me even consider the idea of some affection between them!"

Bingley spoke in low tones again. "She said—and she made me promise not to tell a soul—that Miss Elizabeth is often awake all night writing long letters confessing her feelings. I had wondered why my stores of paper were running so low. But she burns them all in the morning, save one scrap that Jane... Miss Bennet found. And then, upon learning it had survived the flames, Miss Elizabeth grabbed it and sent it into the fire."

"Shall we tell Darcy?" Richard asked. "If the lady likes him, he ought to know."

Bingley was silent for some time. "I cannot think what good would come of it. He has so little liking for her that it would certainly make the war between them even worse."

"Hmmm…" Darcy knew that sound well, and could picture his cousin rubbing at his chin, as he did when he was deep in thought. "Would it not be possible that instead, he might temper his own behaviour if he knew of Miss Elizabeth's true feelings?"

"I cannot say, Colonel. You have known him far longer than I. No matter how great a friend he has been to me, he is a very private person. Perhaps we ought to consider this for some time before coming to a conclusion."

"Yes, Bingley," Richard mused, "I believe you are right. Nothing good can come of haste. They will have plenty of time to learn to come to a truce. A day or so more of this battle can hurt no one, if we can keep them apart."

There was more silence. Then Bingley spoke again. "Where is Darcy, anyway? He was not in his rooms. Could he be out riding in this weather? Let us look in the billiards room…"

A creak told of the door being opened, and the footsteps moved back through the doorway before fading into the hallway.

A great many minutes passed before Darcy was able to move. What strange thing had he heard? That Elizabeth Bennet, who uttered not a word to him except to inflict injury, secretly admired him? Esteemed him, even? Was awe-struck by him? It hardly seemed possible.

And yet, perhaps, it did make some sort of sense. He was not a vain man—although some had slandered him with that epithet— but he knew as well that he was not poorly made. He was tall and with a good form, and he had been called handsome. Furthermore, he was educated and tutored in the finer points of etiquette and deportment, and was said to have excellent taste. Of this, and of his wealth, status, and estate, he was proud. And whilst vanity was a weakness indeed, where there is a real superiority of mind or condition, pride would always be under good regulation!

And Elizabeth had seen all of this and had come to esteem the man beneath the caustic exterior. Of course she would. It spoke of her own finer feelings and discernment that she should uncover these qualities and come to admire him. If Bingley spoke true, that she covered her great regard with the insults she hurled, it only spoke to a particular sensitivity of mind. For, like a tree that encases a sweet fruit within a burred shell, she was protecting her most delicate sensibilities from the possibility of great damage.

He recalled once eating a most unusual fruit called a mangosteen, borne back from the South Seas on a spice trader's ship. It was a round curiosity, about the size of a large plum and similar in colour, but with a tough leathery skin encasing soft white bits of fruit, each encasing a nut. The fruit was not easy to enjoy at first. The skin was hard and thick and when he put a bit upon his tongue, tasted unpleasant and bitter. But the white pulp—oh, what a treat awaited the happy creature who made it past that first unhappy impression!

The texture was delicate, the flavour an exotic combination, sweet and a bit sour at once, and reminiscent of peaches and pineapple, even strawberry. He wondered briefly if such delicacies might grow well at the hothouses at Pemberley.

Like Elizabeth.

She, too, was tough and unappealing upon first encounter. She was pretty enough, despite not achieving her sister's particular beauty. No. He corrected himself. He had, at first, found her only tolerable, but despite his animosity for the lady, he had quickly come to realise that she had a special sort of beauty; she was, perhaps, one of the handsomest women of his acquaintance!

Just as the fruit—unwelcoming at first—so the woman. Exotic, tempting, evocative... when had these words become associated with Miss Elizabeth Bennet? Surely not only now, with Bingley's little speech that he was never meant to hear! Had he suspected it all along? After all, he had cut into the mangosteen to enjoy its fruit. And he had, perhaps, delved a little into the character that was Elizabeth Bennet.

Her insults were clever, inventive. Hers was a creative mind, intelligent and restless. She might, he realised with a jolt, be a worthy companion after all, perhaps even a friend!

But what ought he to do?

Should he go to her and confess what he had heard and offer his friendship? No, surely not. For she was too proud to admit her folly. She would deny it; she could insist he had misheard, or that it was a lie. She would insist he was trapped in delusions, and would torment him as surely as she feared he might torment her. He could just imagine what barbs she would throw at the state of his wits. A small thrill whipped its way up his spine.

Should he, instead, find his friend and cousin and confess his presence in the library whilst they spoke? He could hardly be blamed for being present when they were the ones who did not ensure the room was empty. If asked why he did not speak, he could claim to have been asleep in the chair until it was too late.

But that would not do either. There was surely little more they knew, and they certainly would not tell him anything other than what they had already said, and worse, it might embarrass Elizabeth should she ever learn about it. He imagined himself in that position, having his secrets aired to the world against his will, and having the object of his concealed affection hear of the case from another. He would be mortified! He could never show his face in that society again. No, it would not do.

And Elizabeth, as a woman and so much more restricted in her movements and ability to change her lot in life, would have no escape from a lifetime of pity and mockery. He could never do that to her. No matter how he disliked her, he refused to be the author of her distress. No, he could not say a word to Richard and Bingley. Far better, he considered, to remain silent and let them believe their discussion had been quite private.

What else could he do? For surely he must do something. He sat and pondered for a long while, his eyes staring out at the park through the window, but seeing nothing. The trees with their brown-gold leaves left no trace on his consciousness; the expanse of grass and bloom-bare rose bushes was a void. His entire purpose was enrapt in this great decision he must make.

At the end, when it came to him, it was simple. He would simply be nice.

Chapter Nine

Cupid's crafty arrow

(Hero, 3.1)

Charlotte came by shortly after breakfast. She brought with her a book of charades and two novels with which to amuse the invalid. Elizabeth was, as always, most pleased to see her dear friend, and the three ladies sat in comfortable amusement for much of the morning.

Then, shortly after the morning's tea tray was removed, Elizabeth yawned.

"Oh, Lizzy! You were up very late last night, and you have been so good to help me and sit with me," Jane sighed, "but you will wear yourself to a thread. Charlotte is here to keep me company. I insist that you take a rest."

Elizabeth protested, but Jane was not to be moved. "No, you shall be of no use to me if you do not rest. If I need anything, I can call upon Annie or Miss Bingley. Go to your chamber and rest for an hour. If you wish, I shall send Annie to wake you after that time. There—you just yawned again."

Charlotte cocked her head and pursed her lips. "Jane is correct. You look quite drawn. A rest will do you a world of good. I promise we shall get up to no harm." She took Elizabeth's hands. "Besides, Jane and I can then continue the conversation we began last night about who that tall man was who danced with you!"

Elizabeth joined the others in laughter. "Very well! You are both too cruel! But I admit to being a bit tired. No more than an hour, though. Do I have your promise, Jane, that you will send for me then?"

She took herself to her room and lay down on the bed and, to her surprise, soon found herself slipping into sleep.

She did not move until Annie came in a bit later to wake her up. With the maid's help, she freshened her garb and hair, and soon was ready to reappear in the public rooms of the house.

"The ladies are in the back parlour, Miss," Annie informed her. "I shall bring another tray of refreshments for you."

But Jane and Charlotte were not there. Nor were they in the breakfast room or the large salon where the ball had been held just the previous night. Elizabeth returned to the back parlour in case the two had returned, but the room was still empty. She was about to go in search of Caroline Bingley when there came a tap at the door and Mr. Darcy appeared.

How tiresome! She expected him to take one look at her and stalk away or utter something unpleasant, but instead, he bowed to her and smiled.

She gaped.

Mr. Darcy could smile?

"Miss Elizabeth," he spoke in the most elegant of tones. "I trust you are well."

"Er, yes, very well thank you." She furrowed her brow. What could this be about? Was it some manner of joke? Was he seeking some new means by which to belittle her?

"I trust you enjoyed the dance last night. Was it all to your liking?"

Was he hoping to chide her for her taste in music? "Indeed I did. Did you not?"

He smiled again. He was really quite handsome when he smiled. What a pity about his character. Although, she considered, he was being not unpleasant at the moment.

"I did enjoy the ball. Miss Bingley outdid herself." Had he ever offered a compliment to anybody before? "I particularly enjoyed the music. For so small a band, and engaged so shortly before the event, they performed remarkably well. I hear the fiddle player is a servant in this very house. I must find him and give my compliments, and perhaps a small token of my appreciation as well. Did you dance?"

"Aye, that I did, sir." What a strange conversation. She must make some effort to be polite. "Will you sit?"

He nodded and moved to the chair opposite where she was standing. He gestured for her to take her seat and then sat as well. He was smiling, polite, friendly even, and was exhibiting good manners she never knew he had. Perhaps the man was ill. Ought she to call for Mr. Bingley?

But Mr. Darcy continued. He praised the food, the size of the room, even the pleasant company to be had amongst the officers and villagers. He then lit upon the book lying upon the low coffee table and asked about it as well.

"No, it is not mine," Elizabeth replied. Aha, this was his point! He wished to trick her, only to decry her deplorable taste in literature. "I confess I do enjoy novels, but this particular book is one that Charlotte brought earlier."

"*The Old English Baron*," Darcy read the title. "I have not read this one, although I very much enjoy a good novel." He leaned back and crossed his long legs. "I rather enjoyed *The Monk*, even if I found it quite horrid. Have you read it? It is, perhaps, not quite the thing for delicately bred young ladies, but you seem to be made of stiffer stuff... Oh, do not take that amiss, Miss Elizabeth! I mean it in its best sense. But I—"

He broke off. Annie entered the room, looking red in the face and quite uncomfortable.

"Miss Bennet... I must... that is, if I may be so bold..." She shuffled her feet and stared at the ground before her.

"I am afraid, Miss Bennet, that my presence is excessive to the issue at hand, whatever it may be. I shall take my leave and bid you farewell... for now."

Darcy stood and pulled himself to his full height, then executed a most elegant bow, and with one final smile, left the room.

The man was surely mad! And yet, Elizabeth decided, she did not dislike him so much thus. Still, she must turn her attention to whatever it was Annie had to say.

"Please speak, Annie. Speak freely."

"It is only this, Miss," the young maid twisted one hand in the other, "that I just now heard Miss Bennet—that is your sister, Miss—and Miss Lucas in conversation."

"Aye... they do often converse." She tried to look friendly to encourage the maid to utter the words she knew were not yet said.

"I was... that is, I was tidying up in your bedchamber, and I heard them through the doorway. I didn't mean to listen to their words, honest, but it was impossible not to hear. And what they said..."

"Yes, Annie. Please go on. I shall not be angry."

"They were talking of you, Miss. I know it was not my place to listen, and I wondered if I should just go, but then I heard your name, and you have been so kind, Miss. I think you might wish to hear what they say, for it sounded quite alarming." She dropped another curtsey. "Begging your pardon, Miss." And she darted from the room.

Jane and Charlotte? Talk about her? About some alarming matter? Whatever could it be? She must surely find out. As quickly and quietly as her feet would allow, she hurried back through the halls to the doorway to her private room and slipped inside, then crept to the door connecting her room to Jane's. The door was ajar and sounds filtered through clearly. Indeed, as Annie had intimated, the two women were deep in some conversation.

The first she recognised was Charlotte's voice.

"What, exactly, did Mr. Bingley tell you?" She sounded quite curious.

"I really should not say," Jane's sweet voice came in reply. "It was told in confidence, and I must not betray his trust. Only..."

"Do not be so good, Jane! I dare say, you will quite undo yourself one day with your desire to be so kind and honest. I can see this secret is quite eating you up. I promise I shall not breathe a word of it, if you tell me. You have been speaking at length over your concern about Elizabeth, and now that we come to the nub of it, you must not remain silent."

"Very well..." Jane's voice dropped, becoming almost inaudible. Elizabeth knew full well that she must not listen, but the temptation was too great. Mary, she was certain, would have words of stricture from her sermons admonishing her for this eavesdropping, but Mary was not here, and her curiosity was too great. She took two more steps closer to the door and leaned in towards it.

"...he is quite hopelessly in love with her," Jane all but whispered.

Who? Who was she talking about? Who was in love with whom? Elizabeth wished she could stride in and ask, but of course she could do nothing of the sort. She remained standing half behind the door and listened further, hoping to hear more of what Jane had to say. Her wish was granted.

"You cannot be serious, Jane," Charlotte exclaimed. Her voice was easily audible, even through the door. "Mr. Darcy... in love? I can hardly credit it. He seems so cold, so void of all emotion."

"It is quite unaccountable, I admit," Jane's voice was a bit louder, "but Mr. Bingley swears it is true. Mr. Darcy is deeply in love, and with my sister Elizabeth!"

What? Elizabeth bit back a squeak born of shock. In love? With *her*? It could not be!

Charlotte seemed equally taken aback. "It is beyond reason! Mr. Darcy and Eliza? What joke is this? Is it some strange London custom that Mr. Bingley teases you thus?"

Jane's voice was quiet, but sure. "He promises it is true. He has walked past Mr. Darcy's rooms at night and heard him composing poetry, all with Lizzy's name. He speaks the lines out loud to try the sound, and then writes down what he likes. And in the morning, Mr. Bingley said he finds burned sheets of paper in the grate, as if Mr. Darcy were writing the poems on paper and then burning them. He told me last night at the ball that he had finally confronted his friend, and," Jane dropped her voice again so Elizabeth had to lean towards the door to hear, "Mr. Darcy admitted it. He is in love with my sister!"

There was a long pause. Elizabeth hardly knew what to think, how to react. She was still in shock when Charlotte spoke again, sounding quite as sensible as ever. "Then we must tell her. It is only reasonable that she know."

"Oh no!" Jane cried out. Elizabeth took an involuntary step back from where she hid behind the door. "That is what Mr. Bingley suggested I do, but I could not agree. I urged him to convince his friend to forget Lizzy entirely and learn to suffer his love in silence."

"Surely you did not, Jane! Why would you commit the poor man to such misery? If she can learn to like him..."

"Dear Charlotte, you surely know how proud Lizzy can be. She would taunt him and scorn him, and turn her wit against him even more surely than she does now. If she senses that he is at all weak, even with love for her, she would never permit herself the slightest part of kindness or mercy towards him, but would use him as the target of all her verbal arrows."

"So it is out of kindness to the poor man that you wish him to suffer in silence? This is hardly sensible!"

"How cruel that sounds! And yet, this would certainly be the lesser of the pains awaiting him."

"Would our dear Lizzy be so cruel? I know she dislikes the man, and yet hers is not a hard heart."

"Not hard, but sometimes she makes too much fun of the world. You know how she likes a laugh. If there is not one available, she will make it for herself. And from what I see of her animosity towards Mr. Darcy, I fear she would taunt him without mercy. My sister has a great heart and I love her dearly, but I must confess, I would not wish to be the victim of her tongue when she finds cause for censure!"

All of this and more, Elizabeth heard from her position by the door with a cascade of different emotions. What? Mr. Darcy in love? Impossible! That heart has no room for such tender feelings! He is as cold as a dead fish, as thick as Mr. Hurst's ragouts. But... In love... with me? How could he... but it does demonstrate his excellent taste. I can hardly fault the man for being in love with me, no matter how I have abused him. Perhaps I was correct when he came to converse earlier, and he is ill... but it is no sign of illness to find me attractive. Oh, how should I react? What should I do?

So lost was she in these torrents of thoughts that she lost some of Charlotte's next words.

"...very handsome man, and most wealthy as well. Should she find some way to return his affection, it would see her to a happily settled state."

"And he is one of Mr. Bingley's most intimate friends; for a man with such a happy character to hold him so close speaks only well of the man, despite this persistent argument. Even his pride is not quite so objectionable when one considers where he is from."

"Then we had better be cruel in order to be kind and say not a word to Lizzy. It is better, I fear, that Mr. Bingley counsel Mr. Darcy to hold his own tongue. But oh! Look at the time! Lizzy will be awake and wondering where we are. We had better return to the parlour, should she seek us there!"

And the sound of Jane's chair and Charlotte's footsteps retreated towards the door, where they were lost.

Elizabeth could not move. Little good comes to one who eavesdrops, 'twas sure, but this was news she was strangely pleased she had.

Mr. Darcy loved her. Her! Despite her cruel words and wicked barbs, he loved her. Had she heard these words from his own mouth, she never would have believed it, but if Mr. Bingley knew it from him, it must be true. He would not confess to such a thing were it false, and certainly not if he suspected that Bingley would tell Jane.

A thrill of pride ran up Elizabeth's back, and perhaps something else. Could it be... compassion? It was true that she was not a cruel person, and she never would have assailed Mr. Darcy's character had he not so sorely attacked hers. Perhaps, just perhaps, he was responding in so harsh a manner only to protect his pride.

She could not scorn him for this unexpected but not unwelcome affection. She must find some way to soothe him... dare she think it? Perhaps, if they could see their way to more pleasant conversations such as the one they had today, they might even move towards a friendship of sorts. Indeed, she would have liked to hear his thoughts on *The Monk*. It was rather horrid, as he had suggested, but she took great satisfaction in his opinion that she was no simpering miss to be undone by such a dreadful tale.

She was quite determined! If Mr. Darcy were to come to her with the cup of friendship, she would drink deeply of it.

Chapter Ten

O god of love!

(Hero, 3.1)

How different this afternoon was from all the previous ones Darcy had spent under Netherfield's roof. Before, he had spent the time trying to avoid Caroline Bingley and her acquisitive eye, or was secluded in some office somewhere with Bingley, teaching him how to balance accounts and plan the spring's planting rotations.

These last few days, since Miss Jane Bennet's unfortunate accident and Elizabeth's arrival, he had been desperate to find any place to be other than in her presence so he might avoid becoming the target for her vicious, wounding words. He had walked the parks, ridden the paths, hidden in the butler's pantry and surveyed the stables for the twelfth time, all to avoid meeting her.

But now that he knew the truth, he found himself quite longing for her company. Those stinging barbs, so carefully contrived, were formed to hide a tender heart; the set-downs disguised esteem for him and even (dare he think it) affection. Their discussion earlier today had been... pleasant. That was the word. She had seemed interested in his opinion on books, and had they not been interrupted by that maid, they might have engaged in a stimulating discussion. Did Elizabeth like Mrs. Radcliffe? What did she think of Mr. Lewis? Had she read Mrs. Parsons' *The Castle of Wolfenbach*?

And so, instead of creeping through the hallways seeking refuge, he stalked along them, listening for voices. The breakfast room was empty, as was the back parlour where Miss Bennet was wont to spend her days. Caroline and Louisa were in the cosy front parlour where the pianoforte stood awaiting eager fingers to caress its ivory keys, and neither admitted knowing the other ladies' whereabouts.

"You are... searching... for Eliza Bennet?" Caroline asked in her haughtiest tones. She wrinkled her nose as she pronounced the name 'Eliza.' "Of course!" she snickered to her sister Louisa, "he is hoping to know her whereabouts so he can direct his feet elsewhere. Why do you not sit with us, Mr. Darcy? It is quiet, and the conversation is sure to be superior to anything you might hear from the others."

Darcy controlled his breath. "Thank you for your consideration. Perhaps later. I shall... where is your brother? I had offered to be with him as he took an account of the wine cellars."

He turned to leave, but was stayed by Caroline's voice. "He must be with the ladies and whatever company appears to visit today. But... my dear Mr. Darcy, assure me that you do not intend to spend your time with that rabble. Surely your refined and erudite tastes find little pleasure in that chatter.

"Wait—Louisa, can I be correct? Mr. Darcy, you do not mean to seek out Eliza to wallow in her company? I have seen you two together. Less damage would be done with sword and pistols at dawn! Or perhaps...no. Do I suspect that you like her?" She gave a little laugh. "When am I to wish you joy? How fortunate you will be in your sisters and mother-in-law! The youngest one, Lydia, will be a grand example for dear Georgiana to follow! Oh, how diverted I am!" She gave a nasty little laugh.

Louisa made some reply and the two ladies snickered. "Should you wish for respite, Louisa and I will be pleased to welcome you here. Go, find your little virago. You shall find no joy in her."

He gave a cursory bow and left before she could speak further.

He next went to the billiards room, and then the terrace at the back of the house in case they were seeking some of the last warm rays of the sun. There he saw Bingley and a small group of officers wandering the far end of the gardens and gazing into the woods. Richard was one of the party, and he was pointing at the trees. Were they planning to hunt? The weather was fine for pheasant and grouse. He considered wandering over to join them, but he thought he recognised one of the group. Wickham. His jaw clenched at the very sight of the man and he felt his ire rise. He really must warn Bingley about him. Perhaps after dinner, after everyone had retired for the night, he would tempt his friend into a game of billiards with Richard and inform him of some—and only some—of Wickham's past sins.

Voices from inside caught his attention. He turned back into the house in hopes of finding Elizabeth, but only Jane and Charlotte had returned to the parlour. Where could Elizabeth be? Was she resting? Was she out on one of her long walks? Or in the kitchens, chatting merrily with the cook?

Resigned to a sad and lonely afternoon, he turned back to the stairs to take him to his rooms when he saw the very lady he had hoped to meet heading his way. She carried her bonnet and autumn coat, and he saw her walking boots peek out from under her petticoats.

"Miss Bennet!" He could not stop the smile that spread across his face.

To his amazement, she returned it. "Mr. Darcy."

"Are you... that is, it is a fine day. Were you planning a walk to take the air?"

She held out her coat. "As you see." She was still smiling, her eyes holding a sparkle he had not noticed before.

Now he felt emboldened. They had exchanged a great number of words today, none of which held a curse or insult. He took a deep breath and asked, "Would you be averse to my company on your rambles?"

"On the contrary, sir, I would be pleased. Shall I meet you by the arbour?"

He glanced down at his own house shoes and light coat. Naturally! He would need to change. "Yes. Yes, of course. I shall be but a moment." And hoping that her invitation was genuine, and that she would not disappear into the trees the moment she left the house, he ran off to attire himself for a walk.

She did not disappear. She sat there waiting, a sweet smile upon her face. Her dark eyes shone under her bonnet, and she greeted him prettily when he arrived.

"You are a great walker, Miss Elizabeth," he ventured. He would be friendly and allow her to set the tone of the conversation.

"I am, sir. I cannot claim a great many accomplishments, but if walking is so considered, then I shall profess to be expert in it. I have been practising, you see, since I was only a year of age, and now I am quite proficient. See." She lifted her skirts to show her ankles and placed one foot in front of the other, demonstrating how she moved forward, step by step.

"Remarkable, Madam!" She really could be quite delightful when she was not flinging her poisoned arrows. "Time well spent! You do that exceedingly well."

"And see, I have perfected my technique so I can move thus," she stepped to the side and back again, "and thus," she stepped backwards.

"Admirable. Allow me to try." He executed his own steps sideways and backwards, and then bowed with theatrical elan. Elizabeth laughed in glee and clasped her hands together.

"Oh, bravo, Mr. Darcy! With enough practise, you shall be quite as good as I am! Shall we begin our training? There is a lovely path through the woods to where the stream swells into a pool. Very few know of it, but it is one of my favourite places to walk. One foot before the other, just so, and we shall be there in all good time."

"I am honoured to join you." She strode forward, and he wondered if he ought to offer his arm for her support, as he had been trained to do. Would she see it as a sign of gallantry? Or would she take it amiss, a suggestion that she was not strong enough to walk without the support of a man's arm? By now she was three steps ahead of him, and he rushed after her. What better to do, he decided at once, than simply to ask? This he did, uttering his offer and his reasons for making it, and she chuckled as she refused.

"I thank you, sir. It appears you can be a gentleman when you so choose after all! But I am used to walking by myself with no one to support me, and I am strong and capable." Her smile satisfied him that she had taken no offence.

He must continue the conversation. "Do you often include others on your walks, or do you prefer to go alone?" He moved easily beside her as she led the way.

"I am accustomed to taking solitary rambles, sir, but it does not follow that I am necessarily averse to company. Indeed, when walking with a suitable companion, with a like mind and a similar pleasure in the activity, a walk can become as wonderful as the finest ball or an expedition through a gallery or a pleasure garden."

Ah! Here was an entrée to further conversation. "Do you visit the galleries much, Miss Elizabeth? I had not thought there were a great many in Hertfordshire."

"Alas, there are not. But I visit my aunt and uncle in London a great deal, and we always take advantage of everything the city has to offer when we are there. The galleries, the opera, public lectures at the Royal Society, everything of interest and value."

Hah! Perhaps he ought to reconsider his prejudices against the relations in Cheapside.

As they wandered down the path towards Meryton, and then into the wood, they spoke more and more easily. They talked of London and its galleries, of her favourite artists, and of the Greek and Egyptian statuary at the British Museum.

Eventually they came to the pond and spent some time there before walking back through the fields towards Netherfield. Here was the lane that led past Farmer Smith's pastures, there the path to where the old storage shed had stood before the fire that burned the old tannery, and there the stile which they must cross to return to Netherfield's park.

Here Darcy's old habits could not be denied, and he offered Elizabeth his hand as she climbed over the stile. She accepted it and placed her own hand in his. Even through his gloves, it felt good. More than good. It fit there, as if it had been made for him. Without a thought, he gave her hand a slight squeeze, and she responded likewise, and they both smiled at each other. Something unknown and indescribable passed between them. An invisible string, or a flash of electricity, something strange and wonderful. And as they walked on, they began to talk with the easiness of old friends who had discovered each other again after an absence of many years.

One foot tracing the other, shoulders side by side, they talked now of nothing and everything, of her favourite trees and his old pair of riding boots he would not discard despite their age and wear. They pondered over the weather and what Mr. Ellings would speak about at church on Sunday, and whether strawberry jam was better than peach, or the opposite.

Not once did he insult her, and not once did she throw barbs at him, and he had never spent a more pleasant afternoon in his life. From the smile on Elizabeth's face, he thought she had enjoyed it greatly as well.

It was near dusk when they returned. The party of officers had returned to their barracks, and Charlotte was taking her leave of Jane. Those two ladies were in the back parlour with Richard and Bingley, and all smiled indulgently as Darcy and Elizabeth entered, their faces still flushed from the fresh autumn air, their grins fixed on their reddened faces.

"Have we interrupted some conversation?" Elizabeth asked.

Bingley's eyes grew wide and a pink flush worked its way up from his collar. Thank heavens the man had never tried his luck at the gaming tables; he would surely lose every penny he had within moments. Jane smiled blandly ahead, and Richard made scoffing noises. Only Charlotte Lucas tutted back. "No, not any in particular. We were merely observing the pleasant turn in the weather this afternoon." She turned to Elizabeth. "I was about to leave, my friend. I shall see you tomorrow, should the rain hold off. Now, go and change out of your walking clothes and I shall see if Mr. Bingley would be so kind as to order more tea."

"And so we have been dismissed," Darcy joked to Elizabeth. She smiled back at him and they went off to their respective rooms to clean up with plans to meet in the parlour for the promised refreshments shortly.

"It seems to have worked!" Bingley all but giggled as he heard Darcy's footsteps retreat down the hallway.

"Well, of course it worked," Richard returned. "It was my scheme, after all, and I am never wrong."

Jane shifted in her Bath chair. "You are certain he heard you this morning? Was he assuredly in the room?"

"Absolutely," came Richard's reply. "The maid was following him and went in after him, presumably to check the fire. She inquired about his plans for the day, and then watched the room to be certain he did not leave. He was in the alcove beyond the fireplace. I could see his feet reflected in the glass door of the cabinet opposite him. I only wish I could have seen his face as we talked about how much Miss Elizabeth esteemed him!"

"You are far too devious!" Charlotte still held her bonnet, but seemed determined to stay, at least until this conversation was over.

"At your service, Madam." Richard bowed and winked. "And Miss Elizabeth? How went your plans with her?"

"So very well," came Jane's reply. "After she went for a rest, we again set Annie to watch her once she awoke. When we knew she was listening, we began our little scene about how Darcy is in love with her."

"I believe I even heard her gasp," laughed Charlotte.

"Well, they certainly seem to be more friends than enemies at last." Bingley clapped his hands together. "At the very least, dinners will be less conducive to indigestion now that they seem to have reached an entente. What very great fun!"

"I only wonder what will happen next," Richard pondered. "I cannot believe it will be entirely smooth waters from this point."

"That, my friends, we shall have to wait and see. And now, I must leave. What fun this was!" And Charlotte took her final curtseys and made her way to the door to depart for Lucas Lodge.

The following days were very pleasant ones at Netherfield. The jovial presence of Richard Fitzwilliam brought an air of levity to the residents of the house, and even Caroline Bingley soon decided that he was company worth keeping. Whether this was due to the man's personal attributes or the discovery that his father was an earl—a man of exceptional Quality—she never did say. But she uttered not one complaint about his presence and made certain to talk to Cook about his particular likes and dislikes at the dinner table.

"I say, Richard," Darcy caught his cousin walking the damp park one morning, "Miss Bingley certainly spends a great deal of time seeing to your comfort. Last night, after dinner, I was quite ready to believe she would fetch you your slippers herself. She seems to have set her cap at you, so beware!"

"Lord no!" Richard guffawed. "I have seen her manoeuvres and I am preparing to take evasive action. Have I been cold enough towards her, do you think?"

"Always the soldier. I fear that nothing short of a full and brutal repulsion of her advance will deter her from her course. Although I must thank you; this is the first time ever that I have spent in her company that she has not deployed those same manoeuvres against me."

"There, my cousin, you speak the language as well. I shall try to set her down gently tonight. I admit her dowry is appealing, as is her face, but her temper I never could abide. Give me a hatchet-faced dame with a tender heart over such a pretty young catty mercenary any day. There." He changed the subject and pointed. "The field yonder is where I saw that catch of birds the other day. Would Miss Bennet object to her party being overtaken by a hunt? Bingley claims to be rather a good shot..."

Also pleasant were Darcy's interactions with Elizabeth. She greeted him warmly in the mornings at breakfast and smiled sweetly in the afternoons, and engaged in sparkling conversation at dinner in the evenings. Had he but known she could be so delightful a companion, he never would have made that initial disparaging remark that set their entire little war aflame. And so it seemed that those words he heard whispered were entirely true—that she did indeed admire him and needed only some kindness to allow her better nature to reveal itself.

After dinner on the very day that Darcy and Richard had spoken, the party were gathered in the front parlour, there to amuse themselves until it was time to retire. Bingley was fluttering about

Jane like a fussy mother hen, pushing her closer to, and then further from, the fire and seeing to her every comfort. The Hursts and Caroline were discussing a game of cards, to which Richard seemed doomed to be the unlucky fourth, leaving Elizabeth sitting with a pen and paper at the writing desk in the corner.

"To whom do you write?" Darcy came up behind her. Her neck was particularly graceful from this angle, and he fought the impulse to run a finger up the back of it to where a stray tendril of hair escaped its pins.

"To my aunt in London." She did not turn around, but neither did she seem surprised at his presence.

"Your aunt in London?" Caroline's voice sounded from the card table. "Pray, which aunt might that be? I have heard tell only of one."

Now Elizabeth turned to face her tormentor. "I have only one aunt in London, as you surely know, Miss Bingley. She is Mrs. Gardiner, and she is my mother's sister-in-law."

"Oh yes, the Gardiners," cooed Louisa. "I know him, your uncle. I believe we have done business at his shops, have we not, Mr. Hurst?" She gave a short laugh. It was not a pretty sound.

"Gardiner, wot?" That man blinked. "Good stock he carries."

"So it is," Louisa continued. "We do, on occasion, make the descent into Cheapside to see what is on offer at his warehouse."

"Of course, the uncle in Cheapside!" Caroline responded in mock surprise. "How do they do, Miss Eliza? Is business brisk?"

Darcy shot a glare at the Bingley sisters. He wished, not for the first time, that his eyes could strike them mute. "I am certain," he replied in his haughtiest voice, "that he does an excellent business. Why, I understand he is quite as successful as your own father was in his business up in Scarborough. Bingley has told me something of his affairs; I should like to hear your own recollections. Perhaps you have a great deal in common with Mr. Gardiner. But perhaps not. From what I hear tell, Mr. and Mrs. Gardiner are most elegant, being frequent visitors to the finest cultural amenities that London has to offer."

Caroline's face went white as her lips tightened into a stiff line on her face. "Well! I never!" She then turned to Richard, whom Darcy could see was holding back a laugh. "I am certain your circles in London include people of much more... elevated positions than Mr. Gardiner. Pray, Colonel, I would so love to hear of your acquaintances."

Richard sat up straight in his chair and allowed a broad grin to spread across his face. He stroked his chin with his hand, as he always did when thinking, and then drawled, "Oh, indeed, Miss Bingley, my circle have the greatest respect for Mr. Gardiner! Why, my very own mother—the countess—cannot go two weeks when she is in London without darkening his doorway to procure some treasure or another. She quite adores him, and his wife is one of the most elegant women I have had the pleasure to meet. Present company excepted, of course." He winked at Elizabeth, who choked back a snicker at Darcy's side. "But Miss Bingley, are you telling me you do not know them? Why, all the ton do. Perhaps, when next you are in Town, Miss Elizabeth might introduce you. Miss Bennet, Miss Elizabeth, I must congratulate you on your most excellent choice of relations. I shall tell them, when next we meet at one of Mother's soireés, how fortunate I was to meet you here. I really had no idea!"

With that, he fell back against the plush cushion of his chair and took a deep drink of the amber liquid in the glass that he held.

Bingley looked delighted, Jane flattered, and Caroline looked like she had been slapped.

"Yes, well... I am certain he is everything charming." She began to shuffle the cards in her hands as if they were the very things keeping the world in its sphere.

"Forgive me, Miss Elizabeth," Darcy now purred quietly, "for interrupting your letter. I am certain you have a great many things to write to your aunt, and we are not giving you the peace in which to do it. But perhaps," he raised his voice again so it could be heard across the room at the card table, "you will remember me to your uncle and compliment him once more on the excellent suggestion he had for a birthday present for my sister Georgiana. She was quite delighted with it."

To which Elizabeth gave him the warmest smile ever he had seen on her lovely face.

Chapter Eleven

Food to my displeasure

(Don John, 1.3)

Over the next two days, the rains fell constantly. The sky was leaden and the grounds a sodden mess. Charlotte was unable to visit for she had no carriage, but Elizabeth's mother and sisters came to visit on both days, as did the usual contingent of officers.

Bingley was in fine form as the host of this merry party, having determined, so he announced, to enjoy every moment. His was an unending supply of ideas and suggestions for keeping Jane happy. "I have had boxes from the attic brought down," he announced on the first morning of the deluge, "and we shall plan and present to Miss Bennet a series of tableaux, which she will endeavour to name." This resulted in a great deal of mirth and merriment, and some rather awkward depictions of various scenes from art and history.

"La! I will be with the officers!" Lydia all but shouted. "Shall I be a maiden in need of rescue from a dragon? What say you, Mr. Denny? Will you be my hero? Or perhaps Mr. Wickham. Coo, you shall do very well. I can all but see you on a white horse..."

"Lydia!" Elizabeth called out in horror. Then, more quietly to her mother, "Mama, please try to check her. Her behaviour brings us all into disrepute."

That lady waved a lace handkerchief as she rolled her eyes. "Pish, girl, let her have her fun. It is all innocent amusement. I enjoyed the sight of plenty a red-coated man in my youth, and I shall not deny my daughter that same pleasure. Why do you not join her? There are plenty of men to go around. Perhaps one might take a liking to you and marry you. You could do worse than a major with three or four thousand a year..." She turned her gaze to the small cluster of red coats that surrounded Lydia. "That Mr. Wickham is a good-looking one, and so charming too. He would do well for you, Lizzy."

She turned to look at the handsome soldier. She had all but forgotten his accusations, so charmed had she been by this strange new Mr. Darcy of late. But now all his words of caution came back to her. She had decided that he could not entirely be believed, and yet how could one with such an appearance of goodness speak anything but truth? He had assuredly been injured in some way by

Mr. Darcy and she must discover exactly how. She wished, not for the first time, that she had Jane's temperament where she might see the good and the truth in both of them. A misunderstanding, an ill-spoken word... there must be some explanation that would see both men be virtuous.

And so, when Mr. Wickham came over to engage her aid in planning and executing a tableau, she smiled happily and went with him, eager to learn more about this person who had known Mr. Darcy for so long.

If she glimpsed Mr. Darcy from the corner of her eye, his face black with thunder, she did not speak of it now, resolving only to speak to the man later when time and circumstance allowed.

On the second day, Mr. Bingley had yet another plan for their combined amusement. He had been through all the shelves in the library at Netherfield and had discovered some plays which he proposed the company read aloud. "Look, here are some copies of Sheridan's *The Rivals*," he announced, holding a pile of pamphlets containing the lines of the play. "Let us each take a part. Here, I shall be Jack, unless another wishes to take that role. And Miss Bennet, are you inclined to act a part? Perhaps, as the guest of honour at this little party, you would wish to read Lydia."

"What? Jane be Lydia?" the youngest Bennet daughter cried out. "That cannot be, for *I* am Lydia, and only Lydia should read Lydia!"

"Perhaps you should read Lydia, Lizzy," Jane offered. "You have often confessed to me that only the deepest love would tempt you into marriage, and here is a character who, if I recall the play, desires a deeply romantic *affair de coeur*."

Lydia Bennet flounced off in a huff at being denied and went to sit by a small cluster of visiting officers. Elizabeth kept her sigh internal; her sister would one day come to no good if she kept on this way.

But all thoughts of her sister were cast aside when, beside her, she saw Mr. Darcy blink at Jane's words about her desire for true love. Was he surprised at this? She had thought, after their few days of entente, that he knew her rather well. She wondered if this piece of news would increase the ardency of his devotions to her. For now, she must respond to Jane.

"But what of you, Jane? What shall you read?"

Her sister demurred. "I am no great actress. Let me take a lesser part. Perhaps Julia, who has some very sweet lines. Perhaps I can read her."

"Then you, Bingley," Richard joked, "ought to read Faulkland. He makes some very high-flown speeches, which will sit well with you."

Mr. Bingley clearly did not know the play, for he seemed pleased with this suggestion, and at length the parts were divided up and the pamphlets distributed to all those wishing to participate.

"How unlike Faulkland Mr. Bingley is," Elizabeth confessed to Darcy when they had a moment to talk together. "Mr. Bingley is so open and happy to be pleased, whilst Faulkland is of a very jealous nature, always believing his lover to be false."

Darcy laughed. "Indeed, it is so. But whilst Bingley is not a jealous man by nature, he is easily led. In that way, he is not so different from his character."

"Easily led?" Elizabeth asked.

Darcy pursed his lips. "When first I made the suggestion, so many months ago, that he lease an estate, I meant it in jest, but he took it right to heart and was immediately convinced that this is what he must do. He is always happy where he is, but it takes very little for him to change his mind completely. Why, to see him right now, one would think he never wishes to leave the countryside, but it would take but a breath for him to decide that London is the only place he wishes to be."

"I had not thought him so fickle in his ways."

Darcy looked very serious. "I would not term him fickle, for he always intends to be true to his course. But it takes very little—a comment, or a suggestion, or a joke, even—to turn him to a new path, to which he also intends to remain quite faithful."

"Then," she replied most soberly, "let us hope nothing arises to turn his feet now."

"This is wonderful!" Mr. Bingley crowed when all the parts were set. "Shall we begin? Here, let us set ourselves according to our roles. Miss Bennet and I shall sit here, as we will read Julia and Faulkland, and Miss Elizabeth and Darcy there, for Lydia and Jack. Colonel, you and Mrs. Bennet will do well together in those chairs..." and so he went on until the party was all established to his liking.

Elizabeth scanned the faces now set up in a great circle around the room. Most were excited and eager; there were expressions of anticipation and confusion over the text here and there, and a sea of smiles on all faces but one.

There, across the room on the other side of the circle, sat Mr. Wickham, looking quite as thunderous as ever Elizabeth had seen a man. As his eyes caught hers looking at him, his expression changed in an instant and the storm was replaced with a cheeky grin and a twinkling eye, but she knew what she had seen. What was so eating at the man? Was he that angry to be in Mr. Darcy's presence that it could affect such violence of emotion in him? Was it something quite different?

She resolved, again, to make efforts to further her friendship with the soldier, to better discern his mind and whatever strange thoughts were roiling below his charming surface.

The reading was everything diverting. Even Caroline and Louisa deigned to join the party to enjoy the reading, and they clapped with glee at the end of each scene. Mr. Bingley proved to be a creditable actor, as did Mr. Wickham and—of all people—Elizabeth's sister Mary. Jane was, perhaps, a bit too calm in her manner to truly convey the emotion of her lines, but as the aim was the joy of the reading and not a professional interpretation of the play, this was as nothing to the merriment derived from the activity.

Afterwards, a luncheon was brought in, and the party broke once more into small groups as the actors and audience partook of sandwiches and tarts and pickled vegetables. Seeing her sister Jane well entertained by Lydia and two of the officers, and Mr. Darcy ensconced in conversation with Mr. Bingley and his cousin Richard, Elizabeth drifted across the room to where Mr. Wickham stood, staring out the window.

"Unhappy weather, is it not?" She stood by his side, contemplating the constant drizzle.

"Sadly it is," replied that officer. "It is no fine day to walk or ride, and certainly not to hunt, for even the birds have thought better of it and are in their nests, around a warm hearth and drinking tea."

"We are fortunate, then, that we have this fine house, with its cheerful fires and plentiful tea, in which to sit whilst the rains fall."

"Aye, fortunate indeed." He stared a moment longer at the dreary scene through the window. "I must not lament my circumstances, for I know I am well provisioned, and yet sometimes I cannot help but think of what might have been. I should, perhaps, be sitting in my own home in Kympton. That is the living which I ought to have had, the living in the keeping of Mr. Darcy. It is a most delightful place, an excellent parsonage house! It would have suited me in every respect."

"Why do you not speak to Mr. Darcy about it now? He is here, and at leisure. I have found him to be not entirely closed to new ideas."

But the lieutenant scoffed, "What? Speak to Darcy? No, I am afraid, Miss Bennet, that such would never do. He has it in his mind, I am certain, that he is the wronged party. I would only harm my own cause to raise the matter again. But..." he turned his head to look sidelong across the room, "you seem to abide his company better than you had before. Do you not find his arrogance distasteful? He is a man whose opinions are firmly fixed, and who is unable to change from his place of pride."

Elizabeth followed his gaze. "Yes, he is quite proud, and his natural reserve does not recommend him well upon first meeting. But I am learning that there is more to him than such poor first impressions. His pride is not entirely unwarranted. He is not so unmoving or rigid, and I find that he improves upon further acquaintance."

Mr. Wickham did not look pleased at this comment, but quickly found his smile and affixed it to his face before claiming, "I believe your sister is calling to me. A pleasure, Miss Elizabeth." Whereupon he walked away to where Lydia was tittering on a sofa, leaving her pondering his words and sudden change in mood.

As the afternoon drew on, Elizabeth moved from group to group, enjoying conversations here and there. She always had an eye on Jane, who sat ensconced upon her Bath chair like some sort of throne, and who was never without company and a willing person to bring her what food or drink she desired. Mr. Bingley was often there basking in her light, as were two or three of the other officers. Colonel Forster seemed quite pleased to sit at her side, talking happily of his imminent wedding and future bride, and Captains Carter and Denny, too, were happy to engage Meryton's most lovely lady in pleasant chatter.

Even Mr. Darcy seemed comfortable and at ease. How different he was now from the icy and arrogant man who first had graced Meryton's society at the assembly hall last month. Now he sat with Colonel Fitzwilliam at one side and her sister Mary at the other, his entire demeanour one of relaxation, his one leg crossed over the other knee, his hand gesturing at something with great eloquence. At times Caroline Bingley or Mr. Hurst would wander over to share his company, and not once did she see him stalk the perimeters of the room like a malevolent god, disgusted with his creation.

The other person whom her eye would not leave completely was Mr. Wickham. He flirted with all the ladies with his accustomed charm; first with Lydia and Kitty, then with Louisa Hurst, then with her own Mama, and then with Lydia again. Elizabeth sighed. Lydia, at fifteen, was too young to be out in society, and far too young to be teasing and batting her lashes at a man nearly twice her age, no matter how fine his appearance. She laughed at his jokes in a most outrageous manner, and—Elizabeth gasped in horror—she grabbed at the man's sword and ran her fingers along its long edge with movements that quite shocked Elizabeth, although she knew not why. Lydia ought, instead, to be still in the schoolroom until she could comport herself with the decorum expected of a gently born young lady. Mama would be of no use in trying to check Lydia's behaviour; perhaps Papa could be prevailed upon to exercise some of his paternal duties.

But Papa was not here, and Elizabeth's mother seemed to be all determined to embarrass her daughter as much as possibly she could. For no sooner had she laughed at Lydia's antics and made another comment about the handsome men in scarlet, than she began to discuss Jane with Colonel Forster, who had the misfortune of being nearest the lady.

"I hear you are soon to wed, Colonel."

That officer nodded with a wide smile. "I am indeed so fortunate, Madam. In just a few days, I will be off to London, and when I return, it will be with Mrs. Forster. She is a charming lady, and I am very lucky that she will have me."

"Pish, nonsense, sir! She is lucky to have you. A smart soldier—a colonel, no less! What more could a young woman desire?"

"I prefer to think the lady likes me more for my character than my uniform," he replied good-naturedly, "even that she might love me."

"I am certain that is part of it. But what a lady really desires is not love but security, a place in the world."

"Madam! I must protest. I hope to give my Harriet both."

"Of course, of course, Colonel. But see my Jane over there." Elizabeth saw her mother gesture towards Jane, sitting between Mr. Bingley and Louisa Hurst on the other side of the room. She stifled a groan. Must Mama always crow, and crow so loudly. Her head drooped and she ran a hand over her eyes in shame.

"She is so beautiful," Mrs. Bennet continued, "and for so good a reason, for it seems likely she will soon catch Mr. Bingley. See how she gets on!"

Elizabeth could, indeed, see Mr. Bingley rushing about to get another cup of tea and cakes for her sister. But her mother would not stop. "I do not say there is anything to talk of now, but I advise you not to be surprised should there be an engagement announced soon. How well she will be set up! He is a wealthy man—as are you, I should imagine, and how fortunate for Mrs. Forster—and she will want for nothing. And handsome, and living so close to Longbourn, such things that a mother should most desire. And see how fond his sisters are of her. She shall be a fine mistress of Netherfield, do you not think so, Colonel?"

Colonel Forster opened his mouth to reply, but Lizzy's Mama gave him not the time to draw breath before she carried on.

"And better still, as he is so wealthy a man, so are his friends, who are all likely to come to visit him and his new wife, and they will meet my other daughters. It is such a promising thing for them, as Jane's marrying so well must throw them in the way of other rich men!"

And on she talked, and at great volume, that none near her could escape from the hearing. Elizabeth wished she might vanish through the walls or disappear into the upholstery, such was her embarrassment. And how much greater did that become when she noticed, sitting no great distance behind her, none other than Mr. Darcy.

Oh, how I pray he does not think me like my mother! I am mortified!

She turned away from her mother's terrible display to glance back across at where Lydia was still flirting with Mr. Wickham. She loved her family greatly, but at times she wished she might exchange them for some more decorous models. Such were her thoughts that she did not notice she had company.

"He is a fine looking officer, is he not?"

Elizabeth paused from her introspection to find Caroline Bingley at her elbow. She blinked.

"Mr. Wickham? He is indeed. He looks well in this fine room, surrounded by many other fine looking objects. Your hospitality does you credit, Miss Bingley."

The lady would not be swayed from her purpose, however. "He glances at you a lot, Miss Eliza."

"Does he? I had not noticed. He seems rather well occupied with his present company."

"And I have observed you glancing at him as well. Hush, I shall not breathe a word, but am I to suspect some sort of attachment between you?"

Elizabeth did not know whether to protest or laugh. "What? I and Mr. Wickham? No, indeed! We have met only a few times and have had little time to converse."

"And yet I have noticed you, on those few occasions, engaged in deep conversation."

"I must protest, Miss Bingley. It is nothing like you think. He was merely telling me tales of his childhood in... in the north."

That lady bowed her head and looked at Elizabeth through her lashes. "You would look well together. He would be a good match; the best sort a lady such as yourself could hope for. A dashing officer with a good commission... When your father dies and you lose your estate, you would be pleased with such a man."

Now she was affronted. "I thank you, Miss Bingley, not to commit my father to an early grave. We shall not be in the hedgerows, no matter what my mother may cry."

"Still, you might wish to further your way with him, for you cannot hope for a better sort of situation." Now Miss Bingley's eyes darted towards where Mr. Darcy sat at the end of the room, talking to Colonel Forster.

Aha! So that was the way of it. Elizabeth had noticed Caroline putting herself before Colonel Fitzwilliam since his arrival, but their recent conversation after dinner seemed to have disabused her of any hopes in that line. Consequently, she must now be hoping once again for Mr. Darcy's attentions, and was made unhappy by Darcy's seeming preference for herself.

"I shall marry where my heart leads me, Miss Bingley. I thank you for your concern."

"A word in your ear, Miss Eliza." Caroline grabbed her elbow and pulled her into a corner where they might not be overheard. "I see a slight preference for Mr. Darcy right now, but be warned: When my brother decides, as he inevitably must, that he wishes to return to London, Mr. Darcy will be gone from here and he will think of you no more. Seize your future where it is more secure."

"And do you expect your brother to depart from this neighbourhood soon?" She had seen nothing to alarm her in that respect, but suddenly she recalled all of Darcy's words about his friend from earlier.

"No..." Caroline hedged. "He has said nothing. But I know him well. He will change his mind from one minute to the next. As the wind blows, so does Charles go from fancy to fancy. Do not expect us to be here for any great length of time."

Elizabeth turned to stare directly into Caroline's kohl-rimmed eyes. They were mere slits in a stony face, overhung by forbidding brows. If Caroline had any say in the matter, Lizzy apprehended, she and her party would be gone in an hour, taking Charles and all of Jane's hopes with her. "I understand you perfectly, Miss Bingley." And without another word, she turned and went to seek her sister Jane.

Chapter Twelve

There was a star danced

(Beatrice, 2.1)

Darcy opened his eyes the next morning and wondered if he had left his lamp on all night. Surely the oil would have burned out by now. But no, that was not it at all. It was sunlight, streaming through his open draperies. Had he forgotten to close them? Or had the maid been in earlier? He blinked into the unexpected brightness and waited to come fully to consciousness. After so many days of rain, this sunlight was welcome indeed.

His first thought was that he must go for a ride. How long had it been since his horse had been out for exercise? Spending all that time in Bingley's stables, no matter how well appointed and large, would play poorly on the beast's mood and muscles alike.

His second thought was to wonder if Elizabeth rode. Surely Bingley could find a suitable mount for her. He must find her and inquire.

She was, to his great pleasure, already at breakfast when he appeared. She sat at the table with a steaming cup of tea before her and the newspaper open at her side, the long-missed sunlight that poured through the windows gilding her curls in gold. When she glanced up and smiled at him, he could believe that an angel had descended from heaven just for him.

"Miss Bennet." He went through the expected civilities, asking after her health and that of her sister, and voicing a wish that she had slept well. She responded accordingly, like the lines from a well-rehearsed play, and they chatted about nothing as he took his coffee and eggs. At last, he came to his point.

"I was thinking... that is, I was hoping... Do you ride, Miss Elizabeth?"

Her eyes opened wide. "I? Ride? I can, but I am not a skilled horsewoman; I cannot boast nearly the level of accomplishment as I have with walking." His face must have fallen, for she quickly added, "However, I believe that a good teacher might see me improve my skills. Do you know of a good riding teacher, Mr. Darcy?" Her eyes sparkled. For a moment, they rivalled the sun.

"I should not call myself quite the best in England, but I have some experience in this matter, having taught my sister."

"You shall not get the exercise you wish, I am afraid, if you are coddling me."

He reached a hand across the table to cover hers. It was warm and soft, and it felt very good in his. A thread of energy wound its way through his fingers and around his palm before working its way up his arm. Soon it suffused his entire body. What magic did this strange creature work on him?

"I can ride any time I wish," he responded to her comment. "I shall be quite satisfied being outside in the sunshine, with a beautiful woman at my side. Will you join me?"

She smiled her acceptance, and they made arrangements to meet a short time hence at the stables.

Bingley did, indeed, have a suitable horse; at least, that is what the stable master said. Bingley himself was likely still asleep and unlikely to know or to care. It was a pretty little grey, calm and biddable, and accustomed to taking a side-saddle, for Louisa used it from time to time.

Elizabeth appeared in borrowed riding clothes—from the attics? Darcy wondered, for neither Louisa nor Caroline were of the lady's size—and soon she was mounted and ready.

"You are more adept than you led me to believe, Madam," Darcy observed. They had walked about the enclosure for a time, then attempted a gentle trot over the lawns. "I expected a lady who barely knew one end of the beast from the other, and here you are, sitting tall and strong, with a nice hand for the ribbons."

"I thank you, sir. But I have not your level of accomplishment."

"No, indeed not." Darcy sat up straight in his saddle and pulled his shoulders back, the very image of an arrogant aristocrat. "I have been riding since I was four summers old, and have practised frequently since then. Observe my technique." He came to a stop and then guided his horse to take three careful steps forward, and then three backwards. "And thus." His horse stepped to this side and then to the other, before bending its front knees to execute a sort of bow.

Elizabeth laughed in delight. "Oh, bravo, sir, and bravo to your valiant steed! I am most pleasantly diverted! What skill, what talent! Shall we ride?" And she cantered forward at a moderate pace. "Keep up if you can, Mr. Darcy!"

They rode for a long time. The earth was soft from all the rain, but the roads and paths were dry enough for easy travel, and she led him all about the countryside, showing him one special place after another: the pond where she learned to swim (the images that evoked were best contemplated later—alone), the tree she loved to climb, the lane to the school house that her mother and Mrs. Phillips had helped to establish for the parish children, and the copse in the woods where, in the summer, she would disappear with a book for a great many hours on end, not to emerge until her belly told her it was time for dinner.

The pace was no challenge for him, but he could see she was beginning to tire. Despite her adequate skill, it was clear she was no practised horsewoman.

"Let us rest, Miss Elizabeth. Here is a fallen log we can use as a mounting block later, and the horses can drink from the stream."

She agreed, and they pulled to a stop. He swung off his horse and wrapped the reins about a tree, then went to help her dismount. He stood at the grey's side and held up his arms. She could, he suspected, manage this manoeuvre without his assistance, but she gave no word of complaint and reached forward to slide into his embrace, staying there long after she had achieved her balance on the soft ground.

Oh, she felt good. His arms were around her waist and he could almost feel the boning in her stays beneath the stiff fabric of her habit. He ought to release her, to stand back and let her walk forward, but instead his hands moved of their own accord and slid further around her to pull her towards him. And her hands, at first on his forearms as he lifted her to the ground, were now snaking around his neck. He was a good deal taller than her, and she had to raise her chin to look up at him.

"I should let you go... I should not be standing here like this."

"Oh, no indeed, Mr. Darcy. But the ground is soft under my feet and I fear I might fall. Far better that you support me; it would do no good for me to sustain any injury, since Jane cannot care for me." She looked up at him, batting her lashes like a practised coquette. Good Lord! Her sister Lydia was no match for the allure of Elizabeth!

His voice caught in his throat and when it came, it was almost a rasp. "That would be a great misfortune, Miss Elizabeth. In the interests of your sister's peace of mind, I shall make the sacrifice and keep you steady."

"Perhaps if I lean on you a bit." She closed the small space between them.

"Yes. That is much more secure." His hands reached the small of her back. He clasped them tighter to ensure she would not fall. In response, she moved one of her own hands up into his hair at the back of his head and allowed the other to curl around his neck. For stability, of course. His hat slipped forward on his head and he must look a fool, but nothing mattered now but her.

"What would happen were I to slip and hurt myself?" Those bright eyes flashed. "When I was a child and sustained some injury, my father would make it better with a kiss."

"My feelings right now are hardly paternal. What, pray tell, hurts?"

"My nose... my cheek... perhaps here, by my mouth..."

"You talk too much, Elizabeth. There is only one way to stop you."

And he lowered his head to hers and stifled any further words with a kiss.

It started with a nothing, a mere brush of the air about her lips, hardly enough to feel. But that ephemeral butterfly-touch lit his body like a burning torch and he had to have more. She was ready to meet him, her hands drawing his head towards hers, her lips moving against his so he could scarcely draw breath.

"My God, Elizabeth! What you do to me." He gasped the words, whether aloud or in his head he knew not. She was a bell and she was a symphony, she was the earth and she was the sky, she was this instance in time and she was eternity. She was his undoing.

"Tell me the truth, Darcy. What do you think of her?"

Darcy put down his cup of coffee. It was too early in the morning for so deep a conversation. After returning from that wonderful ride yesterday, he had made every effort to be a charming houseguest, but his mind was still awhirl. Elizabeth had gone right to see Jane, and he had retired early to his rooms. But sleep was elusive and he greeted the morning with something less than yesterday's vigour. And now, when all he wished to do was contemplate Elizabeth, Bingley wished to discuss Jane. Once more, he was compelled to hide his inner fire behind his habitual shield of ice.

"She is very beautiful."

"Any man with eyes can see that!" Bingley rolled his eyes heavenward and helped himself to another slice of ham from the platter. "I am asking, rather, what you think of the lady herself."

"Dare I ask what makes you ponder such things?" He really had no wish to enter into such a discussion.

"I confess I like her a great deal, and am contemplating a courtship. If she agrees... if her father agrees."

Darcy put down his cup. It would be far preferable to have this conversation late at night, preferably over a tankard of strong ale or a glass of brandy. Instead, all he had for fortification was a now-tepid cup of coffee. He walked over to the sideboard to refill the bitter brew with something hot.

"You were equally enamoured, I recall, with a lady in Cambridge two years ago, and then with another in London only last spring. Wherever you go, my friend, you find an angel to adore."

Bingley turned large wounded eyes upon him. "Yes, they were lovely. But they were nothing to Jane... Miss Bennet. I must know, Darcy, if there is anything you know against her."

"Her mother does not always show the greatest decorum. She is the daughter of a country attorney—"

"Which means nothing! I am the son of a tradesman, and I cannot fault my excellent father for his birth, nor should I fault Mrs. Bennet for hers."

"—and she does not always have the manners expected in the circles in which you hope to move."

Bingley let out a quick snort of air. "It is Miss Bennet I wish to court, not her mother. Wherever she is known, she must be respected and valued, and she should not appear at any less advantage for having a less than decorous parent."

"Very well. But the matron has it all in her head to marry off her daughters to whichever gentleman appears among them who might have large pockets and half an inclination thus. Did you not hear her just two days ago? She could speak of nothing else."

"Darcy, you jest! That makes her no different from any other mother in Town, or in any part of society, I wager!"

"Just be aware that Mrs. Bennet's aims might be rather too much taken up by the daughter."

"You believe Miss Bennet to be false? Tell me if that is so."

"Be calm, Bingley. I know nothing to hold against Miss Bennet, nothing ill of her. She is everything lovely and charming as well. I cannot fault her, except that she appears too perfect. She smiles at every one and at every thing, and I cannot detect where graciousness of manner ends and genuine affection begins."

"So you doubt her heart? Could she possibly care for another?" Now he looked quite alarmed and his shoulders stiffened.

"Charles, you tend too much to exaggerate such things. I meant nothing of the sort. I merely said that I cannot detect whether the lady has deeper feelings, not that they are not there."

"But now I have to wonder... She is always so kind and friendly to everybody, to all the officers. Just yesterday she talked for hours with Colonel Forster—"

"Who is to be married within the week."

"—and to Captain Sanders and those others about her. I must double my efforts to woo her, so she forgets all the others."

"You are jealous, Charles, but of no one. If she exhibits no particular signs of deep affection, that same can be said of every man she meets. Do not create monsters where there are none."

Bingley's shoulders eased. "Yes, yes, of course. I shall speak to her and offer a courtship. A courtship is only that, not an engagement. I shall endeavour to learn her mind... and her heart."

"A wise decision." Darcy downed the rest of his coffee and rose. "If you are settled in your thoughts, then, I shall take some air before the ladies arise. Perhaps... Well, I shall see what they have planned for today."

Yesterday's reprieve of bright sunlight had been short, and the skies were grey once more, but there was little threat of rain in the heavens. Today, Darcy decided to ride. Yesterday's outing with Elizabeth had been wonderful, beyond anything he could have imagined, but it had not been the vigorous exercise he craved. Today, he would push himself and his horse a bit harder. He called upon his cousin, who threw a piece of toast into his mouth and a few rolls into a pocket, and then joined him at the stables.

In the few weeks Darcy had been in this part of Hertfordshire, the season had quite changed from the vibrant hues of autumn to the dour tones of early winter. It was not yet the icy weather of winter, but browns and greys had quite replaced the glowing oranges and reds he had seen upon his arrival in this neighbourhood.

He knew the countryside rather well by now and rode the paths and fields he knew would take him on a long circuit around the vicinity. He showed his cousin the town, the lane to Longbourn, the vista towards Oakham Mount, and many other landmarks he had discovered during his stay thus far. His route took him near to the encampment where the militia were stationed until the summer, and as Richard saw the familiar sight, he requested a brief stop to pay his respects to Colonel Forster.

The camp, when they arrived, was in an uproar. Men were yelling and privates were scurrying around hither and yon, some seeming to obey orders, others looking as if they wished merely not to be seen.

"What is the matter? Where is the colonel?" Richard asked one young lieutenant.

"Colonel is in his offices, sir." Richard had on his own regimental coat, his rank emblazoned on his epaulettes. The officer snapped a quick salute to him, then hurried on with his explanation. "Seems money went missing from the treasury last night, and no one seems to know about it. But I'll wager there's one here who does. Sir."

He gave a quick salute and rushed off. Richard dismounted and tied up his horse, beckoning Darcy to follow.

As told, Colonel Forster was in his offices, standing behind his desk and castigating a group of lesser officers with language that made Darcy blush. He was no stranger to strong language, but he had seldom heard this many words strung together for such a purpose.

"And when I catch the bastard—and I shall, believe me, men— he will rue the day that ever he donned a uniform and came calling at my door. He shall hang! Or worse! Now you heard what Nickelson saw. Go and find the man. Now!"

The five officers saluted and turned as one and fled the office as quickly as decorum would allow.

Forster looked up. "Fitzwilliam. And Mr. Darcy. You have come at an inopportune time."

"So I see," Richard returned the greeting. "If I may be of assistance?"

"No joy in it. Come, sit. 'Tis still early for a drink, but perhaps we have earned one. No? Well and good, then. As you have surely heard, one of my men seems to think me his own personal account of the Bank of England. And, worse for him, he made a withdrawal last night. A guardsman saw somebody in the treasury room and set the alarm, but it was too late to catch him. Five hundred pounds have gone missing. Five hundred! Unbelievable!"

"Five *hundred?*" Darcy gasped. That was a fortune. "What on earth was the regiment doing with five hundred pounds in its treasury?"

"The men's wages, provisions for the camp, some equipment we have coming in... Most of our expenses are covered by London, but not all."

Richard nodded, his eyebrows all but meeting at the centre of his forehead. "Will London make up the shortfall until the money is recovered?" Forster grunted. Darcy assumed that meant yes. "And have you any idea who was involved?"

"Not as yet, but we shall catch the damned louse, have no fear. He did us the favour of leaving us some clues to his identity in the form of some muddy boot prints. All this rain has been to some benefit. We shall catch the man. That is certain. If I find a way to use your aid, Fitzwilliam, I shall summon you at once. Now, if I may be so rude..."

"Of course, Forster." Richard rose. "No offence taken. You have duties, and we shall not keep you from them. Accept my offer as standing."

Richard and Darcy took their leave and reclaimed their horses to make the short ride back to Netherfield.

"Five hundred pounds is a frightening amount of money to be stolen like that," Darcy began as they crested a small rise of land at the edge of Netherfield's property. "You do not think...?"

"Wickham? It seems the very thing he would do. But why risk it now? He has a career and good prospects."

"I cannot say," Darcy replied. "He is such a one that never feels he has enough. Perhaps it was merely to supplement his pockets." He nudged his mount to a faster gallop. "There, boy! You see home." He turned back to his cousin. "He cannot hope to benefit from this. If Forster is correct, he will be found, and soon. And then he will lose it all, and a lot more. I only hope that he stays as far away from the Bennet sisters as he can. His is a bad story whose final chapter is still waiting to be told."

But, alas, Wickham was skulking around the stables when they returned. "Darcy!" he hissed from behind an outbuilding as the cousins handed their horses to the grooms.

Darcy gave him no reply other than a long, scalding stare.

"Please, Darcy. Will... we were friends once. I must talk to you." Wickham's eyes moved to Richard. "Alone, if you please."

"We have nothing to say to each other. Leave me."

"Please. I am desperate." And indeed, the man did look in a fix. His eyes were wild and his hair, normally so prettily arranged, was a mess. He must have run worried fingers through those careful curls all morning. Darcy was, contrary to all appearances, not entirely without heart. "Very well. I shall listen to you. For five minutes only." He reached into his fob pocket to check his watch. "There, by the arbour. Richard, please stay close enough to observe us, but far enough not to overhear, in deference to our 'friend' here."

"Thank you, Darcy." Wickham led the way to a small glade by the edge of the woods, with two low benches and protected by a now-bare trellis. He sat, then stood again, and began to pace the perimeter of the compact area. Darcy remained standing. He had no intention of putting Wickham at any sort of ease.

Only after Darcy glanced once more at his fob watch did Wickham start to speak. "I am desperate. I need some blunt. I have made a dreadful mistake and I need a loan."

"For five hundred pounds, perhaps?"

Wickham stopped as if frozen in place and gaped at Darcy with a stricken face. "How... how did you know?"

"We have just returned from seeing Colonel Forster. I hoped beyond reason you were not involved."

"I had no choice. You must believe me. I made... that is, I bought into a game of cards at the tavern the other week..."

"They do not play for such amounts at the tavern. You lie!"

"No, no! Listen. I did well, very well, that night. I quite filled my pockets. Then two of the men told me of another game, a private game, with much higher stakes. They invited me to join them. I felt I was certain to win. My skills at the table must be superior to these country hicks. And so I bought in, and... well, you can guess the rest. I lost everything. And Marlon—from the village past Oakham— threatened me. He said he would send the smith over to break my legs if I did not pay on time, and then gave me the name and direction of the last person who did not pay. Darcy... that man will never walk again. I know it! So I took the money from the treasury. And now I need to repay it. If it reappears, I can say I found it and am returning it, and shall escape punishment. I might even be the hero. It's only five hundred pounds. You will never miss it. Please. I am begging you."

He began pacing again, now wandering further along the wall of shrubbery that still held its browning leaves. His hands were clenched, and he stopped every few steps to turn back towards the arbour where Darcy still stood, unmoving as a statue.

"And why am I to empty my pockets to fill your own?" Darcy had heard too many of these tales from Wickham's lips to feel much sympathy. There was usually a thread of truth at the bottom of them, but far more embellishment than evidence went into their full creation.

"I will pay you back. I promise."

"I have heard that before, George. And where, pray tell, will you find five hundred pounds?" The leaves of the wall of shrubbery rustled in the wind.

"You can spare it. You will not notice the loss of it. You likely have that amount rolled up in banknotes in your stockings. Do this once, I beg you, and I shall never ask you for a single thing again. I am desperate; I do not ask this lightly."

Darcy checked his watch again. "Your five minutes are over. No. I have given you a substantial fortune over the years, and at every turn you come, cap in hand, asking for more. I shall aid you by not telling Colonel Forster of your deeds, but that is all. Confess your actions and you might find some leniency there. But I told you the last time that I would not see you to another penny from my coffers, and I hold with that. If I give you a farthing, you will only come begging for more. It is enough, and I have had my final say. Now goodbye."

"Darcy!" Wickham's panic had turned to anger. "Your pride and superiority are too much! You will do this. I insist upon it."

"No, George. I will do nothing of the kind. You have asked one thing too many, and one time too often."

"You will pay. I will see to it. I will destroy you."

Darcy turned to face his foe fully. His voice dropped to an ominous whisper. "You have no hold over me, Wickham. No one in my family will talk to you; your name is dirt amongst all who know you. Besides which, you have already destroyed my sister. What more damage can you possibly do?"

The handsome face transformed into a twisted mask and the smooth voice wrenched with bitterness. "I will find a way. You will never see it coming—neither the time nor the place, but believe me, I will destroy you. And then you will be sorry."

Without responding, Darcy turned and strode across the lawn to where Richard stood watching and waiting. He had heard more than enough of Wickham's threats. The man had enough bluster to keep a warship on its path. He stormed past Richard, who hurried after him.

"What did he want?"

"Money, of course," he spat back. "Some cock-and-bull story about needing to avoid an unpleasant creditor. I have heard these tales before. I cannot believe a word he says. He admits to stealing the money from the regiment treasury. I advised him to tell Colonel Forster; what he does is really up to him and his conscience. I will no longer be party to his sins."

"He will not be pleased."

"He never is. But after the living... and more especially after last summer, I owe the man nothing. He is anathema to me."

Richard clapped his cousin on the back as they entered the back door to Netherfield. "I grew up with him as well. That I quite understand."

Chapter Thirteen

Constant in the accusation

(Borachio, 2.3)

Mr. Jones came to see Jane shortly after breakfast. He poked and prodded at her ankle and tutted about her for a time, and then declared, with a satisfied smile, that she was healing well. Elizabeth sat with Jane in the large front room; there was little enough involved in this examination that required the privacy of a bedchamber.

He unwrapped the bandages and manipulated her foot this way and that. At times, Jane winced, but quickly regained her serene smile.

"And the pain?" he asked. "Are you able to sleep?"

"Other than a slight ache at times, there is no more pain. There, when you do that, it is less comfortable, but most of the time it gives me no trouble. I have Annie wrap it well before I retire so it cannot move, and I sleep adequately." She added after a moment, "I have no more need for the draughts."

"Good, good." He took her foot in his hand again. "Let us try this... Good. Now do that.... Good. What about this? Fine, fine!"

After some discussion, he proclaimed Jane was sufficiently healed to withstand the short carriage ride and return to Longbourn.

This was met by a cry of alarm by Mr. Bingley, who was sitting at the far end of the room behind a screen.

"I apologise for my outburst," came his voice. "I am most gratified that Miss Bennet is recovering so well. It is just that, well, I have... my sisters and I have so enjoyed your company. Along with the visitors who have come so often to see you, I have never been so pleased, so diverted in all my life. I shall quite miss you once you have gone from here."

"I, too, have been most content, despite the unhappy reason behind our prolonged stay." Jane was everything polite and grateful.

"More talk of that later, Miss Bennet," Mr. Jones cut in. "Here, I wish to see how you do on a crutch. I shall come by with one later today, and perhaps tomorrow you can see about returning home. You will need some assistance there, however. A room on the ground storey, if such can be managed, and a maid to assist you with all things as Annie here has done. Let me call upon your father immediately upon leaving here to see what can be arranged for you. I shall bring his answers when I come with the crutch."

He took his leave of his patient and her host and hurried off to complete his tasks.

Elizabeth watched him with envy in her eyes. After yesterday's glorious ride with Mr. Darcy, she was aching to be outside again. Might she meet him on one of the paths, or in the woods? Her eyes strayed to the window.

"Go, Lizzy. You want a walk, and I shall not stop you from it. Mr. Bingley," Jane called. "Might your sisters keep me company whilst Lizzy takes some air? It seems like another day of no rain, most certainly a day for exercise if one is of that inclination."

"Of course! And I shall sit with them. We shall have a fine morning of it whilst Miss Elizabeth is out."

This was arranged, and only a short time later, Elizabeth found herself walking alone on the path leading around the house, skirting the gardens and running near the stables. She had come to quite like the grey she had ridden yesterday, and thought to stop in to visit the lovely animal and offer it a carrot or two. She wrapped her shawl tight about her shoulders and picked her way along the path.

Before she achieved her goal, however, a figure caught her eye. There was Mr. Wickham sitting in the arbour near the woods, and looking as dejected as ever she had seen him. He had always been kind to her, and she hoped to return the favour. They were in view of the stable hands, and she saw little danger in approaching him.

"Lieutenant," she called out as she neared his bench, "what is the matter?"

He struggled to his feet. "All is well, Miss Bennet. I ought to ask after you. But..." He cast his eyes aside. "But no, you are correct. All is not well. I find I am in a spot of some difficulty."

"Is it some matter in which I can help?"

"I am afraid not, madam, unless you have some great fortune you have been hiding from the world. My last hope has vanished, and I find myself quite undone."

She took the other bench. "Would that I could be of assistance."

He raised his eyes again, and something flashed through them that she could not identify. "I must not speak ill... and yet... perhaps relating the particulars will help to ease my mind."

"Yes, yes, of course," she replied. "Do speak if it will help."

He stared into the blue sky for a moment. "I find myself financially embarrassed. It is shameful to admit, but it is the truth of things. I am in need of a rather substantial amount of ready cash, and I know not where to turn."

She knew but two men with great fortunes, and one had but recently let an estate; therefore, she must mention the other. "Have you not spoken to Mr. Darcy? I know you are not on the very best of terms, but if you were so intimate in your youth, surely he would help you. In memory of what was, if not in current friendship."

Wickham gave a great and prolonged sigh. "Ah, yes. Darcy and his great wealth. I have, indeed, asked him. I came to him, cap in hand, and laid the whole of the matter before his feet, hoping against hope for succour. But the man turned me down flat."

The air rushed from Elizabeth's lungs. Was this the man she was starting to like so much? "He would do such a thing? It sounds so unlike him."

"You have seen him, Miss Bennet, when he dons his robes of arrogance and pride. He thinks himself quite above the world and thinks nothing of lesser men such as myself." He stood and walked as he spoke, and Elizabeth followed him.

"Surely that is not so. If you were friends once, he must hold some affection for you. And he is not so very proud that he only associates with his equals. He holds Mr. Bingley as a close friend, and his wealth comes from industry. I do not believe he distinguishes better and lesser by a man's birth."

"If you knew him as I did, Miss Bennet, your thoughts would not be so forgiving. He is friends with Bingley, to be sure, but... dare I say this? I have heard that he will visit Bingley at his house but will not have the man seen before his own front door, and will certainly not make any introductions to those of his circles." Could this be so? But then why was Colonel Fitzwilliam here at Bingley's estate? She had no time to consider this as Wickham continued. "He is willing to dally with those he deems beneath him, but ultimately he will return to his own class." He lowered his voice. "I would offer caution, even to you and your sister. You are a diversion for him, as I was as a child, but in his true estimation, you are nothing."

The thought sent a shiver through her. Could it be true? Was yesterday's passionate embrace merely a diversion? The man had known what he was about, to be sure. Did he toy with maidens on a regular basis? No! It could not be. And it seemed so unlike what she was coming to know of Mr. Darcy. Mr. Wickham's words did not quite sit well, but why would he lie to her?

Mr. Wickham must have seen the confusion on her face, for he continued. "I even begged him to reconsider, for the people to whom I owe... a rather alarming amount of money.... have uttered threats against me. I quite fear for my safety. I laid it all at his feet, but he was as cold and haughty as ever I have seen a man. He did not give an inch. I know not what I can do."

What could this great amount of money be, she wondered? And who was Mr. Wickham dealing with that would threaten him with bodily harm should he not render his promised payment? It all seemed most alarming.

"I can hardly account it," she responded at last. "We have had our disagreements in the past, but even at our worst stages of enmity, I never imagined him a man so without feelings."

"I could tell you so very many tales of his icy heart, Miss Bennet. Why, only last summer he quite destroyed me." His appealing eyes once more drifted towards the clear blue sky. "It was a matter of the heart then, rather than one of the pocketbook, but he destroyed me nonetheless."

Elizabeth remained silent. It was quite inappropriate to inquire over such personal matters, but Mr. Wickham obliged her curiosity nonetheless.

"I may have mentioned Mr. Darcy's sister."

She nodded.

"She is much younger than me, and I knew her and adored her as a child. She was a lovely thing, but I thought nothing more of her after I left Pemberley for university. I was a man, after all, and she just a little girl. But last summer, fate threw us together once more. She was at Ramsgate with her companion, and I had travelled there for the summer, and I knew her immediately upon seeing her walking along the promenade.

"Imagine my surprise upon renewing the acquaintance, for this was not the child of my recollection, but rather, a young woman. She had grown lovely, and to my delight and surprise, she remembered me as well. Miss Darcy called me by name and spoke warmly to her companion of our childhood together. I was honoured to become a welcome guest at the apartments they had, and as the weeks drew on, my childhood affection grew into something rather deeper. In short, I found myself falling in love with Miss Georgiana Darcy."

"Yet you are not with her now."

"No. Alas. We wished to marry, but feared that Darcy would not approve. We planned, therefore, to elope and were about to set our plan into motion when the worst happened. Darcy, by some stroke of fate, came to Ramsgate to visit his sister only three days before our departure. And dear Georgiana, with her tender and loving heart, could not but tell her brother of our plans. She hoped he would see through his dislike of me in favour of her happiness, but this was not to be. He sent her companion off at once for permitting me near her, and he carried her immediately back to London. We did not even have a chance to say goodbye to each other."

Was this the man who had kissed her so shamelessly just yesterday? Was he that fickle of character? Every insult he had thrown at her in the first weeks of their acquaintance came back to her, and she shivered.

"How cruelly done! I am most ashamed of him." This was insupportable! How could Mr. Darcy, who was now seeming so misunderstood, be so cold-blooded as to break his sister's heart?

Was he in truth such a merciless tyrant? Were her initial impressions of him correct, after all?

"Can you not approach her now?" she asked, tears threatening her eyes.

"I wish I could. But she is up at Pemberley with her new dragon of a companion, and I am forbidden from the property, neither is she allowed any correspondence that even mentions my name. I am quite isolated from her, and she from me." He mopped at the corner of his eye with a handkerchief. "She is young and her heart will heal. Mine will always carry a wound."

There was nothing to say. "I am so very sorry." Those words could not mend what had been so coldly damaged, but they were all Elizabeth had.

"Thank you. I shall get on, even if somehow diminished. But here we are at the house. I would prefer that Darcy not see me right now."

"Yes, I understand completely. Good day, Lieutenant."

He bowed and stood still as she returned to the house.

Elizabeth was in a daze. Could this tale be true? Could Mr. Darcy really be so unkind as to treat his former friend thus? She was not ready to accept every word that Mr. Wickham uttered as infallible, for too many questions troubled her, but how could she not be moved by his sad tale? Was Jane correct in that there was some terrible misunderstanding lying between the men? Could Mr. Wickham have mistaken Darcy's words?

But no. That seemed all but impossible, not if Darcy was all but keeping his sister a prisoner at his estate. And not if he would see his childhood companion in peril and not offer to help with even a small gift or loan. It seemed unaccountable.

She let herself into the house and sat down on the long bench to remove her wet boots. One of the maids would clean them and have them ready for her next venture across the autumn-limned lawns, but she had no need for them in the house. It was no great distance to her room, where she could change her dress and put on her house shoes.

Her footsteps were all but silent and she moved unheard through the hallways when she thought she heard her name.

She ought not to stop, ought not to listen, this she knew. But the last time she had inadvertently overheard a conversation, it proved to be to her great advantage, and she could not walk on now. She slid closer to the doorway whence she had heard the voices and stopped outside to listen.

The first voice she recognised was that of Caroline Bingley.

"... a very sweet girl, but I fear for my brother."

"We must allow him to make his own choices, for all that they might be ill-advised."

That was Mr. Darcy. Could they be talking about Jane? Miss Bingley's next words confirmed that supposition.

"I know he has spoken to you, Mr. Darcy, but what are your thoughts on Miss Jane Bennet?"

Silence. Then, after a moment, he spoke.

"She is, as we have said, sweet." Pause. "But I cannot say with certainty that she loves him. You heard her mother on the afternoon we read the play. She was quite vocal in her opinions that Jane had done well to 'catch Bingley,' as I believe she expressed it.

It might be that she has encouraged her daughter to do whatever she must in order to ensure your brother's affections. Her hope, surely, is of fixing for herself a wealthy husband."

"Shocking! But what are we to do, Mr. Darcy?"

Red spots began to appear before Elizabeth's eyes. Could they really think this of dear Jane? Could they not see her genuine affection for Mr. Bingley? Charlotte's exhortations came back to her now, her advice that a woman ought to show more than she felt to catch her man. *She must act to assure him of her growing affection. Very few of us have heart enough to be really in love without encouragement. In nine cases out of ten, a woman had better show more affection than she feels.* Had those been Charlotte's exact words? At the time, Elizabeth had thought her friend cold and mercenary, but had she been, rather, correct?

Had Jane not done enough to assure Mr. Bingley of her regard? It seemed sufficient for the gentleman concerned, but not enough for his sister or friend. She ought to walk right into the room and confront them...

But of course she could not do that! She must think of what to do. But Mr. Darcy spoke again.

"Perhaps I will speak to him once more. I must try to warn him that Miss Bennet may not truly care for him, that he ought not lose his heart completely to her."

"And I shall do likewise. Perhaps we, together, can make him see reason. Oh, how I should like to go back to London. Do you not miss London, Mr. Darcy? The theatre, the galleries, the fine society...?"

Elizabeth could listen no longer. She slid back to the hallway and carried on to her rooms, rage and heartbreak warring for prominence in her breast. She must talk to Jane, have her somehow assure Mr. Bingley of her affection.

But worse, this confirmed everything ill that Mr. Wickham had said of Darcy. He was, indeed, a cold and arrogant man. How she had been mistaken about him; how his love for her had turned her head and blinded her to the truth. And she had allowed him—encouraged him, even—to kiss her only yesterday. The horror, the shame of it. Her first impressions had been the correct ones, it seemed. Mr. Darcy was no gentleman at all!

She flung open her bedroom door, and as tears began to flow down her face, she threw herself upon the bed and cried until sleep overcame her.

Chapter Fourteen

I am apt to do myself wrong

(Benedick, 2.1)

The sun was very low in the sky when Elizabeth awoke. She cracked open her eyes and tried to identify the sounds that had roused her from her sleep. Rustling, and the creak of wood. She opened her eyes further to see who was about. Annie was busy at the grate, tending to the fire, and Jane sat in her Bath chair at the side of the bed.

"I slept as well," her sister stated. Elizabeth rolled over and rubbed her eyes. Jane continued, "Mr. Jones came back with the crutches and he and Mr. Bingley helped me walk about the parlour for a time. It is rather tiring."

"Mr. Bingley was attentive?"

"Oh, very much so! I do like him, Lizzy."

"Have you told him as much?" Memories of that horrid conversation she had heard flooded her mind. But Jane looked aghast.

"Tell him? Oh, I could not do that! It would be most improper. A lady always waits for the gentleman to speak first. To do otherwise would be far too forward. But I am certain he knows it. I can hardly hide how I feel."

Elizabeth struggled up to sit. At once, her head began to ache and a tightness grew behind her eyes. She fell back against the pillows.

"Oh, Lizzy? Another headache?" Jane knew her too well. "Here is some water. Annie, can you bring Miss Elizabeth some tea? Let me find a compress for your head... oh, but I cannot walk! Annie, can you... thank you."

Jane fussed about as much as she was able, and once Annie had returned with a cold compress and the promise of tea, she spoke more about her afternoon.

"We walked with the crutch for a while. Mr. Jones thinks it is well that I move around, if I put no weight on my foot. It will be some weeks still until I am able to walk unassisted, but I shall be pleased not to be confined to the chair, no matter how much I appreciate its use. Papa returned with him as well, and Mama too, but not our sisters. They are having Mrs. Hill set up the room off the library for me, but Mama insists it cannot be ready until tomorrow. Mr. Bingley has graciously invited us to remain for one final night."

"To which Mama, I am certain, agreed without hesitation."

"She only cares about our futures, Lizzy."

The throbbing behind her eyes intensified. "Perhaps Mama would be better to keep her thoughts to herself. Oh, forgive me, Janey! But she is so open about her wishes and people hear and misunderstand her. I would be most distressed if something untoward were to happen because of her lack of better judgement."

Jane adjusted the compress and began to massage Elizabeth's temples. "Nothing will happen, Lizzy. Everybody knows it is only her way. She means no harm. Here, is this easier? Good."

She worked her slim fingers around the compress to rub at Elizabeth's temples and forehead and Elizabeth moaned at the relief this offered. Jane sighed and worked in silence for a few moments before speaking further.

"Papa had more news for us. He told me of a letter he had received some time ago, which he only recently answered, from our cousin Mr. Collins."

"Mr. Collins!" Elizabeth exclaimed, then winced at the stab of pain this evoked. "Is he not the man who will inherit Longbourn once Papa is no longer alive? The man whom Papa says he will never admit to Longbourn whilst he draws breath?"

"It is he. It seems Papa has had a change of heart. Mr. Collins wrote of the disagreement between his own father and ours, which he claims has always given him uneasiness. In an attempt to heal the breach between the two sides of the family, he proposes this visit as a gesture of good-will. He is recently ordained as a clergyman, he says, and feels this his Christian duty as well as his own genuine wish." Jane moved her fingers to another tender place on Elizabeth's brow. "Furthermore, he makes some comments that lead Mama to suppose he wishes to marry one of us, to fully atone for his sin of being the next in line in the entail."

"Mama would indeed believe that! But it shall not be you, Jane, for you still have Mr. Bingley's esteem, and neither shall it be me!"

The gentle fingers stopped their careful ministrations. "Do you have expectations from Mr. Darcy, then?"

"Mr. Darcy? No, indeed! I fear I have been mistaken about him of late, that my initial impressions were more true to his nature."

"No! Surely you cannot believe that."

Elizabeth pushed herself up to sitting again and squinted at Jane from under the compress. "I have learned things, Janey, that I wish I had never known, but that I am glad I do know. I could not bear to think well of a man who is, at his essence, cruel and heartless. My conscience demands that of me. I shall not tell you what I learned, but not even you could make him good. No, I cannot imagine a man I would wish to marry. I shall remain an old maid and be the happier for it." She allowed herself to collapse back onto the bed. "I am sore at heart, for I had come to like the man I thought he was."

A bell sounded from the main part of the house. "It is time to dress for dinner..."

"You go, Jane, and please give my apologies. Tell them I have a headache, for it is quite true. Here is Annie again. She can help you."

After a moment's argument, Jane agreed. She leaned forward to kiss Elizabeth's forehead and disappeared into her own room, with Annie behind her, pushing the chair. Elizabeth adjusted the compress on her forehead and somehow drifted off into another unsettled slumber.

When next she opened her eyes, it was quite dark outside. Her fire was burning merrily in the grate, and somebody had brought in a tray for her. She washed her face and had some of the cool lemonade and warm stew and felt much recovered, the headache all but gone.

A glance at the clock by the wall showed it was half-past eight, far too late to join the family for dinner. In truth, she had no wish to be with the Bingleys or with Mr. Darcy. What she had heard today, both from Mr. Wickham and from Darcy's own lips, had so upset her that the very thought of him made her stomach roil. To deny help to a friend who was in danger; to ruin his sister's happiness; to work to destroy her own sister's future—all of these singly would be enough to make her wish never to see him again. Worse still was her mistaken affection for him. Her emotions were traitors to her reason! The man who had gone riding with her, who had taken her in his arms and kissed her until she forgot about the world, was a chimaera, an illusion. All this appearance of goodness was nothing but a mask to hide the true devil within. It was far too dreadful to contemplate. Cruel, cruel man.

Tomorrow could not come too soon, when she and Jane might be out of this house and away from Mr. Darcy forever.

Her stomach knotted and her mind awhirl, she paced the floor awhile before selecting a book to try to read.

She had no sooner opened the cover when a knock came at her door, and none other than the dreaded Mr. Darcy appeared.

"Miss Bennet." He bowed and entered the room without asking permission. He was dressed as smartly as ever she had seen him, and his every movement was formal to the point of stiffness. Could he have learned that she had discovered the truth about him? Had he come to confront her about it? He stared at her and stalked to the window before turning back to face her.

"In vain I have struggled," he began. "It will not do. My feelings will not be repressed."

So it was true. He was going to confess all his sins to her! But his next words were quite unlike anything she had expected.

"You must allow me to tell you how ardently I admire and love you."

Elizabeth's astonishment was beyond expression. That he *professed* to love her, she knew, for she had heard it from Richard and Mr. Bingley not so long ago. Perhaps he had convinced even himself. But after hearing Mr. Wickham speak, Elizabeth was certain that the man could truly love no one but himself. He was cold and heartless, happy to ruin the prospects and happiness of everybody about him. He knew nothing of genuine love. His attentions to her had only been in the interests of a dalliance, as men of his station were known to engage in. Fortunate was she that she had allowed him no more than a kiss.

And yet, he was speaking these very words of love and ardour to her, almost as if he believed them. She stood, her mouth agape. But even this was nothing to what she heard next.

"In coming forward thus, I have fought my better inclinations, and have settled on the side of tenderness of feeling. Our stations, as you well know, are quite unequal. My uncle is an earl—my own grandfather was an earl—and we move amongst the first circles. I shall endeavour to bring you up to their level that you may meet them with equanimity, and yet I shall gladly withstand the loss should they choose to refuse you into their society, such is my passion."

And on he spoke whilst she stood there aghast, listening to his recital of her every fault, of her family's every inferiority. "It is only by the strength of my attachment, which I have found impossible to conquer, that I now deign to offer you my hand, which I only hope you will accept."

To which she had but one response.

She quite refused him.

Had he spoken yesterday, she might have accepted him. Had he spoken before she knew the truth, she would have been honoured, despite the cold calculation with which he enumerated his thoughts for and against her. She certainly would have wished not to cause him pain. But now, knowing what she did, such was her anger at him, and such was her own shame at having been taken in by him, that she could not temper her response.

"I have learned such things of you, sir, that I do not desire your good opinion, and if you have bestowed such upon me, I am certain it was unwillingly. No, Mr. Darcy, I cannot accept the hand of one who crows of his superiority, but who displays nothing of the behaviour expected of a man of quality. I am a gentleman's daughter and must marry a gentleman. And you, sir, I state once more, are no gentleman."

She moved to the door to open it for his exit, but he stood there, glaring at her, his face turning now red, now white. At length he regained some semblance of calm and spat out, "And this is all the reply which I am to have the honour of expecting! I might, perhaps, wish to be informed why, with so little *endeavour* at civility, I am thus rejected. But it is of small importance."

"You have offered for me with such offence and insult that I could never accept you. You chose to tell me that you loved me against your better reason, that you consider my condition an abasement. Your insults when first we met were more welcome to me than this contempt which now you show me. But I have other reasons for deciding against you."

"And what might these be?" His voice was as cold as ice.

"I know of your treatment of Mr. Wickham. When first he approached me I thought he was somehow mistaken by your refusal to grant him the living which he had been expecting; I thought there was some legal impediment, or some misunderstanding. But now I have learned that he is in desperate need of help, that he fears some dire consequence for a minor debt, which you refuse to offer to him. You would see a childhood friend suffer in the cruellest way before unbending enough to offer him succour. This is not the behaviour I would see in any man I could agree to marry.

"But there is more. I have also learned of your ruthless treatment of your sister." If she did not know better, she could almost believe he looked confused. But he surely knew exactly of what she spoke.

"I almost wished to believe Mr. Wickham false when he told of how you had come between him and your sister, preventing their long-desired marriage, and carrying her off to Pemberley to be some sort of prisoner so they might never be together.

"But in your very own words, just moments ago, you have demonstrated clearly that your sense of pride and station rate more strongly than the demands of love and attachment. I am scarcely good enough for you, despite being of equal rank; it is now evident that Mr. Wickham is by no means good enough for your sister. Your arrogance and pride are everything to you, worth more than your sister's heart and happiness."

"How dare you..." he began. "The man speaks all lies!"

"And there is one matter more, Mr. Darcy, which quite turns me against you. I did not intend to hear, but happenstance brought me by the room when you were speaking to Miss Bingley earlier. I know that you are seeking to separate my sister from your friend. I heard you discuss her mercenary ways of attempting to catch Mr. Bingley. Have you ever spoken to Jane? Have you attempted even once to discern her heart? Can you know the depths of her feelings when you clearly have never attributed anything fine to anybody other than yourself? My sister is no social-climber, sir, and would never marry for any reason other than affection. That you would seek to dissuade your friend from knowing her better marks you as one of the very last men I would ever be prevailed upon to marry. And now," she swung the door wide, "I beg you to leave me. We have nothing more to say to each other."

He opened his mouth once or twice, as if seeking words that would not come to him. "And this," he managed at last, "is your opinion of me! This is the estimation in which you hold me. I was led to believe, only yesterday, that your sentiments were more generous. I was misled. I thank you for explaining it so fully." She had never seen such thunder on his face, and she was almost afraid of him.

"Then we have both been deceived." She glared back.

He now walked quickly up and down the room, his present agitation quite replacing the icy reserve with which he had entered not so long ago.

"You have said quite enough. I perfectly comprehend your feelings and have now only to be ashamed of my own. Forgive me for having taken up so much of your time."

And with these words, he marched from the room, slamming the door behind him. And for the second time that day, Elizabeth threw herself onto her bed in a torrent of hot tears.

Chapter Fifteen

Into a pit of ink

(Leonato, 4.1)

Elizabeth and Jane were a sombre pair the following morning. Jane, whilst pleased to be returning to her home and family, confessed to a regret at leaving Mr. Bingley's house. "He has been everything attentive to me, Lizzy, and I dare say I have hopes. And his sisters are so kind and charming, I shall quite miss their company when I am home."

Elizabeth could not echo Jane's sentiments regarding Miss Bingley and Mrs. Hurst, but she quite understood Jane's reluctance to leave Mr. Bingley. "Still, some time apart might bring him to thoughts of how much he misses you, and you never know where that might lead!" she teased.

Elizabeth, on the other hand, could not leave Netherfield quickly enough for her tastes. She had little patience for Bingley's sisters and quite dreaded the prospect of seeing Mr. Darcy again. Odious, arrogant, lizard-hearted man! His sin was not accidental, but a matter of pride for him, a veritable profession! With every thought, every recollection, her anger grew.

Fortunately, he was nowhere to be seen when the sisters came for breakfast, Jane on her crutches, Annie walking behind with the Bath chair should it be needed. Only Mr. Bingley was in the room. He seemed to have been waiting for them.

"Miss Bennet!" He leapt to his feet and pulled out a chair for Jane, who gave him a radiant smile and took her seat. "Miss Elizabeth." His friendliness, at least, was genuine. How could so good and kind a man surround himself with such duplicitous companions?

He helped Jane to her breakfast and then, taking his own, sat beside her. Elizabeth sat opposite them with her own morning repast.

"I am so very pleased that you are recovering well," he began, "although I shall be sad to see you leave my house. I have enjoyed our time together. The separation will be an unhappy one." Elizabeth wished she had some excuse to leave the room; surely Mr. Bingley wished to speak only to Jane. But she could think of no reason to rise, and her tea was hot in its delicate cup.

"However," Mr. Bingley continued, "I hope our separation shall not be for long. I propose..." he took a breath, and Elizabeth realised she had forgotten something—anything!—in her room. But as she started to rise, Mr. Bingley continued, "I propose a ball! In your honour, Miss Bennet, in celebration of your recovery. I know you will be unable to dance for some time, but I hope that presiding at a ball will provide some pleasure even if you must sit the whole evening."

His face was so hopeful and eager that Elizabeth could not help but smile.

"Thank you, Mr. Bingley. I am honoured." Jane cast her eyes downward in a display of modesty, but her smile was radiant.

"And, please God, when you are quite healed—and heeled!" he laughed at his joke, "—we shall have a second ball and there, I hope, you will honour me with the first dance."

"Thank you. Nothing would please me more."

"Excellent!" He looked like a puppy dog who had just mastered some great trick to please his owner. "Let us plan our first ball, then. What say you to the Thursday after next? That will give Caroline a full week and more to arrange everything, which I am certain she can do with Mrs. Nicholls' assistance. Will that do?"

Jane blushed. "Most excellently, I am certain!"

"Good, good, then. Here, may I help you to some more eggs? Toast? Chocolate?" He bustled about like a mother hen, seeing to Jane's every need and allowing Elizabeth to finish her own breakfast without the need to speak more than two or three words.

At last, they were ready to go. The trunks were packed, and Jane was sitting with Caroline and Louisa as the servants prepared the carriage. It was a journey of only four miles, the lanes being less direct than the three miles across the fields, but the preparations were equal to those of a much longer trip. Trunks must be stowed, a suitable seat for Jane arranged, and warm bricks prepared. Elizabeth begged their indulgence to walk once more in the gardens until the carriage was ready.

The house, as grand and as elegant as it was, had become oppressive. Even the air in the fine rooms felt heavy and somehow malevolent, and the potential of meeting Mr. Darcy was a leaden weight upon her soul. She found her coat and bonnet and all but ran from the house to wander under watery white skies.

She wandered through the gardens and a short distance through the wooded park when the sound of footsteps stayed her feet. There, a short distance away, stood the last person in the world she wished to see: Mr. Darcy.

He stood absolutely still and looked about to turn and run, when he straightened up and slipped his hand inside a pocket on his greatcoat and withdrew a white envelope with a large red seal at the flap.

"I have been walking these paths for some time in the hopes of meeting you. Will you do me the honour of reading that letter?" He held it out towards her, and in a motion born of instinct rather than rational thought, she accepted it from his hand. And then, with a slight bow, he turned again into the trees and was soon out of sight.

She stared at the package in her hand. She knew this paper well, for she had used some of Mr. Bingley's supply during her own residence in his house to write notes to her family and letters to her aunt in London. She really ought to discard it at once. A lady never receives a missive from a man not a relation or connected by matters of business. It was quite improper, and she wondered if she should drop it in the pond through the woods or consign it to the fire, unopened.

And yet her hand gripped the paper. She could not imagine herself destroying it.

Foolish girl! She chided herself. What was she thinking? Even now, her fingers were picking at the seal, embossed by a crest she had seen on one of the carriages in the carriage house near the stables. No, she really ought not to read it—ought not even to have taken it from his hand—but her curiosity was greater than her sense of propriety. Very well. She would do him this last favour and read it. She was now more impatient than ever for her return to Longbourn where she might retire to the quiet comfort of her room and, in blessed familiar silence, peruse the words which Mr. Darcy had deemed so important to give to her.

Still, her curiosity would not be stifled. The seal broke and she stared down at the letter in her hands. With no expectation of pleasure, Elizabeth opened the letter, perceiving therein two sheets of paper, written quite through in a very close hand, the envelope too being full. Her eyes flickered to the package, but her attempts were forestalled by a call from the house. For good or for ill, she would not have the time now to read it, for the carriage was ready. Before she tucked it away in her reticule, however, she allowed herself to glance at the first sheet. It was dated from Netherfield at eight o'clock that morning. How much had he written? What had he to say that must be consigned thus to paper? She would have to wait until she was alone to learn it.

That longed-for solitude, however, was a long time in coming. Immediately upon the carriage returning Jane and Elizabeth to their home at Longbourn, the entire family rushed out to greet them, as if they had been in Russia or Italy for months, and not across the fields and unseen by their closest relations only since yesterday.

"Jane, Lizzy! You are home!" Mrs. Bennet cried as the carriage came to a stop and the footman opened the door, waiting for Jane so he could carry her from the vehicle and into the house. "You must tell us everything. Everything! How were the beds? Was Mr. Bingley's food good? What of the servants? Did Miss Bingley really make you sleep in the front hall?"

Their sisters were no less exuberant in their welcome. Mary, usually silent unless pontificating upon some point, actually gave both Elizabeth and Jane a hug and welcomed them home. "I shall be pleased to have your good sense in the house once more. I have missed you." And Kitty and Lydia could not stop talking about the officers.

"Did they come often? Who was the most frequent visitor? Was it Denny? I do like Denny, for he is more handsome than Sanders, but he is nothing compared to Mr. Wickham! What of Colonel Fitzwilliam? Is he always in his regimentals? A man is so handsome in a uniform. Is he a real colonel? Has he been to war? Did he show you any scars? La! How I wish we had more officers visiting Longbourn!"

Even their Papa made an appearance, kissing each of his prodigal daughters on the forehead in turn. "I have missed you, Lizzy," he said when everybody else was out of hearing. "I have not heard two words of sense together since you went to Netherfield."

They were ushered into the drawing room where a full luncheon had been prepared for them, despite breakfast having been only a short time before, and there Jane's foot was examined and discussed at length. "Is it still sore? Can you move your ankle? Are the crutches awfully uncomfortable? Show us how you walk with them!" Her sisters could not stop the flow of words, and eventually Jane satisfied them all by taking a turn about the room to demonstrate her emerging skills with the wooden devices. This was followed by the entire family accompanying her to her new bedchamber on the ground storey, so she would not have to take the stairs until her foot was quite healed.

"And this way," Kitty ventured, "Mama will be able to give your room to our cousin Mr. Collins when he arrives tomorrow, which he has promised to do. For the guest bedroom is quite in disarray and it will be easier to fix yours for him instead of tending to the other one."

"Kitty!" their mother hissed, and Lydia laughed.

With all this ado, it was not until much later, when the family retired to their rooms to dress for dinner, that Elizabeth finally was able to close her own bedroom door and withdraw Mr. Darcy's letter from her reticule, where it had been sitting like a hot ember all the long day. She pulled a chair close to the window and wrapped herself in her favourite shawl. Then, unfolding the envelope, she separated the pages and began to read.

Be not alarmed, Madam, on receiving this letter, by the apprehension of its containing any repetition of those sentiments, or renewal of those offers, which were last night so disgusting to you. I write without any intention of paining you, or humbling myself, by dwelling on wishes which, for the happiness of both, cannot be too soon forgotten.

"Odious, arrogant man! Boil! Plague sore! To have cast off our friendship so easily!"

My character required that this letter be written and, I hope, read. You must, therefore, pardon the freedom with which I demand your attention; your feelings, I know, will bestow it unwillingly, but I demand it of your justice.

"He demands? What right has he to demand anything of me? He is a foul-spoken coward to trust to paper what his own lips will not dare to say. I half fear that reading his words will infect my eyes!"

Three offences of a very different nature, and by no means of equal magnitude, you last night laid to my charge. The first mentioned concerned my dealings with Mr. Wickham and your accusation of having injured him in the past and at present. I cannot refute his story, for of what he has particularly accused me, I am ignorant; but of the truth of what I shall relate, I can summon more than one witness of undoubted veracity.

I shall begin with the presumption that Mr. Wickham has relayed his long-standing complaint, that of the living to which he avers he was destined. I shall lay it all out; every word I write can be attested to by others. My cousin, Colonel Fitzwilliam, is only one man of many who know the entirety of the matter.

Mr. Wickham was the son of my father's steward, a most respectable man, and his son was raised with me at Pemberley and sent to the best schools, where he was given a gentleman's education. You have heard,

I am certain, of his long-standing complaint that I have denied him a valuable living on my properties, to which he felt he was destined. This living was, indeed, offered to him by my own excellent father, who died five years ago. It was my father's hope—his wish—that this young man might take the church as his profession. In my father's will, he recommended to me to promote Mr. Wickham's advancement and suggested that if he took orders, he should be given a valuable living on my lands when it became vacant.

It was not half a year from this time that Mr. Wickham wrote to me to say he had resolved against taking orders after all, a decision I supported, for the man's character is not suited to that of a clergyman. But I digress. To the point, Mr. Wickham suggested that since he would not take the living, it was not unreasonable to expect some more immediate pecuniary advantage. He had some intention of studying the law, and the one thousand pounds given to him by my father's will was insufficient for such an undertaking. I agreed. He resigned all claim to assistance in the church and in return accepted an additional sum of three thousand pounds. All connexion between us now seemed dissolved.

For three years, I heard little of him, but tales of his dissipated lifestyle and mounting debts. But on the decease of the incumbent of the living, he applied to me again for the presentation. His circumstances were exceedingly bad, and was now determined on being ordained.

"What? One thousand pounds and then three thousand more? Gone in three years? I can scarcely believe it! Such an amount would be a competence for life for a careful person, and a most comfortable start for one engaging in a career of law."

You will hardly blame me for refusing his entreaty. He has come to me often since then, each time requesting more money for one purpose or another. I have assisted him, but each time he has spent or lost the lot of it within months. I have since informed him without equivocation that I will give him not one penny more until such time as he mends his ways completely.

This most recent such occurrence, of which I am certain he has told you, is a sad matter in which he engaged in wagers of amounts far beyond his purse, and upon losing all, felt compelled to meet his debts by relieving the militia regiment's treasury of the amount, a total of five hundred pounds. It is this debt that he now wishes me to pay for him, and which, in keeping with my assurances to him that I would not subsidise his habits, I refused and advised him to take his quarrel to Colonel Forster in the hopes that this might, at last, turn him from his current path to one more honourable. Blame me for that, if you will.

"Five hundred pounds? Five *hundred?*" Mr. Wickham had not been precise but had intimated to her a far lesser amount. This was a fortune! No wonder the man had spent his way through four thousand pounds in three years! And to steal another five hundred from the regiment? "Can it be believed?"

She rose from her seat and stormed about the room for some minutes before regaining her equilibrium and sitting back down to read further.

I shall now mention the second circumstance which you mentioned, that regarding Mr. Wickham and my sister. As you hopefully now recognise, Mr. Wickham is not a man of strong character and virtue, and his aim was not that of love but of something far more base. I have mentioned my sister to you before. She is more than ten years my junior, about your sister Lydia's age. Last summer she and her companion went to Ramsgate, where Mr. Wickham also went, almost certainly by design, for there proved to be a prior acquaintance between him and my sister's companion at the time. In Ramsgate, he came upon my sister as if by happenstance and thence recommended himself to her until she believed herself to be quite in love with him. She consented to an elopement. She was but fifteen.

"Fifteen!" This was alarming. Elizabeth had known his sister was a great deal younger than he, but she had not imagined Miss Darcy to be that young. She was only Lydia's age, not Mary's, as Elizabeth had thought. "How Mr. Wickham misled me. He is a man of nearly thirty, and she a girl who is little more than a child! How base! How he has lied to me; he led me to think her much older than that. What else has he lied about? That coward, that infinite liar! He breaks promises by the hour!"

That I refused the connexion and took my sister immediately from the place should come as no shock to you; Mrs. Younge was discharged at once, and Wickham immediately took himself far from Ramsgate, to where, exactly, I knew not. All I knew was that I must protect my sister, which I have done by ensconcing her at Pemberley with her new companion. As for Wickham, his intent was clear. He cared not at all for my sister, but for her fortune of thirty thousand pounds. This I know for when I offered to consider his suit if he relinquished all claim to her dowry, he told me so in as many words. I shudder to think of what might have happened had I not come to Ramsgate when I did.

His goal was revenge, and had he succeeded in his plan, his revenge would have been complete.

"How awful! That poor, poor girl! How I have been misled." She imagined Lydia, young and naïve despite her adult mannerisms, being so deceived by such a man and her heart all but missed a beat.

There is one more charge of which I desire to acquit myself. You accused me of conspiring with Miss Bingley to separate your sister from my friend. I must confess to having thoughts of such, but I decided otherwise.

Miss Bennet is everything charming and lovely, but to my eye, showed no particular attachment to Bingley. This I admitted to Miss Bingley when we spoke, which conversation I believe you overheard. I know not which words came to you and which did not, but I assure you that I expressed my concern, but then advised the lady that I would counsel her brother to ascertain for himself the depth of Miss Bennet's attachment.

In these, as in all these matters, I offer you the word of my cousin Colonel Fitzwilliam in corroboration, as he is privy to my innermost thoughts and to the affairs concerning my sister. If your abhorrence of me should make my assertions valueless, you may confide in him. I shall endeavour to put this letter in your hands ere you depart Netherfield. I will only add, God bless you.

Fitzwilliam Darcy

"Oh, how I have been so blind, so easily led! That I had eyes more able to see, and a mind less blinded by my own pride and preconceptions. Poor Miss Darcy! Poor Mr. Darcy! I have had the chance for love handed to me, and I have cast it aside as worthless because of my own foolishness!"

And thus she sat, reading and rereading the letter and berating herself until Mary came to beg her attend the family for dinner.

Chapter Sixteen

Come, Friar Francis, be brief

(Leonato, 4.1)

Elizabeth did not see Mr. Darcy again.

When Charlotte came to visit the following morning, she brought with her the news that Mr. Darcy and Colonel Fitzwilliam had returned to London.

"Father had it from Mr. Bingley himself," she explained. "They left on horseback at great speed, leaving word for their trunks to follow on a cart."

"Will they not return, then?" Jane asked.

"I cannot say. Mr. Bingley did not offer such information and I do not know if Father asked it."

So Mr. Darcy was gone, and with him the chance to speak to him again. Even had he been in the neighbourhood, Elizabeth did not know what she might say. She could hardly hope for a renewal of his addresses to her, but she did wish for an opportunity to apologise. She had been wrong, so wrong, and wished to atone for her mistakes. She tried to smile and be bright for her friend's sake, but this news had sunk her spirits quite low.

In place of Mr. Darcy, however, another gentleman appeared in Meryton, there to amuse and entertain the local society. Mr. Bennet's cousin Mr. Collins arrived, as he had written he would, to pay his addresses to the family and ingratiate himself in the eyes of Mrs. Bennet and, it was widely rumoured, to take a wife from amongst the Bennet sisters.

Mr. Collins was a large man of five-and-twenty years. He was neither handsome nor plain, and within a short time of his arrival at Longbourn, was determined by Elizabeth to be one of the most foolish men of her acquaintance. He dropped meaningless flatteries like autumn leaves, where they were neither sought nor wanted, and he spouted lessons and examples from Scripture that he clearly did not understand.

"How fortunate you are in your family, Mr. Bennet. '*Children are a heritage from the Lord, a reward from Him.*'" How little he forgot that these 'rewards,' all being female, would remove from the family forever the heritage of Longbourn. Mr. Bennet replied nothing in return, other than to invite his relation into the house.

Only Mrs. Bennet seemed pleased with him, for the prospect of marrying off one of her daughters was her greatest aspiration. When Mr. Collins complimented her on her house, the excellent tea, the weather, and singular beauty of her collective daughters, she grew besotted with him to a degree that Elizabeth had seldom seen.

"You have a very fine family of daughters," he announced to his hostess. "And how comfortable is this settee. I have heard very much of their beauty—of your daughters' beauty, not that of your furniture, although that is exceedingly fine as well—but in this instance words fall far short of the truth, for they are all, singularly and plurally, excellent young women."

Mrs. Bennet cooed, and Mr. Collins, encouraged, continued, "I cannot doubt that, with such loveliness, they will all soon be well disposed. Well disposed in marriage, that is. No matter their lack of fortunes, their fair faces must recommend them."

Such words were inanity to Elizabeth, and very much not to her tastes, but her mother replied in kind, "You are very kind, sir. I wish with all my heart it may prove so, for else they will have nothing."

"I am sensible as to the harm my place in the entail brings to my cousins, and I could say more on the subject… but no more for now. But I assure these blossoms of womanhood that I come prepared to admire them. No more for now, but perhaps when we are better acquainted—" He looked from one sister to the other, taking the measure of each in her turn, and Elizabeth felt a rush of revulsion at the sight of it.

Nor was her unwelcome cousin's desire to take a bride solely of his own making; instead, it came out, this impetus was encouraged by another of the man's acquaintance.

"My esteemed patroness, the great Lady Catherine de Bourgh," he pontificated at dinner, "has advised me, and most wisely so, that a man of my station ought by all rights to take a wife, and as soon as possible." He looked at Jane, who was the loveliest of the five pretty sisters, but at a less-than-subtle shake of Mrs. Bennet's head, turned his eyes to Elizabeth.

"Does Lady Catherine often advise you on such intimate matters?" she asked, keeping her voice as serious as possible.

Her cousin folded his hands before him. "Indeed, Cousin Elizabeth, I am most gracious for her ladyship's condescension, for she is a veritable font of wisdom, and I strive to satisfy her desires—that is, her desires to direct matters for their best outcome—for she is most insistent upon having the finest ideas for the management of one's household and one's affairs, which benefit is seen in the meticulous management of Rosings, the great house in which she dwells." He stopped to draw breath.

"I see. How... interesting. And is the great lady herself married?"

"She is a widow, possessed of one daughter, the heir to the grand house of Rosings. Her opinions are everything excellent, and she has counselled me well. She has given me several reasons for marrying, which are commendable and most wise, as is every pearl of wisdom that passes her most excellent lips. It is the duty of a clergyman, so she says, to set the example of a moralistic and Christian life in his parish by taking a good sort of a bride, who will deal well with the parishioners and will make him a pleasant home.

She has advised me to choose a gentlewoman who will make a small income go a good way, and who will attend to her with the diligence which a lady of her standing deserves."

And on he spoke, using expensive words as if they were cheap at the market that week, and fully understanding but few of them. Elizabeth wondered at his willingness to have his patroness manage so very much of his existence, to the point of heeding her suggestion to put shelves in one of the upstairs closets; perhaps he was too childlike to have any thoughts of his own!

Throughout the evening, Elizabeth noticed his eyes always upon her, and soon began to fear that she was his next choice after Jane. She must find a way to disabuse him of any thoughts of offering for her. She could hardly claim, as Jane could, a prior attachment. No one knew of Mr. Darcy's proposal and of her resounding refusal thereof. It would not do to have her mother and sisters learn of her shame, for her mother would think only of the ten thousand a year she had cast away like so many baubles, no matter the character of the man who earned them. In the end, she decided to tell Mr. Collins in no uncertain terms that she had no interest at the moment in marrying.

Her opportunity came the following morning, when the sisters made a plan to walk into Meryton. Lydia and Kitty hoped to see some new ribbons at the haberdashers—and presumably to see some of the scarlet-coated officers—and Elizabeth wished to visit her Aunt Phillips and Margaret Robinson. Jane must, of course, remain at home, and Mary stated her intention to do likewise, to sit with her invalid sister.

Having heard once more that Jane was likely soon to be engaged, Mr. Collins proposed to accompany his fair cousins into the village. As Kitty and Lydia walked ahead, he fell into step with Elizabeth.

"A fine morning this is, and most invigorating and effervescent, as fine as anything I have seen in Hunsford. That is where my parish is in Kent, and a very fine one it is too. It is a fine house with a good prospect, and is separated only by a laneway from the extenuating park around Rosings, that noble house wherein dwells my patroness Lady Catherine de Bourgh. It has a good sort of garden—the parsonage, that is, not Rosings, which has a great many fine gardens all well tended—and a fine room looking over the lane along which Miss de Bourgh, Lady Catherine's daughter, at times drives in her phaeton with her companion. Your mother's fine salon reminds me of that room."

The nerve of that man! "My mother's fine salon brings you to mind of the front room of your parsonage?"

"Indeed—that is, I would not dare to suggest that anything in my own poor home is equal to your own charming and elegant abode, but the proportions of the room and the light coming through the trees does bring some of its finer and most appealing aspects to mind."

And so he spoke with such pompous nothings until they had all but arrived in the centre of the town. As Kitty and Lydia rushed ahead, calling out about some new bonnet in a shop window, Mr. Collins paused, making Elizabeth slow her steps not to outpace him.

"Would such a place as a village parsonage suit your hopes, Cousin Elizabeth? Have you given thought to what your desires for the future might be?"

He surely could not be so forward as to ask her this now! And yet, such was his inflated sense of himself that he likely could not imagine his words to be unwelcome. Now was her time to put all such thoughts out of his head.

"I am certain your home is everything charming, Mr. Collins, and will be a fine home for the proper woman; I, however, am known to be far too outspoken and impertinent ever to suit as a parson's wife, for I am certain to say quite the wrong thing and cause all manner of offence. Your esteemed patroness would find me quite headstrong! No, I have long since resolved not to marry, for no good man deserves the whipping that my tongue would give on too regular a basis. Instead, I shall be the family's maiden aunt and teach all my nieces and nephews to count to seven in Italian and play their instruments very ill."

He gaped at her as if not quite understanding her words.

"The Bible recommends us, Mr. Collins, to answer every man with meekness and fear. This is a virtue which I have still to learn."

He gaped at her, then blinked and walked on. "Ah. Yes. Yes, I see. I quite take your meaning, madam. And your sisters...?"

"Are better to answer for themselves, sir. I am not their master, nor their keeper."

"Yes, yes. So I see. So I see. Look, there are Cousin Lydia and Cousin Catherine. Let us find them!"

And, to Elizabeth's great satisfaction, all such attentions by Mr. Collins were put to an end before they began.

If Elizabeth had expected her cousin's eyes to move next to her sister Mary, she was mistaken. Despite Mary's piety and serious nature, she was unmoved by Mr. Collins' platitudes and dependence on mis-remembered lines of scripture, and—so she related to Elizabeth late one evening—she found his lack of sense quite inimical to any sort of attachment. She completely ignored the parson until he realised that this was not his future wife, whereupon he moved to the next sister in line, Kitty.

Kitty was seventeen, and if not the loveliest of the Bennet sisters, still a beautiful girl. She was not as tall as Jane and Lydia and had more of Elizabeth's colouring, but none of Elizabeth's wit or good sense. She was kind-hearted but silly and was more wont to follow than to lead or to take action on her own behalf.

Therefore, when Mr. Collins transferred his attentions from Mary to Kitty, she did not put him off. She did not encourage him, and once confessed to Elizabeth that she did not like the man and would certainly never accept him, but she lacked the fortitude or determination to tell him so directly. And, Elizabeth suspected, she took some pride in having a suitor—even an unwanted one—when Lydia, prettier, more lively, and far more flirtatious, did not.

In consequence to what he must have seen as quiet encouragement, Mr. Collins took to following Kitty about like a stray dog. He sat near her when the family were gathered in the parlour or at meals and laughed at her jokes. And when the dry autumn air brought about a slight fit of coughing, as it did every year, he was at her side with a glass of watered wine or some warm honeyed tea before anybody else in the family could respond at all.

When the sisters went walking, he was at her side, and before long the village was abuzz with whispers that Mr. Collins had intentions towards the second youngest Bennet daughter. Mrs. Bennet was in raptures.

"Two daughters married!" she crowed to her friend Lady Lucas one afternoon as they took tea. Elizabeth was sitting with Charlotte, talking about what to wear for Mr. Bingley's rapidly approaching ball, but her mother's voice could not be denied.

"Is it true, Lizzy? Will Mr. Collins offer for Kitty?"

Elizabeth sighed. "I believe he will, and I know not what Kitty will do. She does not like him, that I know, but neither does she dislike him enough to find the strength to refuse him, I fear. And, when I think of it, she would not make a poor sort of parson's wife. She is sweet and kind, and biddable enough that she would do exactly what was expected of her. For him, she is really a rather good choice."

"And for her?" Charlotte asked.

"For her, the choice is less good. She would not be happy, not with him. With a better sort of man, such a role would suit her well."

"He is not... unkind, is he?"

Both Elizabeth and Charlotte knew of the sorts of things that happened when the doors closed, even in supposedly happy marriages. Not all men were honourable; not all women found the married state a good one. There were some households where too many bruises were hidden beneath heavy mobcaps and awkward capes, where too many bones were broken for the normal sorts of household accidents.

"No. I do not believe him to be of that sort of rude temper. Rather, he is dull and really rather stupid. He is not the sort to rouse a woman's heart to feelings of love."

"Not all women require love, Lizzy. For some, security is more important than finer feelings."

Elizabeth contemplated her friend. Still single at twenty-seven and plain, and with no great fortune, Charlotte must feel the weight her continued presence at home placed upon her family. She would surely accept security and the prospect of a kind, if foolish, husband over any hopes of a grand passion.

"You are very wise, my friend. But Kitty is only seventeen. She has time enough to seek love before deciding that security is a better choice. But for now, she must abide Mr. Collins' never-ending devotion. I even believe he walks outside at night purely to sit below her window for a time in a mimicry of a love-lorn lad from times of old. It is—"

"—Affected?" Charlotte supplied.

"Indeed! And a grown man, and a parson at that! He plays the role of himself upon the stage of our lives. I am well relieved he did not settle upon me as his future wife! If he and I were wed, our every conversation would sap his few wits until, after a week, he would have not one left for himself."

"You are too sharp of tongue, Lizzy! He is the fortunate one that you like him not."

Elizabeth laughed at Charlotte's jest and pitied poor Kitty for her undesired beau.

Chapter Seventeen

A canker in a hedge

(Don John, 1.3)

As the day approached for Mr. Bingley's ball, excitement grew throughout the neighbourhood. The shops in Meryton were kept busy selling ribbons and lace and sending lads on fast horses to order extra supplies from London, and the town's bakers and brewers were overwhelmed with orders to ensure that the assembled guests would be adequately refreshed. Netherfield's own kitchens were busy late into the night, and the icehouse in the woods behind the property was filled with treats waiting to be brought out for the enjoyment of all the guests.

A larger band of professional musicians had been engaged and extra servants brought on for the event, and Mr. Bingley even had the floor in the large salon chalked for the benefit of the dancers. There were candles and cards and plenty of wine and punch, and at last even Miss Bingley was satisfied that not a detail had been overlooked.

Everybody of standing had been invited, from the baronet's family from Oakham to the wealthy merchants of Meryton, and Colonel Forster's officers were no exception. That fine gentleman himself had recently returned from London with his new bride and everybody was eager to make the acquaintance of the new Mrs. Forster. Mr. Bingley was even heard to suggest that she might open the ball. It promised to be the grandest affair Meryton had seen in a great many months.

Only Mr. Wickham was unhappy. Colonel Forster still had not discovered whose boot print had been left in the mud outside the regiment's treasury, but he had caused a cast to be taken of the print, and it was only a matter of time before somebody discovered Wickham's old boots now hidden under a pile of dirt just outside of the encampment. He had them made when he was flush with Darcy's money and his initials were embossed into the leather; furthermore, he could not bring himself to burn them for he had none others except for his uniform boots, neither could he hide them further afield, for every man was being watched by his fellows.

With every dawn, his anxiety grew. With every meal, he knew his freedom was soon to be curtailed. With every breath, he cursed

Darcy for bringing him to this state, and he renewed his intentions to destroy the man and everything he loved.

An angry man is not wise, nor is he kind, and after one particularly sleepless night, he set upon a plan.

Darcy, he knew, had taken a liking to the impertinent Miss Elizabeth Bennet, and she, so he believed, returned Darcy's sentiments. That Elizabeth had chosen to believe Darcy over him— George Wickham—gnawed at his gut. Oh, she had listened to his tale with sympathetic enough ears, but her smiles had grown cool when they were in company together at some evening of cards or on the streets, and she seemed to avoid him where possible. No, she must have been swayed by Darcy. That she preferred the arrogant bore over him turned his admiration of her into dislike, then disgust, and then fury. With every thought, her sins grew greater. With every recollection, her culpability in his predicament grew. She was a canker that gnawed at him, giving him no rest. It was not long before Elizabeth was as much the target of his anger as was Darcy.

And now Darcy was gone from Netherfield, and there could be only one reason why: he must have proposed to the lady and been accepted, and was now in London making such arrangements as were necessary for the engagement and eventual wedding. He listened for rumours of the engagement on the streets, but all excitement was for Bingley's ball. Mrs. Bennet must be waiting until that event so her victory would have no competition. And for Darcy, he was a taciturn man at the best of times, not one to crow of his success, but to hold himself even higher and more haughty and preen with greater arrogance. He was, Wickham was certain, meeting with his lawyer and his banker, seeing to the arrangement of his house in town for his wife, preparing his noble relations for the occasion, and otherwise doing what a prospective bridegroom must do to make the settlement needed.

Such a supposition was only confirmed when, the day before the ball, Darcy and Richard Fitzwilliam returned. They would, Wickham believed, announce the engagement at the ball, just as Bingley would announce his engagement to Jane Bennet at that same event.

This latter he knew almost for certain, for he had heard Bingley inquire at the jewellers after a suitable ring to commemorate that betrothal.

And the notion he had, that germ of a thought that sprouted into a vile weed in his fevered imagination, began to grow and develop. He turned it about in his mind, examining it this way and that, considering its strengths and weaknesses and how to bring it all into fruition. If he did this, spoke to that person, acted in such a way, it just might work. He had once seen some French prisoners of war playing at the game of Domino, not in the usual way but setting the tiles up on end in patterns, one close to the next. With a flick of a finger, the first tile would fall, tapping the one before it, and so on, until all lay on their flat surfaces. The effect was fascinating, an enthralling display of inevitable consequences.

He now was ready to set up his tiles. And then, at the right moment, he would flick the first tile and set the events underway. And when the tiles all lay still at the end of their little trick, Darcy would lie crushed beneath them all.

He could destroy them all—his old nemesis, Elizabeth, Bingley, and Jane—with one solitary deed. Once his plans were firm in his head, he needed to pay only one visit, and for that, he needed a haircut and some extra polish on his brass uniform buttons. And the act was as good as done.

Darcy had not intended to return to Netherfield for Bingley's ball. He had said his good-byes ten days ago and departed for London with every thought of travelling thence up to Pemberley to spend Christmas there with his sister, never to darken Meryton's streets again with his presence.

But Georgiana had sent him a letter claiming that she was still heart-sore enough that she wished him to stay away for some time longer, and Richard was eager to return to Hertfordshire. "There are a dashed lot of pretty girls there, Darcy. Do let's go, and I shall see you dance." They were playing billiards in Darcy's town house, neither bothering to keep any sort of score.

"But Elizabeth Bennet will be there."

"As she should be. I had thought you rather fond of the lady."

"I am. I was."

"Darcy?" Richard balanced the end of his cue on the floor and fixed Darcy with his gaze. "Enough of this. You have been a bear all week, and scowling at me every time I mention Miss Elizabeth. No more avoidance. Tell me what occurred or I shall take home two bottles of your best brandy."

Darcy glared at him.

Richard placed his cue ball on the large table and took aim. The ball struck Darcy's cue ball, and then, in the rebound, the red target ball. "There! I score a cannon. Now, I am waiting for your account. Shall I take your turn as well?"

Darcy retrieved the red ball and placed it in its spot before examining the table. He lined up a shot, but missed it and gave a great huff. "Very well. I have been quite ill at ease over the matter."

"Ill at ease? You have been a dragon. I have asked your valet to check your neckcloths for scorch marks."

"Do you wish me to speak or not, Richard? Oh, very well. Talking about it might make it easier to bear." He walked to the sideboard and poured two sherries, taking one for himself and giving the other to his cousin.

"I spoke to her. I declared myself and offered for her. I asked her to marry me."

Richard raised his glass in a toast. "Then I wish you great joy! But why the Friday face all week? You ought to be elated."

"She refused me."

The glass almost hit the table. "She what? After all we did, she refused you?"

"All you did? What did you do? What might that import?" He scowled. Something was amiss. "But it is the sad truth. That blackguard Wickham approached her with his sad tales of woe, and she believed him before me. She cursed me and accused me of every crime under the sun and then spurned my proposal."

He moved back to his cue ball and tried once more. The red ball slipped into the corner pocket. "Hazard." In slow, painful tones, he recounted his ill-received proposal and Elizabeth's vicious refusal. "Wickham's debt, Georgiana's planned proposal, even Bingley's attachment to Jane Bennet—she quite skewered me with slander and half-truths about all, and I was too humiliated, too infuriated, to counter her."

Richard sipped his drink and then replaced it on the mantel to take his shot. "Ah. That, then, is why we departed with such speed the next day. I had wondered. And the lady still believes you to be the worst cad that ever walked the earth?"

"I wrote her a letter."

The cue ball missed its target and bounced harmlessly off the opposite bank. "A letter? Indeed!"

"It was badly done, perhaps, but my honour demanded it. I could not have my name thus sullied without any rebuttal. I explained it all. Including the sad account of Georgiana. Should she ask you about it..."

"Yes, I shall answer. And her response to your note?"

"That I do not know. We left, and I have heard not a word from her or from Bingley, other than Bingley's message today requesting our attendance at his ball."

Richard finished his sherry and sank his next shot. "Hazard. Then we must, by all means, go to this ball. You owe it to your friend, and perhaps to yourself, lest Miss Elizabeth have come to a different opinion about you."

"That I cannot imagine. She was quite... vocal in her accusations. My ears are still ringing from it."

Richard tutted. "The lady is sharp of tongue, that I warrant, but she is not unintelligent and not unfair. Present her with your case. At least you may part as friends, rather than as the bitter enemies you were before."

"And if she does not listen?"

"Then you will be no worse off than you are now."

There ensued a long period of silence. A cloud of thoughts lowered above his head, threatening everything dark and gloomy, but fretting and stewing were solving nothing. He should refuse to go. He would learn to forget her. When he forgot how to use his hands and the sound of his own name. No, he would never forget her. And perhaps Richard had the right of it. Even if she refused to look at him, it could bring him no more harm.

"Very well. My worst pain is that she is in the world and thinking ill of me. I shall do this for Bingley... and hopefully it will bring me some peace. I shall bid my valet pack. We leave in the morning."

Thus it was that Darcy's fine carriage rolled to a stop in front of Netherfield Park shortly after noon on the day before the ball. Bingley had been notified by a fast messenger and rooms were ready for both men.

"The Bennets will come early to dine before the ball," Bingley enthused, "as will the Lucases. Here is the room for cards, and here the ladies' withdrawing room, and here is where we shall set up the supper." And so he paraded about his house, preening as he led them from familiar room to familiar room. "It will be a most special celebration, Darcy. I had not thought to tell anybody, but you are my closest friend, and I did not promise Jane to keep it a secret. We are—that is, I asked Jane Bennet to be my wife and she has accepted me!"

This was met with a round of felicitations from Darcy and Richard, before Bingley continued. "I took your words to heart. I looked at what I knew of her and of her character, and then I considered her mother. But Mrs. Bennet is no worse than any of the matrons in Town, and I have come to know Jane well over the time she resided here during her convalescence. I cannot believe her to be false. I love her, and I have absolute faith in her when she says she loves me too. And tomorrow night, at the ball, we shall announce our engagement to all the local society. Is it not wonderful?"

"Very much so, my friend." Darcy clapped Bingley on the back and Richard shook his hand mightily. "If you know her heart is true, then I am most pleased for you. You will be very happy together, and I wish you everything good in life. May I presume to be invited to the wedding? Excellent. Then I shall celebrate with you there, and—yes, Richard—if there is music at the party, I shall even dance."

Both Caroline and Louisa expressed their great pleasure at Darcy and Richard's return. How they had been deprived of the right sort of company! How starved of elegant conversation! How bereft of the fine manners of the *ton*! They took their refreshments in the music room, where Louisa played first, and Caroline after, as if to demonstrate what accomplishments were to be found in the better homes in England, and then went to dinner. "Cook apologises for a simpler meal this evening," Caroline oozed false modesty, "for she has put all of her forces into tomorrow evening's repast." Still, plate after plate of fine meats and rich ragouts appeared on the table, satisfying even Mr. Hurst, who seemed to think of little other than hunting and his belly.

At last, the evening was coming to a close and Darcy announced his wish to retire for the night. "Tomorrow will be a long day, and we had an early start."

As he and Richard were about to head to their rooms, there came a great knock at the front door and within moments, Mrs. Nicholls led in Captain Sanders, looking most agitated. His coat was misbuttoned and his hair was in great disarray. He looked as if he had been called to action without time to prepare or arrange his *habille*.

"Mr. Bingley, most terribly sorry to charge in like this, so unannounced, so unexpected. But something has happened— something you really must see."

"What is it, man? Tell me at once!"

Sanders shook his head, causing a lock of hair to fall over his eyes. He brushed it back distractedly. "It is beyond the telling. I could not... I dare not. And what I heard might be wrong. But if it is true... I beg you, for your own good. We must ride."

"Is it far?"

"No, not far. Only over at Longbourn. Three miles over the fields, four by the lanes. There is enough moon to ride safely. But time is of the essence." He stood still, his hands now thrust into his coat pockets, but his one foot bounced up and down in its muddy boot, needing to move again.

"Yes. Very well. It sounds dire." Bingley swung his head around wildly, as if searching for something in the room that would give him answers. "Fannow, my horse!"

"Mine too," Richard roared. "My coat! To the stables, now."

"Longbourn?" Darcy echoed. "Ought I to... no. I had better not. I am certain to be most unwelcome. It is best that I remain here. If I am needed, send word at once."

"So I shall," Richard nodded. "Ah, my coat. Bingley, let us be off."

Richard and Bingley followed Sanders' quick steps out of the house. Darcy could already hear the horses whinnying as they were being readied for the short ride. The sky was clear; they would travel quickly over the fields. But all thoughts of an early night were now gone. Whatever could have happened that required such frantic and hasty action? Were all the Bennets well? That must be, else Sanders would have called for a doctor, not Bingley. Darcy sat up a very long time, turning all sorts of dire events over in his thoughts, waiting for the others to return.

It was very late when Bingley and Richard returned. From their walks and the aroma that accompanied them into the house, Darcy suspected their late journey home had taken them past Meryton's public house, where a great deal of ale had been consumed.

Bingley staggered into the house and down the hallway to the stairs without saying a word, uttering only a groan when the steps proved a challenge in his inebriated condition. His eyes, from what Darcy could see, were red-rimmed and his normally cheerful face was tight and emotionless.

Richard was grim. He held his drink better than Bingley did, but was no more voluble on what had transpired. "Everybody is well, but it was an unhappy thing that we saw. I promised I would say no more. To bed."

"Richard?"

"No, Darcy. It is well you were not there. You will learn of it soon enough. Do not ask me."

He let out a world-weary sigh and threw his coat down on a chair. One of the servants would pick it up and have it cleaned and ready for when next he needed it. Without another word, he turned away and trudged down the hallway as if the weight of the world lay upon his shoulders.

With no better option, Darcy followed to his own chambers, but sleep was evasive and he spent the night with a terrible sense of foreboding pressing upon him.

Chapter Eighteen

O mischief strangely thwarting

(Claudio, 3.2)

Elizabeth opened her eyes to bright sunlight. The maid had opened the drapes and a dancing fire warmed the room. It was later than her accustomed hour to rise, but she wished not to spend the latter part of Mr. Bingley's ball yawning. She dressed quickly and twisted her hair into a suitable knot at her nape before descending to see who else was awake.

Jane sat at the breakfast table with her father, her crutches at her side, and a cup of chocolate before her. Papa's eyes were barely visible over the top of the newspaper he held, and from time to time, a pink hand would snake around the broadsheet to pick up or replace the cup of tea, which was his morning choice.

As Elizabeth took her seat, Mr. Collins slid into the room as well. He looked like the cat that had swallowed the canary. He greeted his cousins in his accustomed overblown manner and then announced to the room, "I have requested the first two dances of Cousin Catherine, and she has accepted. I am most looking forward to tonight's ball. Cousin Elizabeth, may I have the second set?" He gave an oleaginous grin, which quite put Elizabeth off her plate of eggs. But there was nothing to do but accept. She did not like her cousin, but had no cause to be uncivil to him. All the more so if he was to be her brother, and more important, the man who would decide whether or not to evict her from Longbourn when he assumed its control, hopefully many, many years away.

"Thank you, Mr. Collins." She rose to replace her eggs with the warm muffins that sat on the sideboard.

"I have been enjoying your gardens at night, Mr. Bennet," the parson spoke around his mouthful of porridge. "The little garden between the west wing and the folly is a particularly charming place to walk after dinner. It brings to mind the path between the kitchen garden at the stables at Rosings..."

"So you have told me." Papa's voice from behind the newspaper was dry.

"I was surprised to see Cousin Catherine walking there last night."

"My daughters are good strong country girls, Mr. Collins, and are not afraid of the moonlight in the safety of their own gardens."

"A wild spirit in a young lady is a trait not to be encouraged, sir. Better that such delicate blossoms be tended and pruned and trained to stay in their places. One might develop... unnatural notions about a young lady who is out of the house alone in the dark."

Papa put down his newspaper. The glimmer of a sarcastic smile limned his lips. "Then, Mr. Collins, when you have daughters, I advise you to raise them accordingly. But please leave the rearing of my own children to me."

"Sir!" Mr. Collins objected. "I intend only to have sons."

"And I wish you well with that thought." Papa picked up the broadsheet and disappeared behind it once more.

"I do hope that you are not so wild as to traipse about in the gardens at night, Cousin Elizabeth."

Elizabeth stifled a snicker. "No, indeed, sir. When I traipse about at night, I am careful to keep to the shaded laneways where I may not be seen." She finished her tea. "Now, Jane, shall I help you to your room? We have a great deal to do to prepare for the ball this evening. Mr. Bingley expects us all for dinner at four."

She helped Jane manage her crutches down the passage to the room, now set aside for her bedroom. There they could talk without fear of being heard, and there Jane ushered her into a chair.

"We had thought to keep this a secret until tonight, Lizzy, but—"

"I knew your face had an extra glow, Jane! Is it Mr. Bingley?"

Jane nodded, her eyes all but shining with joy. "He asked me, just yesterday morning when he came to call, and I said yes! We wished to tell everybody at the ball tonight, but I cannot keep this from you.

I would burst if I did not tell somebody. I am so happy! Why can everybody not be this happy?"

Elizabeth rushed from her chair to embrace her sister. "What news! Oh, what wonderful news! You are so good, my pet, that you deserve all the happiness in the world! My only hope is that Mr. Bingley is of a good enough sort to deserve you."

"He is, Lizzy, he is. He is the very best man in the world."

They talked now, curled up in the warm room, about Jane's hopes and dreams, her expectations and her plans for her wedding. The hours passed all too quickly before it was time to start preparing for the ball.

They arrived at Netherfield in grand style. Even Mr. Bennet elected to appear this evening, for once eschewing his books and folios in preference of society. He was, when garbed in his finest evening dress, a fine-looking man. He was of a good height and his figure showed no evidence of his preference for books over activity. Likewise, Mrs. Bennet, although the mother of five grown daughters, still presented an admirable appearance, and it was little wonder that she had been the beauty of the area in her youth. Her gown was in the latest fashion, cut to best flatter her maternal figure, with—for once—not too much lace and trim to render the elegant obscured.

Following the parents from the carriage came five daughters, each in a lovely gown best suited to the colouring and figure of each. Even Mary, usually the plainest of the five, all but glowed in her soft green frock. There was Elizabeth in pale yellow, Kitty in blue, Lydia in a delicate pink, and last, needing help in her descent from the carriage, Jane in white. They were each lovely, and as a set, striking. They made a most admirable parade as they entered the grand house of Netherfield.

Only Mr. Collins, the very last to enter the house, was less than excellent in appearance. He had not exchanged his parson's garb for evening wear, and looked quite the poor cousin, despite the actuality of affairs.

Mr. Bingley, for his part, seemed quite subdued. There was no hint of the mirth that so often graced his face, no sign of the smile that usually threatened to burst through his most sober thoughts. He was serious, grim even, although he greeted each guest with formal and civil words.

Elizabeth wondered at this. It must be, she mused, due to the enormity of the evening: it was not every day that a man held his first grand ball in his first manor house, and announced his engagement on that same evening. Such would bring any gentleman, no matter how happy of character, to a serious mien.

To her alarm, Mr. Darcy and Colonel Fitzwilliam were present. When she heard that Mr. Darcy had left for London, she had expected him to remain there. His return to Meryton both shocked and bothered her. She felt deeply ashamed of her behaviour towards him, and equally unable to approach him and confess her terrible mistakes. She attempted, as the party sat in the salon before dinner, to catch his eye, to try somehow to convey her thoughts to him, but he studiously avoided looking towards her, focusing intently on his conversations with Miss Bingley or Hurst, or staring out of the window. He smiled at nobody and had the air of a man who was deeply dissatisfied with what he observes. He exhibited, for all she could see, exactly that haughty and cold demeanour that had so disgusted the people of Meryton when first he arrived with Mr. Bingley before Michaelmas.

Despite her glances his way at every opportunity, Mr. Darcy seemed determined to avoid looking at her and seemed to take pains to be needed everywhere she was not. Consequently, no conversation between them was possible, much to Elizabeth's relief and regret.

Dinner was a formal affair. Miss Bingley presided over her table as an empress, and plate after plate of excellent food was presented upon fine white table linens. The Bennets and Lucases were of the party, as were Sir Francis from Oakham and the Robinsons. With so large a gathering at the table, conversation was general and limited to those immediately in proximity.

Eventually, the dinner ended and guests for the ball itself filtered through the front door and into the ballroom. The band set up on a dais at one end of the large salon, and soon enough the room was filled with all the best of the local society, garbed in their finest and all eager for a fine night's entertainment. A thousand candles glowed in their sconces and candelabras, and punch and ratafia flowed copiously.

Elizabeth marvelled at the sight. She had enjoyed the little masquerade ball Bingley had held to entertain Jane, but that event was nothing to the splendour displayed this evening. She caught a glimpse of herself in one large mirror set along a white moulded wall. For a moment, caressed by candlelight and set against a backdrop of a hundred elegant people, she felt herself to be a heroine in a play, or a princess at some grand palace. A flash of light caught the yellow topaz stones on her ears and at her neck and she stood there, staring at herself.

As she gazed at her image, she saw another shape enter the field of the reflection. Mr. Darcy stood there, at the edge of the crowd of guests, neither moving towards her nor retreating into the throngs. She almost felt his eyes pierce the back of her head, and in a moment, he seemed poised to step in her direction.

How ought she to react? What ought she to say? There were so many words that defied the speaking. She thought to turn around and beg his conversation with her eyes, and began to turn in her place. But at that very moment, the band struck its first chords, and the assembled guests started to shift about the room, all intent on finding their promised partners for the first set. Elizabeth had agreed to stand up with Charlotte's brother John; she knew not who Mr. Darcy had selected for the set, but he too looked up sharply at that first chord and swivelled his great head in search of somebody.

That moment of possibility, whatever it might have been, was over. She quite despaired of another such opportunity that evening and, with a deep fortifying breath, went off in search of John Lucas.

The band was fine and the music lively and the set progressed with pleasure on the part of all, participants and observers alike. The dancers traced their patterns on the chalked floor, moving up and down the set as the steps required, talking and laughing and revelling in the luxury of the evening.

When the music ended and the set dispersed to find refreshment and talk for a while, Mr. Bingley himself mounted the dais. A servant brought up a comfortable chair, and Richard helped Jane up the two low steps so she might sit there. "Ladies and gentlemen," Bingley called out, "friends! I beg your indulgence for a moment of time."

The buzz in the room dulled at once to the faintest murmur.

"I am delighted to have you all in my home this evening. Welcome to every one of you. I had hoped, this fine evening, to make a great announcement, concerning myself and this beautiful lady at my side."

A rush of sound replaced the silence, but immediately Bingley quieted them with a gesture.

"I had hoped to make the announcement of our engagement, for only two days ago, Miss Jane Bennet accepted my offer and agreed to be my wife. However," he cut off any exclamations of joy, "I have something else to say.

"Jane?" He turned to the lady seated at his side. She looked quite confused. Elizabeth began to push through the crowds. Something was not right.

"Jane, do you have anything to tell me?"

"Charles?" Her voice wavered.

"You told me you loved me."

"As I do."

"You promised to love only me."

"As I do."

"You assured me your affections were true and not some charade enacted to trap for yourself a wealthy husband."

"As they are." Her voice, always soft, started to shake.

"You lie!" Bingley roared. Jane swayed on her chair. Her face was pale, and Elizabeth feared she would swoon. Elizabeth pushed forward until she was nearly at the front of the mass of people, all holding their breaths, the room silent and forbidding, the tension all but throbbing in the heated air.

"You are no maid!" Bingley shouted from the dais. "You do not love me. You have tricked me, and I curse you for it. You have given your heart—and your body—to another! Do not deny it. I saw you, you and him, only last night. Oh, you thought to hide your little secret, your tryst in the woods, but I was warned and I was there, and I saw you!"

A low rumble of sound filled the room.

"Can you deny it?" Bingley called out.

Jane's face was as white as her dress. She opened her mouth, but no sound emerged.

"See! See how she cannot deny these accusations. She is as guilty as any harlot who ever graced a stew doorway. Here, Bennet! Take back your rotten orange! I will not pollute my house with her." He pushed her, and she almost tumbled from her chair.

"Now what, Bingley?" Papa cried out from somewhere in the crowd as a chorus of protestations arose from the company. Elizabeth at last made it through to the first row of guests to stand gasping right before the dais.

"What can you mean by this, Mr. Bingley?" she called to him. "You cannot believe such things of Jane, of sweet Jane! She has the best soul of anybody I know. She could not do something like this. You have been misled."

"No, Miss Bennet. I saw her, and with my very eyes."

"But she is injured! She cannot walk. You said she was in the woods, but she could not walk that far. Please be sensible."

"She walks well enough when it pleases her. And last night seemed to please her a great deal. I know the man. I heard her call him by name, and in turn I heard him name her. Deny it, Jane. Face all these people, face me, and deny it."

Jane's eyes were wide with horror, her face wet with tears. "Of course I deny it," she choked. "I was never outside the house last night. I would never meet with another in the woods. I was in my bedchamber all the night. Alone."

"With nobody to prove your words?"

"No! Why should I have such a person? I did nothing to bear watching."

"Again, lies! You were with George Wickham, acting the harlot, and bringing shame to yourself and to me. I repudiate you. You sicken me. Get out of my house. Now!" And with that final roar, he pushed at the weeping woman again, shoving her from the chair onto the floor.

"Out! All of you," he bellowed to the guests. "Out of my house!" And then he stormed off through a set of doors behind the dais, leaving chaos and disbelief in his wake, and Jane Bennet, sobbing and unable to move, on the cold marble floor.

Chapter Nineteen

There is some strange misprision

(Friar, 4.1)

Darcy stood in the corner of the room. He could not have been more horrified if Bingley had struck him across the face. Indeed, such a physical assault would have been more welcome than what Bingley had done. What had that silly pup been thinking? What had caused him to turn on Jane Bennet so completely and in so public a manner? If he had a quarrel with the lady, he ought to have spoken in private and not as an announcement to the denizens of the neighbourhood. This was not the man he had called a friend. All around him, the murmuring mass of guests melted away to seek their outer garments and call for their carriages. It was a scene from a bad opera.

Richard appeared at his side. He stared straight ahead to where Jane still lay unmoving on the floor. Elizabeth knelt at her side, and Mrs. Bennet fussed above with a large shawl which Elizabeth now used to wrap about her fallen sister's shoulders. "I saw her as well," he stated. His voice was flat.

"What?" Darcy blinked.

"This is what Bingley was summoned to observe last night. Sanders had news that Wickham had planned a tryst with Miss Bennet, and Sanders came to warn us. He said it was for Bingley's own good." He dropped his voice. "This is what he made me promise not to say."

Darcy turned on his cousin. "You knew he was going to do this?" He clenched his hand into a ball; how would that fist feel hitting his cousin's face?

Richard must have sensed the imagined blow. "No, no! I had no notion he would be so cruel. I thought... I know not what I thought. That he had decided to marry her regardless, that he loved her enough, or that he had already spoken to her... I had no idea at all of what he planned."

"And what of Sanders? Wickham is a known seducer, but he does not crow, neither does he announce his plans to his comrades. This was a plot, a well-planned scheme. But how could he convince Miss Bennet to do such a thing? I questioned the sincerity of her affections, never her character. Unless..."

He faced Richard directly. "Tell me what you saw. Tell me exactly what you saw."

Richard closed his eyes and bowed his head. "Sanders led us to the glade behind the folly. You know the one, at the back of the garden at Longbourn. There was room to walk our horses in silence. There, inside the folly, we saw them. They were... intimately engaged."

"That folly is enclosed, and it was a cold night. Surely they were inside the building."

"Aye, that they were. But the light inside cast clear shadows on the thin curtains. There was no mistaking Wickham's profile or his voice. Likewise, Miss Bennet's. He called her by name, Will! And she responded in kind."

"You saw their silhouettes?"

"As clearly as I see you before me."

"But you did not see the lady herself."

The soldier shook his head. "But her profile is unmistakable. Her height, her figure..."

"I cannot believe this of Jane Bennet. It must have been a trick of some sort. We must find Wickham and learn what horrible game he has played. Forster! Where's Forster?" Darcy swung around. "Where is the man?"

"Be calm. I shall find him. But I know what I saw. It was Miss Bennet's profile I saw against that window."

Darcy narrowed his eyes in a scowl. "Do not say that! We will discover the truth. Find Colonel Forster now, and then together, bring me Wickham!"

Richard all but leapt backwards and dashed from the room.

By now, Mr. Bennet and Mr. Collins had arranged for a litter to be fashioned from some sheets and cushions, and were instructing two strong footmen on how best to carry Jane to the carriage. She seemed to be lost in a swoon. Mrs. Bennet and her three youngest daughters were huddled about, the matron wailing and wringing her lace handkerchief into shreds, the younger daughters looking shocked. Mary stood rigidly by, and Darcy thought he heard her mutter platitudes about loss of virtue and the importance of a lady's good name. Kitty looked about to cry, and Lydia like she was about to be physically ill. In a few moments, the footmen hoisted the litter with Jane, immobile, upon it, and the family filed out of the room like mourners at a burial.

Only Elizabeth remained, unmoving as a statue, streaks of tears catching the bright candlelight as they traced their way down her face. She made no attempt to staunch the flow, but stood there weeping freely.

Darcy could stand it no longer. Ten long strides took him to her side, and he handed her the linen handkerchief from his coat pocket.

"You are crying."

She sniffed back a sob.

"Have you been crying all this time?"

"So I have. And I will cry a little longer as well."

"Here," he took the unused handkerchief from her hand and used it to dab at her eyes. "I do not want you to cry."

"Why not? It seems to be the one thing which I can do, over which I have some agency."

"Oh, my Lizzy. I am so sorry. I am so very sorry. If I had known... If I had any notion, I would have stopped him."

The white cloth caressed her damp cheeks, only to be replaced with his large thumb. He traced the line of her cheekbone and then moved down her cheek. At the gentle pressure of her face against his hand, he dared take that one step closer, and in a moment gathered her into his arms and pulled her against his chest. For a moment she stiffened, but then melted against him and allowed him to hold her close. How long they stood there, he knew not. What his valet would think of his tear-stained coat, he cared not. There was no anger in him now, nor ardour, nor any thought other than comforting Elizabeth. There would be time enough later for fury and retribution. For now, his entire purpose in life was to allow this beautiful and heartbroken woman to cry into his chest for as long as she needed to do so.

In time, the tears slowed and then stopped.

"Your family?"

"All gone home, I imagine. I told them I would find my own way."

"Even now, so late at night?"

"I would steal one of Bingley's horses... or one of his donkeys. He will not miss it unless he looks in a mirror and finds himself missing. For he is the biggest ass in the county."

"Oh, that barbed tongue! There's my Lizzy."

She gave no reply to his gibe other than to nestle deeper into his embrace. If anybody were to discover them like this and raise the alarm, he would be honour-bound to marry the girl. The thought did not distress him at all, and he half hoped Richard or—God forbid!—Caroline would appear. But no. That would not do. He had offered for Elizabeth once and with any encouragement would do so again, but the choice must be hers alone. He would no more force a marriage upon this rare creature than he would destroy a woman before her friends and family, as Bingley had done.

The very thought was abhorrent.

"Come. I will see you home, and in greater comfort than on Bingley's ass."

"Mr. Darcy! What language," she protested. "There are ladies present."

"No, my dear, only you."

She laughed. It was a small laugh, and weak, but it was there and it gave him hope.

"I have missed your wicked wit, love. Come. I shall call for my carriage."

He held out his hand and she took it, allowing him to lead her out of the dreadful, sparkling, fatal room.

Netherfield's grand hallways were empty, deserted of all but a handful of scared-looking servants scurrying about trying to remain unseen. Longbourn's, however, were quite the opposite. Candlelight blazed from every window, and cries and shouts emanated from every doorway. Mrs. Hill opened the door to Darcy and Elizabeth when they arrived. She said not a word about the two having been alone in an enclosed carriage at night. Mr. Darcy, it seemed, was deemed honourable enough that Elizabeth's virtue was secure.

The loudest noises came from the parlour at the back of the house, which Darcy believed was the family's chosen room for their own purposes. He had been in it but once, and recalled several comfortable chairs and two or three large sofas. It was on one of these that Jane lay, her head on a pillow, the rest of her wrapped in an assortment of blankets.

Mr. Bennet and Mary sat at her side, the former looking a decade older than he had mere hours ago, the latter holding her sister's limp hand and trying to spoon some liquid into her mouth. Jane's eyes were closed and Darcy could not see whether she was conscious or not.

On one of the large armchairs sprawled Mrs. Bennet. Much of the noise in the room came from her as she wailed and lamented and cried out for tea! a shawl! her salts! Kitty was bustling to and fro, tending to her mother, and Mr. Collins stumbled awkwardly in her wake, offering to help but having no idea what to do. And on a chair by the far corner, Lydia sat with a stricken look on her pretty face. She wrung her hands together, and she had chewed her bottom lip almost raw. A thought coalesced in Darcy's head, at first a mere feeling of discomfort, then a question, and then a more concrete idea.

Nobody greeted them as they entered the room, but he had not expected such. This was no social call, after all. "How may I help?" was all he said.

A sea of eyes turned to him.

"Mr. Darcy." Bennet bowed his head but did not rise. Another wail issued from Mrs. Bennet's lips.

"Have you come to crow over us in our humiliation? Have you come to lord it over us and preen about how fortunate you are not to be associated with us in any way? Leave us!" Bennet ran a hand over his eyes.

233

"Nothing of the sort. I cannot believe Mr. Bingley's lies and I wish to be of assistance. Elizabeth will vouch for me."

"Lizzy?"

She nodded. "Indeed, Papa."

"But you hate the man."

"I did, but not anymore. Not since I discovered who he really is. He is good and honourable. Listen to him."

"But what are we to do?" Mrs. Bennet wailed. "Oh, we are all undone! Quite undone! We shall be cast from society. Destroyed! It would be better had Jane died!"

"Madam!" her husband exploded. "Guard your words!"

A new voice, little more than a whine, was now heard. "If I may dare, in this most unsettling of circumstances, to offer a thought—which, I do admit, Lady Catherine does not often enjoin me to do, having such excellent notions herself—I might suggest something to help remedy this most unhappy occurrence."

"Mr. Collins," Bennet acknowledged him.

"Your charming lady wife, may the good Lord bless her, has an idea that might be of some merit." Bennet glared at him. "Er, that is, if we let it be known throughout the neighbourhood that Cousin Jane was so overcome by grief and horror at Mr. Bingley's baseless accusations that she lies near death, it might occasion on his part some sort of regret to the point where he will reconsider his vile actions and speak to the townspeople about his abominable error."

Bennet said not a word.

"It might work, Papa." Elizabeth's voice cut through the silence. "We need to learn why Mr. Bingley was so very convinced about what he saw. Perhaps, if he thinks the very worst happened, he will reconsider everything. I cannot imagine this was by accident."

"Not if Wickham was involved," Darcy added.

"Mr. Wickham? Why, he is the most gentlemanly of men." Mrs. Bennet roused herself enough to speak intelligibly. "Always so polite and friendly. He was here to visit only the other day. Here, when everybody else was running about preparing for the ball, he came to call upon us."

In her corner, Lydia grew very still and very pale. With her white skin and elegant hairdo now in disarray, it struck Darcy anew how much she looked like Jane, especially in profile. She was not as beautiful in many ways, but her features were similar enough that the two might, from a distance, be mistaken for each other. Why, Bingley himself had mistaken one for the other on at least one occasion. From a distance, or—

The notion that had struck him earlier became more insistent.

"I only now had another thought, if I may interpose my suppositions, Mr. Bennet." Mr. Collins interrupted Darcy's musings. "I have often, as I believe I mentioned before, walked along the paths in that lovely patch of garden which even now, in the cold autumn months, is resplendent with a beauty that reminds me of Rosings."

Rosings? Oh, heaven forbid! This was the sychophantish new parson Darcy's aunt had selected for the Hunsford parish. He would chastise her later.

"On my walk last night, I was brought to wonder why Cousin Lydia was crossing the green towards the folly, and not Cousin

Catherine, who most often wanders through in the evenings after dinner."

Darcy followed his host's eyes as they lit upon his youngest daughter.

"Lydia?"

She went so pale Darcy thought she might swoon.

"And whilst I wandered in the area, I do not recall seeing anybody else from the house leave the premises; I looked particularly at the bedchambers, for..." he blushed and cleared his throat, "I always like to ensure that my fair cousins are safely ensconced for the night. I would have no harm come to them, you see. Cousin Jane's candle was extinguished a great time before Cousin Lydia appeared in my view. I had quite imagined Cousin Jane to be asleep."

Bennet rose and moved towards his youngest daughter with a rush of passion and energy that Darcy had never seen from the man. "Lydia? What have you to tell us? Speak now. I demand it."

The young woman on the chair no longer looked like the fashionable young debutante who had teased her way around the ballroom earlier. Now she looked more like a little girl who had been caught being naughty. Very young and very foolish and quite afraid.

She stared at her father for almost a full minute, opening her mouth and then closing it again without making a sound. The words, when they did come, tumbled out in a rush.

"I didn't mean it! I didn't mean it at all. It was meant to be a joke, only a joke! He assured me it was a joke, and that Mr. Bingley would laugh and laugh when he learned the truth."

"Tell all of it, child." Mr. Bennet had never sounded so much like a father in all the time Darcy had known him.

Lydia slid down to the floor and sat there, leaning against the wall, arms around her knees, and there she told her tale. Mr. Wickham had come around often to visit the sisters, and when it seemed that Kitty had a suitor in Mr. Collins, Lydia began to encourage Wickham's attentions. "He has never done anything but steal a kiss or two! I swear it, Papa!" Three days ago Wickham had come by and had managed to get Lydia alone, when he proposed his plan. She was to meet Wickham late at night in the folly, and when Bingley came by she was to pretend to be Jane enjoying a tryst with Wickham. "He told me how to act and what to say, and I did it very well. He told me so! But he promised it was a joke. He promised he would tell Mr. Bingley and that we would all have a great laugh. He promised!"

Darcy's fist curled into a ball again. "I will kill him! When I find him, he will rue the day that ever he came into my life. He has done this to revenge himself upon me, and as I am the cause of your distress, so I will fix it."

"I do not know why it is so wrong," Lydia spoke again. She sounded more the coquette now, the teasing, wheedling note back in her voice. "It was a joke. It was not so different from the joke they played on Lizzy and Mr. Darcy."

Darcy spun about to face her. "What joke?"

"I heard Jane and Charlotte talk of it. They did not know I was listening, but they thought it funny, and they said that Mr. Bingley and Colonel Fitzwilliam were part of it as well."

Damn Richard! Is this what he had meant by his aside in London? What had he done?

"What joke?" Elizabeth echoed his thoughts. She did not sound pleased.

"It was a silly thing. They played a trick on you to make you think Mr. Darcy loved you. And Mr. Bingley and the colonel played a trick on Mr. Darcy to make him think you were in love with him! I did not see how that is any different than Mr. Wickham playing a joke on Mr. Bingley."

Elizabeth turned slowly to gape at Jane, who was just now struggling upright on her sofa. "Jane? Tell me this is a fabrication."

Her sister's tear-stained face was a mask of misery. Her eyes were red and her mouth fell in despair. "Do not ask me this, Lizzy. Do not make today worse than it has been."

But Elizabeth was not a lady to be put off. She went to kneel at the side of Jane's sofa. "Janey, I need to know."

Jane squeezed her eyes tightly. "It was in fun. We did it not to deceive you, but to stop the constant bickering. It was so uncomfortable to have you both at dinner or in the parlour, always fighting and insulting each other. You could not spend five minutes together without a squabble. Colonel Fitzwilliam made the suggestion, and we agreed. We needed to find some way to bring some peace. We meant no harm. You must believe me, Lizzy."

Elizabeth looked up at Darcy with a stricken expression. "You arranged for me to hear you and Charlotte talking?"

Jane gulped. "We enlisted Annie's help to let us know when you were there."

"You wished me to believe that Mr. Darcy liked me, despite his behaviour?"

Another nod.

"Then he did not like me at all? You played me for a fool!"

Jane's face crumpled.

So this was what Richard had alluded to in London. A flash of red anger threatened to overcome him, and for a moment, the room swam. He fought for control of his passions and drew in a great breath. With the air came self-regulation and the shield of ice that he used for the purpose. That ice was the cold fury; it was now his sole purpose, impenetrable, and it froze his heart.

"And Bingley and Richard did likewise to me?" The ice in his veins lent its bitterness to his voice.

Another weepy nod.

"And Miss Elizabeth held no affection for me?"

Silence.

He slid his eyes to where Elizabeth knelt at Jane's side. He could read nothing in her face. It was as blank to him as an empty canvas. What was he hoping for? Some sign that Jane was wrong? A smile? A nod? Some reflection of that passion he had seen on that day he had kissed her in the woods?

Insult me! his mind screamed. Curse me for my impudence. Tell me Jane is wrong. Show me you care, even a bit.

But she just sat there, immobile, saying nothing at all.

He was lost in a sea of pain and misery. Every face around him was painted with one shade or another of agony. Sorrow washed over every feature. They did not need him here. He fought for something civil to say. He was a gentleman. He was in control. A gentleman always found the proper words.

"I am afraid you have been long desiring my absence, nor have I any purpose in remaining here other than to show my genuine concern. I shall torment you with my presence no longer. See to your family, Bennet, and know that I believe entirely in Miss Jane Bennet's honour."

Not daring to look again at Elizabeth, lest he vary from his purpose and run to her once more and beg her to consider him like a lovesick boy, he bowed stiffly and turned from the room.

He rode back through the town and stopped briefly at the inn before continuing on to Netherfield. Upon reaching that house, his first move was to find his cousin's room. "Richard, pack your trunks. We are away at once. I can stay in this house not a moment more."

"What? Back to London now? It is past midnight!"

"To the inn in Meryton. I have taken rooms. Pack up. Have my valet do likewise. The carriage is waiting below. I must see Bingley."

Without another word, he stormed down the hallway to the suite that Bingley called his own. He crashed his fist against the door hard enough to set it rattling on its hinges and then barged in without awaiting a response.

Bingley was sitting in a chair by the fire, half dressed and wholly drunk. He staggered to his feet, only to meet Darcy's fist. The blow stung Darcy's knuckles, but he relished the pain.

"What have you done? What terrible, terrible thing have you done?"

"I saw her," Bingley wheezed, holding his hand over his reddening cheek. Good. He would sport a fine bruise for a while.

"You saw what you wanted to see. You saw what you were told to see. Did you think to ask the lady what had happened? Did you think to ask Sanders how he knew of the assignation? What about Wickham? Did you blindly trust what he told you without asking a question? Have I not warned you about him? How could you have thought so little of the lady you were going to marry that you could accept this ruse without questioning a single thing? I am heartily ashamed of you."

"But I saw her…"

"You saw nothing of the sort. You saw Miss Lydia playing a game with Wickham behind a thin curtain. I have a witness who swears he saw Lydia walk that path and nobody else. And Lydia admits freely to this deception. You have publicly destroyed an innocent young woman and humiliated her entire family."

"But…"

"Nothing. On behalf of the Bennet family and on behalf of Elizabeth, I demand justice. Your other sins pale beside this. Get your sorry self to bed, Bingley, for I will see you at dawn. Pistols or swords, I care little which."

"Darcy…" The plaint was more desperate. "What of Jane?"

"How come you to care for her wellbeing now? You have eviscerated her before her friends. She was overcome by your slander. She lies insensible, maybe near death. Yes, you foul-spoken coward, should she not live, you will be the one to blame."

"But Wickham was the one to seduce her. It is his fault, not mine. Why not blame him?"

"I shall deal with him later. You are the one who acted in so vile a manner. To bed, you piece of used rag. Dawn at the river bank. I shall be waiting."

The door splintered as Darcy slammed it shut.

Chapter Twenty

I will protest your cowardice

(Benedick, 5.1)

Contrary to every one of Darcy's expectations, Bingley appeared at the river bank at dawn. His eyes were red and his face green, but he was there. He had somehow wrestled Hurst from his bed to be his second. Darcy stood with Richard.

"What have you to say for yourself?" was Darcy's greeting. The air was damp and cold and the ground tinged with frost. It would melt as soon as the sun's feeble rays touched it, but for now, the dead grass looked grey and menacing underfoot. It would be slippery. He must watch his step.

"Is it true she lies near death?" If Bingley were as weak as his voice, he would fall to the ground before Darcy picked up a weapon.

"It is in God's hands whether she lives or dies. And the blame lies with you."

"But she humiliated me, Darcy. In front of all those people." Bingley was sweating despite the chill in the air. He was still drunk, or possibly regretting his excess from the night before. Darcy cared little.

"Choose your weapon. Swords? Here." Richard had somehow procured a set of foils from the regiment's armoury. He picked up one of the weapons and tossed it towards his former friend. It landed in the mud near the man's feet. "You humiliated yourself. Had you not spoken, it would have been all about nothing. But you—you announced it to all present, and in doing so, proclaimed that you are a coward without compassion, without principles, and without foundation for your slander."

"But I saw her."

Darcy stepped forward and picked up the fallen sword to shove it into Bingley's unsteady hands. "We have spoken of this. You saw nothing but what Wickham wanted you to believe."

"But he came to me the very next morning. Yesterday morning. He came and warned me about Jane; he told me she was false. That he could not stand to see a fine man like me shackled to a whore."

"You truly believed that he had no other motive? Surely, if he cared that much for your welfare, he would not have begun an arrangement with your betrothed. There is no sincerity in him; no truth."

"He wanted me to know..."

"Was that despicable display last night his idea?"

Bingley looked down to the frost-rimed ground and gulped. "It was. He said it would show everybody what sort of person their precious Jane Bennet really was. He said it would be a lesson for the whole neighbourhood."

"You believed him?"

Bingley sniffed. "Yes."

Darcy moved to face the snivelling man. "Stand to!" He shifted into position, waving the point of his own sword towards Bingley's heart.

"Cannot we talk about this? Can we not discuss this calmly?"

"On the count of ten. Richard?" He made some practice lunges; with each one, Bingley's face grew more and more grey. "I have yet to hear a single word of remorse from you, Bingley. I demand justice. How I achieve that is up to you."

Bingley stood there, looking at his sword with such horror on his face Darcy was almost tempted to laugh. Almost. "Stand to!"

At a shout, Darcy lunged again, and in earnest now. He knew Bingley had trained at Cambridge and was adequate with a blade, but he was no match for Darcy when calm and sober; now, terrified and likely still inebriated, he was as ineffectual as a stuffed pillow. The younger man flailed about with his sword, flicking it here and there in Darcy's direction, but never attempting even to approach. Then, with another shout and a side step, Darcy knocked the weapon from Bingley's hands, and with a well-aimed kick, sent him sprawling into the icy mud. He moved closer and waved the point of his foil near Bingley's throat.

"Will you kill me? Will that make amends?" Bingley panted on the ground.

"Unlike you, I do not attack unarmed people," Darcy spat and stepped back, gathering Bingley's lost sword from where it lay. "You will make amends. This I am commanding you. You will go to every household that was present last night and explain your mistake. You will beg the forgiveness of each family. And you will write, in your own hand, a message that will be pasted on the assembly room doors admitting to your egregious error and declaring Jane Bennet to be completely without blame in this matter."

"But I saw—"

"Enough!" Darcy roared. He must have been heard in the village. "Did you not hear me the first time, or the second or the third? You saw Lydia pretending to be Jane. I have a witness in the form of Mr. Collins, the clergyman, who saw Lydia go to the folly. I have Lydia's own word that Wickham tricked her into the ruse. And I have Sanders' corroboration that he was involved in the prank, thinking it a joke, as Wickham wished him to do. And when we find Wickham, he will admit to it all. I shall see to that."

Bingley rolled onto his side and curled up like a babe. Unaccountably, he started to weep. "I was so sure... So sure. I thought she loved me. I loved her."

"You loved the idea of being in love, and Miss Bennet was an admirable object for your attentions. If you truly loved her, you never would have treated her this way. That is not love. That is control. The two are very different." He began to walk away from the bawling coward, but turned back after a few steps. "To think, I was concerned that Miss Bennet's affections were false. How wrong I was. It was your intentions I ought to have been more concerned about. Come Richard. We are finished here."

He placed the two swords back in their case and led his cousin to the waiting carriage, without another glance back at the sobbing man on the ground or the large second who hovered uselessly about, not having uttered a single word all morning.

For three days, the Bennet family saw nobody. They accepted no callers, took in no mail, and were quite unavailable to any who dared to inquire after them. Mrs. Bennet took to her rooms, where she wailed over Bingley's infamous treatment of her eldest daughter and wept and flailed, calling for more fire, less heat, warmer blankets and more air, and quite relying upon her salts. Kitty and Mary tended her; they had both been confined to the house, not allowed even to venture into the gardens or to walk out onto the lanes within Longbourn's park. Mary took this stricture in stride, although Kitty was less complacent. "It was not my fault," she constantly badgered her father. "It was all Lydia's doing. She only told me about it on the very afternoon before it happened!" And then, realising her mistake, ran up to her rooms to avoid further punishment.

Mr. Bennet kept largely to his books, having secluded himself in his study. To all appearances, he was taking solace in ancient Latin texts and modern English ale, emerging only to dine with the family and refuse Kitty's pleas for leniency.

Of Mr. Collins, the family saw little. He had, for once, the presence of mind to keep his admonitions to a single sermon on the necessity for virtue, and then refrained from more. By day, he stalked the grounds, daring neither to bother his hosts nor to venture into Meryton, and by night he wrote a great deal at the desk in the parlour, although of what or to whom, Elizabeth did not ask.

As for Lydia, she had been immediately sent back to the nursery. That very first night after her confession, her father had ordered her bedroom to be locked and her basic needs moved upstairs, where she was to remain without company but with a great supply of edifying texts—suggested by Mr. Collins—to contemplate until such time as a governess could be engaged. Her wails of protestation went unheeded, and at length, one of the strapping lads from the stables was called in to sit outside the nursery door to ensure she did not leave.

Elizabeth condoled with Jane, who ate little and slept less and grew very weak and pale. Elizabeth began to fear that there might be some truth after all in the rumours they had set about concerning Jane's very precarious state. Never had she seen her sister so ill and listless. If she were to die, Elizabeth swore she would hunt Bingley down herself and see him suffer as her sister had suffered. "He is not fit to spit on," she cursed to her mirror one evening.

Her own broken heart, she kept to herself. Whom could she tell, after all? Jane had her own miseries with which to contend, and Charlotte was kept from the house. But when alone, late into the night, Elizabeth saw Mr. Darcy's face again and again as he went cold and turned from her.

How could Jane and Charlotte have done this? How could they have toyed with her to make her think Mr. Darcy in love with her? She had responded only as a decent person could, by offering kindness to soothe a lovesick heart. Was it any wonder, then, that Mr. Darcy had responded in turn and that they had grown into some sort of friendship?

But—and here was the rub—he had been under the same misapprehension about her! He had only been charming and civil because he thought she loved him! He, too, was acting only in such a way as to be kind. Surely there was no real affection in him. His final words had shown that to be true. He had never cared for her at all!

But what of that delicious kiss? That was not feigned! *Pah!* Elizabeth chided herself. She knew what men were about. She had enjoyed a kiss or two from the village lads over the years, and always had to disabuse them of any thoughts that a kiss might lead to more. Surely Mr. Darcy was only toying with her in hopes of satisfying some of his more... manly urges.

In that light, even his horrible proposal made some sort of sense. He wished to court her, but not engage her heart. Had she accepted him, he would be permitted more licence with her. Engaged couples were not chaperoned as carefully as courting couples, and everybody knew that a first child could come any time after the wedding. It was only subsequent children whose arrival took nine months or so. He was hoping to attach her just enough to have his way, but not so much that he could not jilt her before the wedding.

It was humiliating.

But more shameful still was the realisation that, over their time together, she had come not just to like him and esteem him. She had come to love him.

Despite the humiliating scheme, despite Mr. Darcy's obvious disdain for her, she had fallen in love with him. His initial behaviour to her notwithstanding, he had shown himself to be a man of charm and character, with deep penetration and a sparkling wit. He was committed to his obligations, firm in his decisions, and dedicated to doing the right thing. He had given Mr. Wickham more than the man had ever deserved, and acted only to help him finally set his feet on an honourable path. He was loyal to his friends—even if they did not repay the sentiment—and wished the best for them. If he had cautioned Mr. Bingley about Jane's supposed attachment, it was with Bingley's heart in mind, and he advised the man to judge the lady for himself. As for his sister, what brother could do anything else? He had rescued her from a scoundrel who wanted only her wealth and then set about protecting her the best he possibly could manage. He had set her up in her own home with a caring companion, where she could recover from Wickham's predations.

But what marked him most honourable in her view were his actions on the night of the ball.

Bingley had accused Jane of horrible things, and the guests had gaped and milled about and then left without a word to any in the family. Bingley had stormed off and the militia seemed to believe him completely. Even Colonel Fitzwilliam had corroborated Bingley's slander from what she had heard.

But Mr. Darcy had stayed. He was the one person, the one man, who had not fled the scene or rallied around the slanderer. He had been there to stand with her and hold her whilst she sobbed out her agony, and he had voiced his confidence in Jane's innocence. He had come home with her to support her family and vow vengeance.

And—if rumours were to be believed, for even rumours had crept through chinks in the armour around Longbourn—he had done just that. He had challenged Bingley and met him on the field of honour. No matter that such things were against the law and punishable most terribly, he had challenged his former friend to a duel in her sister's honour. Nobody ever had fought a duel for Jane before, and she hoped that one day, when this initial pain had subsided, Jane would see the grand gesture for what it was.

When everybody else had abandoned her, Mr. Darcy was there. No matter that he did not really love her, no matter what his aims might be in his pretence at wooing her, he had been there. And this, above all things, marked him as the very best of men.

And now he was gone, never to return. This was the turmoil, the confusion, the pain with which Elizabeth must live, and for the sake of her sister, she would bear it in silence.

And so, for three nights, Elizabeth waited until the house was quiet and everyone asleep before allowing her tears to dampen her pillow.

Then, on the fourth day after the ball, things began to change.

Mrs. Bennet came down from her rooms for breakfast, and Mr. Bennet requested the mail be brought in. Mrs. Hill placed the teetering stack at his side on the breakfast table, and with excruciating care and precision, he picked up each letter in turn and examined it before placing it into one of a number of piles he was creating.

After far too many minutes of complete silence, broken only by the clink of a china teacup settling onto its saucer, he raised his eyes to his family and, looking over the rims of his spectacles, addressed them.

"These are bills." He waved his hand at a small pile. "I shall attend to them later. These are about my library and the magnifying glass I have commissioned, and these matters of the estate. But these," he indicated a growing stack, "are from our friends and neighbours in the vicinity, each stating without reserve a complete faith in Jane's innocence and shock at that man's vile and erroneous accusations."

Mrs. Bennet let out another wail, but this time it was one of relief. "Then we are saved! Oh, Mr. Bennet, we are saved! How fortunate that Jane is so beautiful and so good, that no one can believe this evil of her. Oh, we are saved!"

This news was relayed to Jane, who relieved her relations by hobbling on her crutches from her room to the breakfast room, her maid at her elbow, and who proceeded to take tea and some bread and cheese for the first time in days. A tinge of colour crept back into her cheeks, and Elizabeth breathed a great sigh of relief at her sister's return from the brink of death.

When Charlotte arrived late in the afternoon, the family were in far better spirits than they had felt since the cataclysm of a ball. Elizabeth glanced up when Mrs. Hill led her into the parlour. Jane was napping in a large armchair with a soft shawl wrapped about her, looking tired but no longer like a wraith from a Gothick novel. Elizabeth herself had been sitting in the sunlight with some discarded embroidery at one side and a neglected book at the other, a creature of light. A tray of uneaten sweet rolls sat on the low table, and several empty tea cups decorated various pieces of furniture.

"I brought you some biscuits," Charlotte greeted her friends in a whisper. Jane's eyes fluttered open and Elizabeth happily abandoned her employments. "Lemon and lavender. Food cannot help everything, but neither does it hurt." She glanced at the untouched tray. "Perhaps I should not have done so."

"You are very welcome, my friend." Elizabeth rose to embrace her friend. "Your biscuits are welcome too. Jane, here, do take one. Nobody makes such excellent biscuits as Charlotte. Susie is bringing more tea; it seems that much as I have little taste for food, I wish for the teapot never to be empty."

The three exchanged such meaningless pleasantries as were expected before Charlotte asked after Jane's wellbeing, and that of the entire family. Susie came with the tea, and Elizabeth set about serving a fresh cup to each, as well as two of the excellent biscuits, before settling down to respond.

"Today we are all much improved. Indeed, we are doing better than I would have expected. Mama quite lamented the destruction of our family's name in our local society, but it is quite the opposite. Townspeople and friends alike have been sending regards and even coming to call with flowers and cards and gestures of goodwill. Where in Meryton so many people managed to procure flowers in November, I never will know. But it seems we will not be the pariahs we had expected to be."

"I have even received three offers of marriage just this morning," Jane added. Her voice was quiet and weak, but firm. "One from Adam Jones, who will take over his father's apothecary when Mr. Jones deems the time to retire is at hand." She looked up at Charlotte. "And one from your own brother John!"

"Aha!" Charlotte clapped her hands. "So that is where he went so soon after noon, and in his best coat, too. You know he has been in love with you for a great long time, Jane."

"I do. He is a sweet man, and I wish him well. I thanked him kindly and refused him. He deserves a woman who will love him. He ought," she dropped her voice, "to think of Miss Harriet Robinson, who I believe quite dotes upon him. She is pretty and sweet and will make a good wife."

Charlotte nibbled one of her biscuits. "I shall endeavour to let that be known! You did well to refuse him, for much as I love my brother, he is not the man for you. But you said three had come by. Who is the third?"

Jane's eyes moved about the room, lingering at the doorway for a moment. Then she whispered, "Mr. Collins!"

All three ladies dissolved into girlish giggles.

"It is true," Elizabeth chuckled. "He came in, right after breakfast, and seeing Jane up for the first time in days, requested an audience with her. May I tell her, my sweet? Mama, of course, hurried us all out of the room as if it were afire, but then stood at the door whispering encouragements to the man as if he could hear them."

"No!" Charlotte clapped her hands again. "What did he say, Jane?"

"He was very sweet. I admit he is a bit pompous, and perhaps more than somewhat weak in understanding, but he is a kind man. He acknowledged my broken heart, which he is certain can never heal, and then made a speech about how the loss of virtue in a maiden is permanent and irrevocable—"

"No! He did not!"

"But he admitted that he saw no blemish on my character, for my sin was not of my own making, and offered to heal the grave injury done to my name with the excellence of his." She gave another weak smile. "He was sincere in his sentiments; he genuinely believes me innocent and truly wishes to help me. I cannot fault him for that; on the contrary, I laud him."

"And what was your answer?"

"I refused him, of course. Can you think it otherwise? I am of no mind to marry now. I am rather not fond of men at the present. But I did not wish to cause him pain. I suggested that whilst I was most appreciative of his own faith in me, Lady Catherine de Bourgh—"

"His esteemed patroness," the others supplied in unison.

"—might find my presence in the parish to be less than salutary to the spiritual health of the community, and that she would prefer he take a bride with less stain upon her name."

Charlotte leaned over to put an arm about Jane's blanket-clad shoulders. "Nicely done. Was he satisfied?"

Jane nodded. "I believe he was relieved. I think he really quite prefers Kitty, if you can believe it."

"Will he offer for Kitty?"

Elizabeth chuckled anew. "I can hardly say. It is a strange thing to court one sister, offer for another, and then propose to the first afterwards, but Mr. Collins is no ordinary man."

"Oh, how true!" Charlotte laughed in response, and even Jane let out a small giggle.

They talked a while longer before Jane could no longer stifle a great yawn. Charlotte began to stir as if to take her leave, but Jane stopped her. "I am a little tired, but do not mind me. You have come to visit Lizzy, and I shall let you do so. Susie can help me back to my room." She reached for the crutches that leant against the table by her chair and pulled herself to standing. Immediately, the maid was at her side, and she bid good afternoon to her guest before hobbling from the room.

Charlotte now moved closer to Elizabeth. "And what of you, Lizzy? The family shall survive, and Jane seems in a fair way. But how do you manage?"

"Oh, Charlotte, I hardly know what to think. I am at once happy and relieved and furious and simply sad. All of these sensations wash over me in succession, but all are also present at once. I can hardly sort between them." She fell back into her chair. "I ought, by all accounts, to be very angry with you."

Charlotte's eyes widened. "With me?"

"I know of the ruse you played on me. Lydia overheard you and Jane talking and Jane confessed to it all."

Charlotte collapsed against the back of her chair and closed her eyes with a loud exhalation of breath. "I am sorry, Lizzy. We did not know what else to do. We only hoped to bring about some peace. We had no idea of the two of you falling in love! Are you very upset?"

Elizabeth's eyes closed in resignation. "I do not know! It was a naughty trick, and yet I discovered that there was something truly honourable in the man. I grew to like him a great deal."

"And he likes you!"

She shook her head. "I cannot believe so, Charlotte. He might have fancied a dalliance of sorts, but he was quick enough to leave."

Charlotte sat up straight. "But surely not! Have you not had the news from Meryton?"

"Only what whispers the servants have brought in. Is it true that there was a duel?"

Charlotte, being very much at home at Longbourn, poured more tea for them both. "So we all believe. Nobody witnessed it, save Mr. Hurst, who says nothing, but some secrets will not be kept. It seems Mr. Darcy challenged Mr. Bingley, and quite defeated him."

Elizabeth clenched her jaw. So that rumour was true. "Was Mr. Bingley injured?" A very wicked part of her hoped he had been, but she would have heard of that. Would she not?

"No, he was merely humiliated. Mr. Darcy charged him with visiting each family in the neighbourhood and explaining his own guilt in this whole affair. He has also set down an accounting of his actions and posted them at the assembly rooms, for all who can to read."

Suddenly, the spate of well wishes made a great deal of sense.

"Then we have Mr. Darcy to thank for the grace we have seen from our neighbours. He is the author of our salvation." Elizabeth stared into the distance, far beyond the merry fire and the delicate porcelain statuettes upon the mantel. "When I think about how I taunted him, how I abused him! I called him the vilest of names and was ready to believe horrible things of him, just as Mr. Bingley was ready to believe horrible things of Jane. And how has he responded? By risking his life and safety for us and by forcing a villain to confess his crimes. He is the very best of men, and I never was able to tell him how sorry I was for my abuse of him. And now," her eyes filled with tears, "and now, from all I have heard, he is gone."

"It is true." Charlotte nodded and shifted on the sofa. "He and Colonel Fitzwilliam returned to London that very morning after the duel. I had it from Julia at the inn where they had spent the night. She said they returned from their appointment quite early and covered in mud, took their breakfasts, and called for the carriage to be prepared. They made no arrangements to return, so we must assume their departure is final."

"Then I shall never see him again."

The bottom fell out of Elizabeth's world, and the tears that had misted her eyes now came in great floods. Charlotte came near to hold her friend whilst she sobbed, but all Elizabeth could think of were Mr. Darcy's strong arms around her and how he had been the comfort she had so sorely needed on that horrible night.

Chapter Twenty-One

To one thing constant never

(Balthasar, 2.3)

The following two days passed with increasing ease. Mrs. Bennet began to entertain her closest friends and relations, allowing both her sister Mrs. Phillips and Lady Lucas into her chambers to sit and discuss how terribly Jane had suffered and how remarkable she was to have survived this horrid ordeal with so much of her beauty intact. Mr. Collins announced he must soon be returning to Hunsford, for Lady Catherine could only do without him for so long, but promising to return soon.

Before he departed, he requested to speak alone with Elizabeth. This could mean only one thing, which Elizabeth was not eager to hear, but her mother insisted. It was ten o'clock in the morning; the hired chaise, which was to take him to St. Albans, there to catch the mail back to London, was to come at eleven. She had, therefore, only an hour of his time to abide.

"Cousin Elizabeth," said he the moment the door to the breakfast room closed, "you can have no doubts as to what I wish to say to you. I have searched my heart and consulted the scriptures, and have decided to act according to the dictates of decency and the milk of familial duty, which governs my every deed. I have, as you must surely know, offered my hand and my name to your excellent sister Jane, who was so maligned only last week."

He paused and Elizabeth satisfied his need for a response with a nod. Thus encouraged, he continued, "Cousin Jane has refused my most generous offer, citing the discomfort which my esteemed patroness Lady Catherine de Bourgh would likely feel in considering an accused adulteress as my wife within the parish. I have considered her words and I believe she is correct in her assumption, and I am grateful for her refusal.

"Since it seems most unlikely that your sister should ever marry—for this stain, no matter that it is not of her making, will be ever affixed to her name—I am therefore honouring you, Cousin Elizabeth, with that same offer which was so delicately refused by your sister not long ago. Namely, I will condescend to marry you, so that one day—long may it be—when Longbourn passes on to me, you will remain mistress of your familial home and may offer a home and companionship to that same sister who is too blemished by shame for a family of her own.

"With your permission, madam, I shall now approach your father, and shall return as soon as my patroness permits to conclude the formalities of an engagement."

He stopped to draw breath and stood there, chin held high and shoulders back, as if expecting a torrent of gratitude and agreement.

She must disabuse him of this expectation at once.

"I thank you for your generous offer, sir, but I am afraid I cannot accept."

"What?" His eyes flew wide open and he blinked twice in rapid succession as he gave his head a quick shake. He looked like a surprised owl. "Cannot accept? But surely, with the blemish of this event staining your family's name, this is the best offer that you ever will receive. You cannot turn me down."

"But I must, sir. Your generous heart and gracious offer do you credit, and in turn that does credit to Lady Catherine for her perspicacity in endowing the rectory upon you, but still I assert I cannot accept it. I have..." She took a deep breath and searched for the words she needed. "I have come to the conclusion that I never shall marry. I have met the man who most suits my heart and have lost him through my own foolishness, and no matter how excellent another might be, he cannot meet that place in my heart and soul that only one person can fit. You must forgive me but my refusal is final."

"You speak of Mr. Darcy. Your name has been linked to his in the village."

"Since any connexion between us can never exist, I would prefer not to mention his name."

"He is, you must surely be aware, the nephew of my esteemed patroness."

"So it might be, but you will understand my reticence here."

Mr. Collins paced up and down for a moment. Elizabeth could all but see the thoughts forming and reforming in his head as he tried to complete the picture she had begun to paint.

"Yes, then. Very well." He bowed to her. "I understand. I believe... it is too confabulous to be imagined, that I might be turned down by two sisters within days of each other."

"No more so, sir, than offering for two sisters within that same short time."

He cocked his head and blinked at her. "What? Oh, indeed! Very much so. Very much so. And to offer for a third would be quite outside the bounds of what is expected of a man."

"My sister Kitty?"

"Cousin Catherine is a charming young woman. Perhaps in a year or two, when she is less a child and more fit to step into such a demanding role as a parson's wife, she might consider me."

"That, sir, you must ask Kitty herself. It is not for me to speak for my sister."

He nodded as if a sage thought had made its way into his head. "Not your sister's keeper. Yes, indeed! That is the very thing. You are not your sister's keeper. I shall ponder your words and I might return soon. Not your sister's keeper, indeed. I wish you well, Cousin." And he left the room, leaving Elizabeth feeling relieved at his departure and heartbroken once more over the loss of Mr. Darcy.

To everybody's greatest surprise, there came an unexpected caller on Thursday morning.

"Who is it, Hill?" Mrs. Bennet asked from her armchair in the family's parlour. "If it is Mrs. Phillips, please beg her to enter."

"No, madam. It is not her, nor any lady. Mr. Bingley has come."

This statement was greeted by complete silence.

Mr. Bennet, who was still in his chosen chair by the window, was the first to speak. "Send him away. He has nothing to say that we wish to hear."

"Begging your pardon, sir," the housekeeper replied, "but he quite insists upon being heard. He has stated that he will stand by the door all day and night and as long as need be until you will hear him." She had been housekeeper at Longbourn for long enough that she was all but a member of the family and was known from time to time to talk back to the master.

"Then let him stand there. We are expecting rain, I believe. I hope the man enjoys being wet."

A flurry of objections met this statement, and Mr. Bennet glared at each of his daughters in turn. "The man deserves no better. Very well, Hill. Have him sit on the bench by my study. Remove the cushions first. I shall join him soon enough. More tea, Mrs. Bennet?

Perhaps Cook could send up another cup of coffee. And I should enjoy another of these Chelsea buns that she makes so well."

In due time, Mr. Bennet ambled down the hallway to where Mr. Bingley had become one with the hard wooden bench and reappeared just minutes later. "Jane, dear, would you join us?"

Jane cast a glance at Elizabeth, who shrugged.

"May Lizzy come too?"

Their father nodded. "If she wishes. We could use some sense in these proceedings. Very well, Lizzy. Come along."

Mr. Bingley was standing in her father's study when they arrived. He was shifting his weight from foot to foot, and it was evident that Papa had not invited him to sit, nor had he taken the presumption to do so himself. He went very red as Jane swung herself into the room on her crutches, and then went white as Elizabeth followed her. Jane moved to the armchair by the fire, and Elizabeth took a wooden chair to sit next to her. Mr. Bingley remained standing.

"Miss Bennet, Miss Elizabeth." The young man's voice was little more than a whisper. "I have come to understand the full weight of my error. I was played upon by a scoundrel seeking to cause trouble, but I accept full culpability for my own actions. I cannot expect your forgiveness, but I do hope you will find it within you to offer it, regardless."

Jane said nothing, and Elizabeth reached over to grasp her hand.

Mr. Bingley cleared his throat and kept speaking. "I will never be easy until I find some way to somehow atone for my actions, to make things right, as much as possible. I would like to propose... that is, I would like to propose. Marriage, if Miss Bennet will have me. No, please, listen, and do not answer me now. Think about what I have to say. I know you must be very angry with me, and I would prefer you consider this carefully before replying."

Jane spoke for the first time. "Angry, sir, does not describe the first of it."

Bingley's eyes closed and he fell into himself. "I understand." He took a deep breath before speaking on. "I would be honoured to be your husband, to show the world that I have repudiated those evil thoughts that overtook my mind. That I trust you and believe in you completely. That you are everything good and innocent. I shall not demand anything of you, however. If you wish to live with me as my wife, I shall be delighted; if you wish to set up your own home apart from me, I shall accept that. You will have a secure income to dispose of as you will and I shall arrange a settlement in such a way as to provide it exclusively for your use. I shall retain no control over it whatsoever. If we have children, and if you decide later on to establish your own home, I shall allow you the decision over where they live and where they are educated, and shall establish suitable funds for them as well. I shall have this all written and made legal. If Darcy..." he swallowed, "If Darcy ever deigns to speak to me again, perhaps he can direct me to a lawyer who can make this happen.

"This is what I have to say for now. Think about it and give me your answer whenever you will. I will impose myself upon your presence no longer. Thank you for listening to me, Miss Bennet."

He said his good-byes to Mr. Bennet and to Elizabeth as well, and bowed out of the room.

"Well, Jane? Lizzy? What do you make of that?" Their father took his comfortable chair behind his desk, but sat forward, arms on the deep wooden surface.

Elizabeth blinked. "I hardly know what to think. It seems very pretty, but..." She trailed off and looked at Jane. Jane stared back at her, shaking her head slowly from side to side.

Mr. Bennet sighed, "If you accept, Jane, I shall have your uncle Phillips look very closely at any document he produces. I will not have you tormented by anything from this man again."

"I liked him once; I liked him a great deal. I loved him. Can love die this quickly? Or is it my pain that hides an affection that still lives? I cannot answer him one way or the other."

"Nor do you have to, dearest." Elizabeth squeezed her sister's hand. "Think, and think for as long as you must. Consult your reason and consult your heart. This is no decision to be made in haste. When you are sure of yourself, whatever your answer, that is when you reply."

Jane turned her sad eyes from sister to father and back again. She looked composed and certain, but Elizabeth could see the turmoil that churned just beneath the placid surface. "Yes. I shall do exactly that. I shall wait and I shall think, and if I leave Mr. Bingley waiting for longer than he wishes, so be it."

Chapter Twenty-Two

Suffer love

(Benedick, 5.2)

It had been two weeks. Two entire, long weeks. Two weeks since he had left Bingley in the mud, two weeks since he had returned to London from Hertfordshire. Two weeks since he had seen Elizabeth. Fourteen short days. A blink of time.

Darcy thought he would surely go mad.

He should put the entire sad story behind him. Christmas was coming; he must make plans to return to Pemberley to celebrate the season with his sister. Whether she wanted him there or not. He must search for presents for Georgiana, as well as for her companion Mrs. Annesley, and for his relations. Nothing would satisfy his aunt Catherine other than her new parson's snivelling and pandering, but he had seen a charming music box that the earl and countess would enjoy, and a particularly fine pair of riding gloves for Richard. A shawl for cousin Anne, some sheet music for his cousin Frances, and some painted tin soldiers for her children. And for Elizabeth, that fetching winter bonnet with the green trim...

No! He must not think of Elizabeth. She, too, was from a chapter that had come to a close. They had been enemies, then friends, then... something more. And then she had set him down firmly and accused him of every vice when he found the courage to declare himself to her. Even after that letter, in which he had laid bare the innermost parts of his soul, she had responded not at all. What he had expected from her, he could not say. It had been beyond the bounds of propriety to give her the letter; for her to respond would be more improper still. And yet she was hardly a lady to be shackled by the expectations of society. He thought back to their initial war of words, to all the slurs and insults she had hurled at him, so unladylike and yet—in their way—so alluring. What quickness of mind she had, what spirit and wit! Surely a woman who would insult a foe to his face in the midst of company would find some way to pass encouragement along to a friend.

He had not known what to expect when he returned to Netherfield for the ball. Had he wished to see her, or had he hoped to avoid any conversation? No, he must admit it to himself, he had hoped she would grace him with a look, a smile, something to give him hope. He had even hoped for a dance, although he had hardly confessed as much to himself.

Such was his affection and faith in Elizabeth that when Bingley made his catastrophic announcement and all the world seemed turned against Jane, it did not cross his mind for even a moment that the accusation had any merit to it. Elizabeth was everything good and true; if she believed her sister pure and innocent of these charges, that must be the truth. He had stood by her, and when she allowed him to hold her whilst she let go of those tears that tore his heart, he had thought, for that brief and shining moment, that she had forgiven him. She had clung to him and welcomed his embrace and had gone willingly with him back to Longbourn, bringing him into the bosom of her family at their lowest moment.

And then she had scarcely glanced at him when he took his final leave.

No wonder, after what Lydia had told them. She had never really cared for him, after all. She had been tricked—as had he—to believe him in love with her, and being the kind-hearted lady she was, she decided to respond to love with kindness. Just as he had requited her esteem with friendship. There had never been any genuine affection between them... except that there had been. She might never have loved him, but he had fallen quite irrevocably in love with her. And what of those kisses they had shared? She had not objected to his display. Nay, she had encouraged it! But was that, too, just a kindness she had offered him, a salve to soothe his love-sore heart?

No wonder she had turned down his proposal. Even without the sins she laid at his feet, she had never loved him.

No wonder she had spurned him on that last night after the ball.

It was as clear as anything she could have committed to paper: She had no more use for him.

And right she was. He was known to be Bingley's most intimate friend, the one Bingley had trusted to establish him in his new estate, the one who was known to have guided the man into society and who had put his name and pedigree behind the newcomer and his family. If Bingley had committed so gross a transgression, the weight of it must come down upon Darcy's very shoulders. If his protégé had erred, the sin was the mentor's. He had failed to instil in Bingley those attributes that would forbid a man from treating a woman—anybody—as he had done, and he bore the full blame for Jane's downfall.

No wonder she hated him.

But he loved her and his honour demanded he see full justice done.

And consequently, for two weeks, he had sought to atone for his sins. He could not make right what was wrong. He could not erase Bingley's cruel words or the injury done to sweet Jane Bennet. But he could root out the evil author of this vile plot and bring him to justice, and this is exactly what Darcy had set out to do.

For where else in England could a man hide so completely as in London? Where better could Wickham be but in this teeming city of more than a million souls, whose slums and stews hid more filth than what flowed in the gutters, whose dark and foetid alleyways harboured more rats than the vermin who crept on four feet in the dark?

He would find Wickham in the muck where he belonged, and would bring him to justice, if not for the slander on Jane's name, then for the fortune missing from the militia's treasury. It would suffice for Colonel Forster to exact that justice; but he would then look the miscreant in the eye and let him know his games were finally at an end. For Darcy had a notion of how to find Wickham, and how to bring him to bay. He would roust this rat from his pile of rubbish.

For two weeks, Darcy had skulked about Seven Dials and the 'Mint.' Dressed in threadbare worker's garb with a woollen cap pulled over his hair and his unshaven face covered in dirt, he had moved about unremarked. His height and size lent him some protection; the blade in his pocket lent him more. For two weeks he had plied urchins with small coins in exchange for the information he sought, which he gathered and pored over when he was, at last, safe again in his fine Mayfair house.

And now, at last, he had success. He had begun with Mrs. Younge, that faithless companion who had led his sister Georgiana so far astray last summer. That she had some connexion to Wickham was established; Darcy believed her to be the man's lover, or perhaps some near relation. Regardless, she had supported him in the past, and would likely do so again. If he could find Mrs. Younge, it was a matter of time before that woman led him to Wickham.

She was easy enough to find. He had her former direction from when she was in his employ, and a series of questions over a day or two led him to her present abode. From there, he had her watched. Within days, she met with Wickham to hand him a pouch, presumably filled with coin to pay for his food and his room. Then the watchers Darcy had hired kept their eyes on the man himself, who led them just today to the rooming house in the Devil's Acre, where, like the rat he was, he was holed up.

Darcy had not accosted his prey; he would leave that for the colonel. He had taken note of the location, assured himself that Wickham felt secure and had no plans to leave, and sent a message at once to both Richard in London and Colonel Forster in Hertfordshire. The rat was trapped.

And now, this moral duty discharged, he could sit back in his comfortable study and dwell on his regret and broken heart at leisure.

He took another drink from the half-empty decanter at his side and fell back into his chair, staring blindly at the fire. The flames licked and wove, leaving their ghosts dancing in his eyes. His eyelids, heavy with the brandy that he had been enjoying, dropped lower and lower until he drifted into a fitful doze.

Elizabeth flitted in and out of his scrambled dreams. She smiled at him, taunted him, danced with him, and showered him with invectives. Each of these latter he tried to deflect with his own assault, but with every renewed volley his own defences grew weaker and weaker. She had won. She had conquered him. He lay wounded at her feet and waited only for the final blow to come and end his sorry life.

That blow came with a loud bang.

Startled awake, Darcy all but dropped the brandy-filled goblet he still held in his hand. A drop of the liquid sloshed out and fell upon his hand, and he stared at it whilst his mind struggled to full consciousness.

"Colonel Fitzwilliam," the footman at the door intoned.

Richard sauntered in and stopped a few steps away, hands on hips, lips twisted into a grimace.

"By God, Darcy, you're foxed!"

"You're not my mother, Richard."

"No, but I can chide you nonetheless. I received your message. There are men around the rooming house. Wickham won't be escaping this time. You look dreadful."

Darcy blinked, and Richard swam in and out of focus. "I feel dreadful. Come and sit, and for the love of all that is holy, stop swaying about in that manner. Have a drink. If I am going to feel maudlin, I might as well have some company."

"Miss Elizabeth Bennet?" Richard found another glass and helped himself to some of his cousin's brandy.

Darcy nodded.

"My mother had an interesting visitor this evening. Prepare yourself, for she shall surely come knocking at your door at first light."

"Who? The countess?"

"No, not Mother. Our Aunt. Aunt Catherine."

Darcy fought the urge to swallow the rest of his brandy.

"She appeared at the door, demanded a room for the night, and complained throughout dinner about you 'not knowing your duty.' She would say nothing more." Richard stretched his long legs out before the fire. "What is she about? Do you know?"

Darcy shrugged. The motion made his head hurt. "I cannot account for it. I have done nothing other than sit here and search for Wickham."

"And drink brandy, so it seems. Perhaps she disapproves of you in rough clothing. But come, tell me how you found him, and I shall tell you what we have planned!"

Lady Catherine de Bourgh appeared at Darcy's front door at exactly eleven o'clock the following morning. Darcy watched from the top of the stairs as she paraded inside like an empress into her palace, throwing her hat at the housekeeper and her great fur hand muff at a shocked footman. The staff had been apprised of her expected arrival and led her to the drawing room. Darcy would let her sit there for some minutes before deigning to appear. There was little she could say to him that he wished to hear.

He stepped before the large mirror and took careful stock of his appearance. His eyes—thankfully—were clear and unshadowed from last night's drink. His hair was perfect, his whiskers shaved just so by his careful valet. His garb was everything suitable for morning wear, elegant and relaxed. He was master of his home and owed nothing to unwanted old women who came unannounced and uninvited. With a final tug at his cravat, he descended the stairs and strode into the parlour.

"Fitzwilliam. It is most ungentlemanlike to leave me waiting for so long a time. You owe better duty to me, your mother's sister and your closest relation. I am quite put out."

Darcy cringed at the memory of another lady calling him ungentlemanlike, but he would not let any weakness show.

"Aunt. I had not expected you." That was all he would give her. But civility required he invite her to sit, which he did.

"You cannot fail to understand the reason for my journey here," she began without the first inquiry into his health or that of his sister. "Your conscience must tell you why I have come."

"On the contrary, Madam. I cannot imagine any reason why you would wish to call upon me at my house."

"Fitzwilliam Darcy!" his aunt all but barked at him. "You, of all people, ought to know that I am not to be trifled with. A most alarming report has reached me. It must be a scandalous falsehood, and I demand to know the truth of it."

Darcy felt his jaw clench and with effort brought himself under enough regulation to respond. "I cannot think of what you are speaking, madam. I know of no such reports or rumours of anything which I have done that would so affect you."

"Your name, nephew, has been linked with that of a young woman of most questionable character. I have been told, in great detail—"

"Ah, the egregious Mr. Collins. Indeed, aunt, tell me what he has said, that I may hear it and deny it forthwith. Should it prove to be, indeed, a falsehood."

"Mr. Collins has written to me at length about the unthinkable goings-on in that family of which he must, in due time, become the head. I know all. I know all about the eldest sister and her wanton behaviour; I know all about the youngest, playing the strumpet; and I know all about... one of the others," she waved her hand as if shooing away a fly, "who seeks to ensnare you in the trap of matrimony."

Darcy sat up and blinked. Whatever had Collins written about Elizabeth?

"I fail to understand what you are about, Madam."

"My parson has told me," she spoke slowly as if to a child, "that he offered to save the family by offering marriage to this second daughter, Elizabeth, and that she turned him down."

Darcy let out a breath of relief. Such a disaster had not occurred to him. His aunt continued.

"She let it be known that her affections were already engaged, and when asked to deny the rumours linking her name to yours, she refused to do so. You know your duty, Fitzwilliam Darcy!" Her voice now rose; the servants must surely hear her from the entrance hall where they must surely be waiting. "You are destined to marry your cousin Anne. You must deny these false rumours at once and hasten back to Kent with me to fulfil your familial obligations."

"If the story is false rumour, I wonder that you came so far to tell me about it."

"So far! You know nothing, Darcy! I have just yesterday come from Hertfordshire, where I confronted the lady herself."

"You did what?" Darcy leapt to his feet. "I must command you never to interfere in my affairs."

"This is not the respect due to one of my status. I shall be heard! And that young woman—what there is in her that draws you, I cannot say. She is obstinate, headstrong, rude even! She spoke too liberally by far of her thoughts and quite refused to deny any understanding between you. When I informed her of your engagement to Anne and demanded she give up all thoughts of you, she uttered invectives against me that ought to make her blush for shame, and replied that if you were engaged to Anne, you would never offer for anybody else. Well! The impudence!"

"She insulted you?" A thread of something bright began to work its way up Darcy's spine.

"Quite infamously. She speaks nothing but falsehood and called my expression tart enough to sour grapes."

Darcy felt the urge to laugh. He could not stop the smile that spread across his face.

"How dare you, Darcy! This... this foul-spoken wretch informed me I spoke too much, and too much of nothing! The ignominy of it!"

The laughter bubbled up stronger until it could not be controlled.

"And she refused to give up the acquaintance?"

"Pig-headed, sullen child."

A great beam nearly split his face in two.

"Then, Aunt, I do beg your forgiveness, for I have some most important business to which I must attend at once. Mrs. Pearce will see you out."

He dashed from the room without a bow and shouted for his valet. "Pack a trunk and call for my carriage. We leave for Hertfordshire within the hour!"

Chapter Twenty-Three

None is left to protest

(Beatrice, 4.1)

Two weeks. It had been two weeks since the ball. Two weeks since Mr. Darcy had left, that one final, terrible parting. Two weeks of sleepless nights, two weeks of regret, two weeks of wishing the past could be undone.

And what a strange two weeks it had been at that!

Jane had received three proposals of marriage and Elizabeth one, and then there was Mr. Bingley's most unexpected offer of a lifetime of security for Jane, to which she had not yet responded. But strangest of all was that visit yesterday morning from a lady so pompous and dictatorial she could only have been Mr. Collins' esteemed patroness, Lady Catherine de Bourgh.

Elizabeth had thought, at first, that the grand lady was there to urge her to accept the parson's offer. Then, after Lady Catherine had spoken her opinion of Jane and the family name, Elizabeth had thought she would, instead, forbid such a union. But nothing could have been more of an astonishment to Elizabeth than Lady Catherine's demand that she not marry Mr. Darcy!

Whatever brought that imperious dame to think of this? It was certainly nothing Elizabeth had said, for she had never thought of the woman before in her life, other than as her ridiculous cousin's patron, and had certainly never communicated such a thing to her. Could Mr. Collins himself have let such a notion form in that overly festooned head? Whatever would bring him to make such a suggestion?

Could it possibly be that his own sense of importance was great enough that her rejection of his offer could only be understood if she were somehow attached to a man even Mr. Collins must deem superior? It was quite amazing to think of, but it must be so! And Elizabeth had laughed aloud as Lady Catherine had bullied and blustered her imperatives.

How she had gone on! How she had ranted. Eventually Elizabeth had given up all hope of controlling her sharp tongue and had given the woman the haranguing her actions deserved. That lady's face had gone pale with shock and effrontery; how much more so it would have been had Elizabeth allowed full voice to her thoughts! Vile cream-faced loon! Obsequious toad! Cawing harpy! But what had been said was sufficient, and the lady had uttered in the iciest of tones, "Very well. I shall now know how to act. Depend upon it, I will carry my point," before departing without a further word.

What, exactly, to make of this most unusual visit, Elizabeth knew not. Nor, when she spoke of it to Jane that night, did her sister have any wise words to offer.

"She came all this great distance, from somewhere in Kent, to enjoin you not to marry Mr. Darcy, a man with whom you have but little connexion and no understanding?"

Elizabeth shrugged in confusion. "And a man whom, sadly, I expect never to see again."

"Oh Lizzy." Jane leaned over to wrap an arm around Elizabeth's shoulders. "Are you very angry with us? We only engaged upon the ruse to bring some peace to the house."

Elizabeth's eyes fluttered shut and the air rushed out of her. "I ought to be. It was not very nice. And yet you also taught me something; that when given a chance, kindness brings out the best in people. When I was kind to him, Mr. Darcy in turn became kind, and I saw in him the very best of men."

"He was kind not only to you, but to all of us. How brave he was! He need not have challenged Mr. Bingley and made him confess to the entire neighbourhood of his misdeeds. He might have been gravely hurt! But he acted and by his actions, I am saved. We all are saved. I might have any man I please in Hertfordshire now!" She laughed, but it was hollow.

"I miss him, Jane. I ought to be angry, but all I am is sad, because I grew to... to think very well of him. But it was all a scheme and whilst I thought he liked me as well, I see now that I was mistaken. I think my heart shall never be quite whole again."

"If it is a hole in your heart, Lizzy, that we might hope to fill. But if there is enough of a hole, then only the right person can make it whole."

Elizabeth gave her sister a playful swat on the arm. "You have been reading too much of the Bard and playing with your words like our sisters play with their ribbons. No, there can never be a piece to fill the gap that has been left. He is gone and shall not be back. Lady Catherine even informed me that he was engaged to her daughter Anne, which I had never heard before. But surely, if that were the case, any supposed engagement to me would be out of the question."

"Perhaps," Jane's brow creased in thought, "the lady is disturbed in her mind. Some of the greatest ones are, you know. I believe it rather runs in some families."

This brought about a series of girlish giggles and the conversation moved on to matters much lighter.

Despite the lingering weight of Mr. Darcy's desertion, Elizabeth was pleased. This last week had seen Jane recover much of her accustomed spirits. She was, perhaps, a bit quieter and slower to smile, but the heavy weight of gloom that had hung so oppressively about her slim shoulders had lifted. "I believe," Jane had mused as the sisters sat together drinking chocolate late that evening, "that I am better knowing exactly what Mr. Bingley is. Had he merely departed the neighbourhood without a word, I should be far more low, not knowing whether he cared, or whether he intended to return or not. Now I have a certainty, and this gives me some peace. There is still the pain of his slander, of course, but the burden now is his and not mine. Yes, I have peace."

"And what of his offer?" Elizabeth pulled the shawl about her shoulders and watched as the flickering firelight gilded her sister's delicate beauty in gold.

"I have not decided. No matter how I answer, I will do so with a complete understanding of the man. His offer is tempting, I admit: a lifetime of security and independence, should I wish it, is something to be longed for. Many women would wish for nothing more. Independence, the sort that men enjoy! But can I tie myself to a man I cannot respect? I need not answer now. I can let my heart heal and consider my true feelings. When I come to an answer, I shall know it deep within myself."

Jane's ankle, too, was growing stronger by the day and she was permitted now to put some slight weight upon it with her crutches, if it did not give her discomfort. She moved cautiously about the house and even ventured out onto the terrace on days when the wind did not blow.

Today was such a day. After the strange visit with Lady Catherine yesterday, Elizabeth wished only to be outside, and the bright sunlight, despite November's chill, beckoned her outside of Longbourn's walls. She sat with Jane in the lee of the house for a while, as Mary and Mrs. Knowles, Lydia's new governess, sat with them, talking of literature and pianoforte sonatas and whether muffins were better with currants or without.

"Your fingers are twitching, Lizzy, and you keep staring out over the lawns." Jane flicked a dried leaf in her sister's direction. "You are longing for a walk, but feel you must keep me company here. Go. I shall be perfectly happy with Mary and Mrs. Knowles."

"Yes, I can help Jane," Mary added. "We shall be perfectly happy here."

There was nothing else to do. Elizabeth smiled her thanks and went in search of her warm coat and bonnet.

The day was fine. It was one of those bright autumn days when the sunlight turned the leaf-bare trees into gilded statues, tall and majestic against the clear blue sky. The air was crisp but pleasant and the ground dry enough for a long ramble through the woods and across fields. After two weeks of sitting at home with Jane, Elizabeth let her feet show her the way and she skipped through the countryside, swinging her arms at her side and twirling with the few leaves still dancing on the outer limbs of the tall hornbeams and oaks.

There was the stream that wound its way through the fields, there the bridge, and there the stile over the fence that marked the boundary of Farmer Leeson's lands until it met with the hedgerows. And there, beckoning and not too distant, was Oakham Mount. She climbed over the last stile and picked her way to the path, and soon achieved the top of the hillock that looked out over the vast fields and woods of the area. How fresh the air was up here; how it filled her body with energy and wellbeing. She breathed deeply of it and twirled slowly around, taking in the vista that was spread out before her.

She could see the village of Longbourn, back the way she had come, the small cluster of cottages and the smithy at the edge of the estate's park. There, in that direction, was the patchwork of fields marked out with hedges, some flocks still grazing on the grass that remained on the ground. That way yonder, if she turned her head but a touch, she could see the road leading to Meryton, and just by the bridge, the lane towards Lucas Lodge. There was a cart, a tiny toy to her eyes, moving towards the town, laden high with goods, and there, heading the other direction, her own family's carriage— Mama, driving home from a visit to her sister Mrs. Phillips, perhaps. And there, galloping across the common, a dark horse with a single rider.

She placed her wrap upon the fallen tree that served as a bench and sat herself upon it, then closed her eyes to let the sun bathe her face in its warming rays. There would not be many of these grand days before winter came; she might not come here again until spring.

Gradually she became aware of the thunder of hooves on the hard ground; the horse she had seen was approaching. She opened her eyes and swivelled in the direction of the sound, and watched the rider as he urged his beast up the path leading to the top of the small hill.

"Mr. Darcy!" She scrambled to her feet. Nothing could have surprised her more; indeed, after yesterday's visit by his aunt, he was the very last person in the world she expected to see.

"I have come all this way to find you," he panted as he swung himself off his mount. "I departed London immediately upon hearing of it... I stopped only at the inn to procure a room for the night. I had to see you."

"Me? You had to see me? But wait! What did you hear? For I had a most unusual visit yesterday."

"My aunt?" She nodded, mute with amazement. "So she told me. She came to harangue me only this morning and to warn me off a most 'obstinate and headstrong girl.' I could think of only one person to whom those charming epithets best apply." He stepped towards her and reached out for her hands, which she willingly held out to him.

He was holding her hands. The grasp was gentle, not fierce. He must not, therefore, be too angry with her for her dealings with his aunt.

She blushed at the recollection. "I said a great many things that I ought not to have done. Oh, had she only heard what I did not say to her! Please, offer her my deepest apologies. My sharp tongue does not always recommend me to others." The heat suffusing through her face now had little to do with the warm sun.

The grasp tightened. "Do not say you are sorry! Her account of it, your barbs, are what taught me to hope. Had you no further wish to know me, you would have informed her at once; you are no simpering fool to mince words. Those very darts and thistles that prick and tear, those very same ones that first aroused my disdain, are now what draw me to you. When she told me of it, I knew that I might still find joy in my life! Do tell me, Lizzy, that I might still hope!"

He caught his bottom lip between his teeth, and she stepped closer. Mere inches separated them now, and she raised her hands, still grasped within his, until they were at the level of her heart.

"I believe, Mr. Darcy, that you might still hope." Her eyes met his and she could not pull away.

"Even though you are only tolerable, and I am no gentleman?" His eyes challenged her, and she grinned at him. He had learned to tease her back.

"Those are foul words, sir!"

"But only foul words, and not foul feelings. I am sorely tempted to kiss you!"

She gave a saucy grin. "Foul words are foul breath, and I do not wish to kiss foul breath! And I do say, you smell strongly of horse. But since it is you, and none other, I shall forgive the foul and beast alike. For you, and you alone, I believe I will allow a kiss." She closed the distance and separated her hands from his so she could wrap them around his neck. He pulled her close, and when his lips touched hers, the entire world melted away. Gone were the fields and the roads and the hedgerows. Only he existed, and she, and she lost herself in their reunion.

They stood a long time, thus embraced at the top of Oakham Mount. When, at last, they separated, her hands had worked their way into his hair and his had made their way under her coat. His eyes glowed with an inner light; Elizabeth imagined hers did likewise.

"Then you do like me, Will," she teased, drawing him to her bench on the fallen tree. "It is as they told me."

"Oh, all those things they told you. All the stories they told me! Dash it, Lizzy, when they told me you liked me, that you greatly esteemed me, I thought them mad. But as I endeavoured to be a friend to you, I discovered that my own heart was not untouched."

"And when they made me overhear that you were sick of love for me, I too chose kindness over cruelty, and learned what an excellent heart beats within your breast! We have both been the fool, Will, but how much luckier are we for it?"

He bit his lip again. "Then you love me?"

"Only as much as is reasonable, sir." She could not stop her lips from forming a wide grin.

"Fine. Then I love you only as much as is reasonable as well." His own glorious smile belied the carelessness of his words, and made his handsome face even more appealing, if such was even possible. "But I cannot begin to measure how much love is reasonable for a woman so incomparable as yourself. Therefore, if you will permit me the great liberty, I shall declare myself." He turned towards her and cupped her chin in one large hand. "I do declare that there is no one I can ever love as much as I love you."

"And I," Elizabeth breathed, "can never love any one as much as I love you."

"What are we to do about this?" Darcy leaned towards her.

She looked up at him, her words but a breath. "I can hardly say. Have you any ideas, sir?"

"I suppose," leaning closer still, "I could make some grand speech. I could enumerate my noble qualities and describe what it is about you that I love. I could write poetry about your beautiful eyes and sing songs on your lovely face. Shall I write a speech, Lizzy?"

"I think not, Will. The last speech you made for me was not so enticing."

"I shudder to think of it!"

"And I shudder to think of how I abused you for it. And yet you proved your worth then, and again at Mr. Bingley's ball, and the day afterwards. Perhaps I am the one who should make a speech about how wrong I was."

"Then your opinions have changed?"

"Oh, Will, they could not be more different than they were that night."

"Then you will marry me?"

"Only if you ask me. But could you bear to be married to one as impertinent as I?"

His lips were nearly touching hers, so close was he. "I cannot imagine being married to anybody else. Your wit will bring joy and vibrancy to my staid life; with you, I shall never be bored or complacent."

"Then I shall make a speech accepting your proposal. I shall enumerate your attractions, the warmth of your eyes, the depths of your pockets..."

"Speak no more, wench, else I shall have to stop your mouth with my own."

She leaned forward and kissed him first, rendering his threat moot.

Chapter Twenty-Four

Nothing in the world so well as you

(Benedick, 4.1)

"There you are, Darcy!" Richard was pacing up and down the walk by Longbourn's stables when he and Elizabeth returned to the house much later, Darcy's horse in tow. "I have been up and down every pathway in this county, and have inquired at every drawing room and tavern, and none had seen hide nor hair of you. It was only when I learned that Miss Elizabeth here was also out in the world that I thought to bide my time on this little acre. Madam." He bowed, looking every bit the son of nobility that he was.

Elizabeth dropped a curtsey, and Darcy glanced over to ensure that not too much evidence was left on her pretty face of their amorous encounter on the hillock.

"What are you doing here, Richard?" Darcy dropped Elizabeth's hand that he had been holding, and passed the reins of his horse over to a stable hand, who dashed out to care for the beast.

"As fine a day as it is, I would prefer to tell this tale sitting down, preferably with a cup of something warm before me, if such would be acceptable, Miss Bennet. My tale might be of some interest to your family, hence my impertinent request."

"Of course, Colonel. You are very welcome." She led them into the house and called to her parents whilst Darcy and Richard shrugged off their heavy outer coats. Soon they were all assembled in the family's parlour with the Bennets gathered around, waiting to listen to Richard's tale.

"You will all be pleased to know," he began, "that Mr. Wickham has been discovered and taken into custody in London, and is even now being brought to Colonel Forster's regiment in chains. He is culpable not only of the heinous crime of hatching the plot to destroy Miss Jane Bennet's reputation, but also of the theft of a substantial amount of money from the militia's treasury."

"Bravo, Colonel!" Mr. Bennet exclaimed. "Such news deserves more than a cup of tea. Brandy? Port?"

"I can take no credit for this, sir. I must thank my cousin Darcy for the information that led us to Wickham, for he has been crawling through the darkest alleyways for two weeks in search of the man. Only yesterday he passed along what he had found, and today the miscreant was taken. It is Darcy who deserves that brandy."

"And he may have all the brandy he desires," chimed in Mrs. Bennet.

"Is it certain that he was the thief?" Mary asked. She was perceptive, if quiet, and it was a good question.

"Indeed, it is, Miss Mary. The man's boots match perfectly a print found outside of the treasury on the night the money was taken, and when presented with that fact, Wickham confessed to the whole thing. He had got himself into a great deal of trouble at the gambling tables and felt this theft was his only hope. Now, he considers his only hope is Colonel Forster's mercy, which he may discover is not as generous as he wishes."

"And the plot against Jane? What of that?" Mrs. Bennet sat upright in her armchair, fluttering a white lace handkerchief.

"He has admitted that as well. It was all in the pursuit of revenge, not against Miss Bennet, but against my cousin Darcy." This was met by a flurry of exclamations, and Richard hastened to explain.

"He held a long-standing grudge against my cousin and blamed him for everything that had gone wrong in his life. The theft of the militia's funds was the most recent event, for he asked Darcy to deliver the money he had stolen, and was furious when Darcy refused. When Miss Elizabeth spurned his advances in favour of Darcy's friendship, he expanded the breadth of his grudge to include her. He then hatched this vile plot to destroy everyone and everything they both loved.

"He was successful at first, but his victory was short-lived. For Miss Bennet's name has emerged unsullied, and my cousin and

Miss Elizabeth seem to have established a firm friendship... or is it something more, Cuz?"

Every eye in the room turned to him, and Darcy's face grew warm.

"Er, well, perhaps I ought to have a word with Mr. Bennet. If you please, sir?"

Bennet raised his bushy eyebrows but said not a word as he led Darcy down the hallway to his study.

"Well, lad? Out with it. The others wish to hear it as well, I dare imagine." The older man settled into his comfortable chair by the desk. Darcy, by his own wishes, remained standing.

"You know what I wish to ask you?"

"Of course, but I must hear you say it. Good to see a man squirm."

"Your daughter comes by her temperament honestly, I see."

Bennet threw back his head and laughed. "I ought to have stifled her caustic wit when she was a child, but I saw so much of myself in her, I had not the heart, nor the stomach, to do so. Has she finally met a man who can stomach her bile?"

"I have quite developed a taste for it. It sits easily upon me now."

"It did not always, I gather."

"No," Darcy shook his head, "but the most complex flavours, those that offer the greatest reward, are not always the ones most readily appreciated. Think of that fine whisky you have." He gestured to a bottle on the chest by one of the bookcases. "When first you tasted it, I imagine it tasted quite foul."

"Unpalatable," Bennet returned.

"But with exposure, you learned to pick out different essences within it. Toffee, perhaps, or pepper, or fresh herbs." Bennet nodded, so Darcy went on. "And in time, what was unpalatable became acceptable, then pleasant, then anticipated and longed-for. So it is with Elizabeth. What turned me against her at first now draws me to her. She has agreed to be my wife; we request only your permission."

Bennet twisted his lips into a half a grimace. "And if I agree, I must demand one promise from you."

"Very well. What is it?"

"If you find you can no longer abide her, that you will not bring her back."

Now it was Darcy's turn to laugh. "I cannot imagine the day when I will no longer be able to abide her. She grows more charming every time I see her. Her allure is stronger, her wit more acute. I can promise to keep her for as long as she will have me."

Bennet rose and walked towards the bottle of whisky that had just now been the subject of their discussion. He poured two glasses and handed one to Darcy. "Then, sir, I believe we are in agreement. Here is to a fine whisky..."

"And a fine woman!"

The family were all delighted to hear the news. Even Lydia was permitted to come downstairs to join in the celebration. Darcy and Richard stayed for dinner and well into the evening before returning to the inn quite late that night.

"Will Darcy, the married man," his cousin jested. "Whoever would have believed that? I have so many memories of you swearing up and down that no woman could tempt you."

"I had, at that time, no notion that one as remarkable as Elizabeth existed. And yet, by your own trickery, you all but ended this amour before it truly began."

"You were never meant to learn of it. All we wished for was an end to the bickering that over-salted every meal. But none of this. I am heartily overjoyed for you. Mother will love her, and Georgiana will delight in such a sister."

"I must only beseech her to hold the worst of her words in Georgie's presence, else I shall have two such harpies in my life. I am not certain Derbyshire is quite ready for such a presence!"

Over the next week, Darcy was a frequent guest at Longbourn. He spent two days in London, conferring with his solicitor to draw up a marriage settlement, and then returned to Hertfordshire. Richard accompanied him, to the pleasure of every mother of a certain class who hoped to procure an earl's son for any unmarried daughters.

Mr. Wickham was dragged through the streets of Meryton in shame. Colonel Forster had been more than pleased to finally have his hands on the thief who had laid his coffers bare, and was convening a court martial to try the man. Rumour swirled over what punishments might be in store for the lieutenant. Would he be stripped of his rank? Would he be flogged? Was such a torture not too savage for civilised Englishmen, or was it a punishment that fit the crime? Mr. Phillips, the town's lawyer and Mrs. Bennet's brother-in-law, opined that since the crime was grand larceny, the five hundred pounds definitely being greater than the twelve pence the law described, Wickham might be hanged for his troubles, or face a firing squad.

No matter, now that he was in chains, every merchant in Meryton and some beyond came forward with claims against him, telling of how he had left a trail of debts in his wake, and more than one daughter seduced. Even should he avoid the gallows, there would be no happy ending for George Wickham.

Only Jane and Bingley's fate remained unclear.

Bingley had, to the best of Darcy's knowledge, remained at Netherfield. He did not venture into the town, nor did he accept social invitations—if, indeed, he received any. He was said to be hunting and riding, but remained within the bounds of his property. He had not sent any message to Darcy at the inn, nor had Darcy visited Bingley. The friendship, to all intents and purposes, was over.

But neither had Bingley returned to London. This was a matter of some interest. There was, perhaps, little enough there for him. It had somehow become known, in a matter of days, that he had falsely accused an unnamed lady of terrible things, and Darcy's break with the man had likewise been told in every drawing room in Town. There would be no invitations for the Bingleys: no balls, no dinners, and no welcome at the clubs. The Hursts might repair to their estate in the country, impoverished as it was. But Miss Bingley must now forever give up hope of establishing herself in society or marrying well.

What did seem clear was that Bingley had been sincere in his proposal to Jane. Elizabeth and Jane together had told him of the unusual offer, and Bennet had shown him some preliminary paperwork that Bingley had sent over for his consideration. Everything looked in order, and the young man seemed to be genuine in his attempts to atone for his grievous error. If Jane accepted, she would be secure for all her days.

But Jane had given no answer. Nor had she told Elizabeth—as far as Darcy knew—what her thoughts might be. Every day Bingley sent some token over to Longbourn, be it some flowers from the greenhouse or some fresh-baked pies, with no request for any response. And each day, Jane looked upon his offering and smiled blandly and said nothing.

It was now a week after their engagement had been announced, and Darcy was more in love than ever with Elizabeth. Jane, too, was much improved. She saw Mr. Jones once more about her ankle and was given permission to put full weight upon it, using her crutches only as needed. Her first attempts were short and marked with little gasps of pain, but soon she could manage to cross the parlour, then the hallways, and then the short expanse on the terrace outside. Since the day was cool and the exertion more than Jane's delicate constitution was accustomed to, she, Elizabeth, Richard, and Darcy took themselves to sit in the little-used drawing room where Mrs. Bennet and the younger sisters seldom visited. A tray with some hot elder wine stood on the table between them, a glass of the same in each person's hand.

"I have decided," Jane said when the conversation came to a natural pause.

"About Mr. Bingley?" Elizabeth moved closer to her sister. Darcy was, as ever, intrigued by the closeness between the two. Jane nodded.

"I have been giving his generous offer a great deal of thought, and I am still not certain I have the very best answer to it. But it is the answer he shall have, and then everything will be concluded. It is, I believe, the response that will set me up in the best way for my future happiness."

"Am I to believe you will accept him?" Richard asked. He leaned back in his chair and stretched out his legs before him.

Jane frowned. "It was not an offer to discard lightly. It would give me everything I need. But not everything I want. No. I have decided to turn him down." Elizabeth gasped and put an arm around Jane's shoulders.

"I need not explain myself," Jane continued, "and yet I feel I need to say these words. Mr. Bingley has offered me security and independence, but he has not offered me the one thing he stole from me when he spoke so rashly at the ball. He has taken away my happiness, and he cannot replace it. Not he. I cannot live my life with a man who would destroy something he claimed to love, who would think so little of another that he could inflict such damage without pause.

"No, he cannot restore my happiness, but perhaps some other person can. And whilst I might never meet that person, if I do, I wish to be able to pursue that happiness and—if I am lucky—attain it. I have seen you, dear Lizzy and Mr. Darcy, and I wish to find such satisfaction for myself. I am resolved to act in that manner which will constitute my happiness and not console another's guilty conscience. And this is why I shall tell him no."

There was silence in the room. Each of the four seemed lost in his or her own thoughts. Then Richard spoke up in jest. "You could always marry me, Madam."

Jane laughed. "No, indeed, for you are too expensive for me, Colonel. I am not made for your sort of society. Even as a second son, you live amongst earls and barons. I am a country girl, happier in a barn or a stillroom than in a grand salon. I should want a husband for every day and not only those occasions when I must impress the neighbours. You will find a lady with a purse to meet your needs, and I shall find a husband with a character to meet mine."

"Well said, Miss Bennet." Richard raised his glass and drank to her. "And I wish you every success."

"How will it be if Mr. Bingley remains in the neighbourhood?" Elizabeth asked. "Will you not feel uncomfortable?"

Jane took up her glass of hot wine. "It is not for me to be uncomfortable, Lizzy, but for him. This is my home and always has been. He is the newcomer who has not endeared himself to our society. I shall go about my way as I have always done."

"And when you meet him again, for you know you must at some point, even if only passing in the streets?"

"Then we shall meet as common acquaintances. The first time will be difficult, I admit. Once that is done, it will be easy."

Darcy glanced over at Elizabeth, who met his eyes and understood the question he asked with them. Was this love, to be able to understand each other without a word? It was a little frightening, and quite wonderful.

She blinked her own fine eyes and gave a small nod, almost imperceptible to one who was not looking. He understood her as perfectly as she understood him. He grinned with a deep satisfaction.

"We have a proposal of our own, then, Miss Bennet. Once we are married, come to Pemberley and live with us there. My sister Georgiana would greatly benefit from not one, but two charming sisters, and there you may meet an entirely new society. No matter that you are loved and believed here, there is a shadow over you. In Derbyshire you will be new and interesting and entirely unsullied."

"And as Darcy's sister and my new cousin, you are certain to be welcomed most warmly," Richard added. "Indeed, I can think of a good dozen or so men of suitable age and station to introduce to you, and many fine young women as well to include in your circles."

"And I shall be completely and incandescently happy," Elizabeth added, "having everything my heart desires: the one man most perfectly suited to me, whom I love with my entire being, and my dearest sister, without whose company my joy would be incomplete."

Jane smiled. It was an easy smile that shone from her eyes, and the first such one that Darcy had seen.

"I shall be happy to accept!" She leaned over to hug her sister, and was soon caught up in brotherly embraces by both Richard and Darcy.

"How a few weeks have changed everything." Elizabeth tucked her hand under Darcy's arm as they walked along Longbourn's bare paths the next afternoon. "Only last September I should never have imagined what great things were on their way. And then I met a rude man—"

"And I met an equally rude woman." He beamed at her.

"—and nothing was ever the same." She glanced about and, when satisfied that they were not observed, pulled him closer to press a kiss against his welcoming lips. "Do you wish I were less of a harridan, Will?"

"Not at all! I wish nothing of the sort. I had met so many beautiful, charming, and quite insipid ladies in London that I swore I would never marry. I required something else, an accomplishment of wit that I saw nowhere else but in you. Never stop teasing me, although I might beg you to be kind!" He kissed her nose, her cheeks, and then turned his attention to her mouth. After a time he asked, "Do you wish I were less hot-headed?"

"And be another Mr. Bingley, happy to hear whatever anyone tells him, or another Mr. Collins? No, indeed! We shall quarrel and spar, and be absolutely delighted with each other as we do so."

He pulled her behind the folly where Lydia and Wickham had so deceived Bingley, and enfolded her in his arms. "We are too wise to woo peaceably, you and I. But despite all this ado about nothing, I believe we shall be as happy as ever two people were on earth."

And he kissed her again.

The End

⊘otes

⊘uch ⊘do ⊘bout ⊘usten

William Shakespeare's *Much Ado About Nothing* was probably written in late 1598. The play involves the entanglements of two couples—Beatrice and Benedick, and Hero and Claudio—whose journeys are very different. Beatrice and Benedick have a bitter past and their constant bickering provides much of the play's wit. In a trick by their friends, each is duped into thinking the other is secretly in love with them, with predictable results. Hero and Claudio, however, are a case of love at first sight and their wooing is quick and seemingly smooth. But Claudio himself is tricked into thinking Hero unfaithful, with almost tragic consequences.

Much Ado About Nothing is classed with Shakespeare's comedies, but it is not the light-hearted offering of Twelfth Night or *A Midsummer Night's Dream*. Yes, it fits with the comedies in that there are plenty of moments of mirth and outright humour, and everybody gets married at the end – just like a Jane Austen novel!

But there is a darker side to the play as well. Don John is about as unrepentant a villain as Shakespeare wrote, almost on a par with Iago, willing to destroy innocent people for his pleasure. And while the love story between Beatrice and Benedick is a delightful romp, that between Hero and Claudio is far less smooth, and ultimately, for the modern reader at least, far less satisfying. This latter story is almost more suited to his tragedies than his comedies, if not for the supposedly happy ending.

Much Ado is not the only time Shakespeare crossed genre lines in his magnificent plays. *Romeo and Juliet* is cast as a tragedy because (spoiler alert) they die. But on first reading, it is a very funny play almost until the end. Likewise in *Hamlet*, arguably Shakespeare's greatest tragedy, the laughs come fast and often.

There are clear parallels with Austen's Pride and Prejudice. I am certainly not the first person to see echoes of Beatrice and Benedick in the initial antagonism between Elizabeth and Mr. Darcy. Their path to a happy ending is different to that of Shakespeare's couple, but in broad strokes, they learn to see the good in each other and move from disdain to affection.

Echoes of Hero and Claudio can also be seen in Jane and Mr. Bingley. Like the two lovers from the play, Austen's characters fall in love almost at first sight and seem to be heading towards an early happy conclusion when a word in Bingley's ear (like Don John's word in Claudio's ear) sets things very wrong.

It was, therefore, a joy to take these two classics with their common threads and different slants and combine them. I do hope you have enjoyed the result.

About the Author

Riana Everly was born in South Africa but has called Canada home since she was eight years old. She has a Master's degree in Medieval Studies and is trained as a classical musician, specialising in Baroque and early Classical music. She first encountered Jane Austen when her father handed her a copy of *Emma* at age 11, and has never looked back.

Riana now lives in Toronto with her family. When she is not writing, she can often be found playing string quartets with friends, biking around the beautiful province of Ontario with her husband, trying to improve her photography, thinking about what to make for dinner, and, of course, reading!

If you enjoyed this novel, please consider posting a review at your favourite bookseller's website.

Riana Everly loves connecting with readers on Facebook at facebook.com/RianaEverly/.

Also, be sure to check out her website at rianaeverly.com for sneak peeks at coming works and links to works in progress.

Also, be sure to check out her website at rianaeverly.com for sneak peeks at coming works and links to works in progress!

More from Riana Everly

From: The Bennet Affair: A Pride and Prejudice Variation

A tale of secrets, sweethearts, and spies!

Elizabeth Bennet's bedroom in the ancient tower of Longbourn has always been her private haven. So what are those footsteps and shuffling noises she's now hearing from the room above her head? Drawn from her bed one dark summer night, her clandestine investigations land her in the middle of what looks like a gang of French spies!

William Darcy's summer has been awful so far, especially after barely rescuing his sister from a most injudicious elopement. Then he is attacked and almost killed nearly at his own front door in one of the best parts of London. Luckily his saviour and new friend, Lord Stanton, has a grand suggestion—recuperate in the countryside and help uncover the workings of a ring of French spies, rumoured to be led by none other than country squire Thomas Bennet!

Drawn together as they work to uncover the truth about the Frenchmen hiding in their midst, Elizabeth and Darcy must use all their intellect as they are confronted with an ingenious code machine, a variety of clockwork devices, ancient secrets and very modern traitors to the Crown. And somewhere along the line, they just might lose their hearts and discover true love—assuming they survive what they learn in the Bennet affair.

$\mathcal{P}$rologue

E lizabeth Bennet's eyes flew open. The previous moment she had been in a peaceful sleep, and now, an instant later, she was wide awake. Something must have happened to so disturb her slumber. Had it been the storm outside? Even through the heavy draperies that fell from ceiling to floor at her windows, she could hear crashes of thunder punctuating the soliloquy of rain that pelted the window, and the accompanying shards of lightning lit up her room through the chinks between the folds of fabric. The rains must be heavy indeed to create such a noise; only a very desperate man would be out on a night like this one. She folded herself further into her blankets, relieved to be warm and dry and safe.

A hint of another noise tickled her ears from the other side of the window. Perhaps a horse had been spooked by the noise of the storm and had whinnied its alarm, or one of the dogs had barked his disapproval. Such was the crash of rain and thunder that she could not discern any more than that the courtyard was not quite devoid of life. Now she thought she heard something in the house. Had a cat yowled? Or had one of her sisters cried out in alarm at the storm? Her own chamber was separated from those of her family by some distance, but sounds did carry through the building. At times, when she sat at the top of the stairs, she could hear conversations from the kitchens as clearly as if she were in that very room! But it mattered not whence the sounds came, for now she was awake, and quite completely so. She closed her eyes, but sleep eluded her, and after a while, she gave up her attempts. Resigning herself to a long few hours until the sun crept fitfully over the horizon to cast its weary rays upon what remained of the storm, she threw her head back upon the pillows, and then she heard another noise.

This time the sound came from directly above her: a tentative footstep, and then another, and the noise of something sliding across the floor. This was most strange, for that room ought, by all rights, to be quite empty, and especially so at this darkest of hours. What hour could it be? It was impossible to tell from the darkness of the night and the intensity of the storm. Out of instinct, her eyes sought the small clock that sat upon the mantelpiece in her bedchamber, but it was too dark to see the hands. Two quick steps took her from her bed to the fireplace, and then it was little trouble to light the lamp. Three o'clock.

As she contemplated returning to bed, another sound came from above. Had somebody dropped something? Whoever could be up there? This would not do! She found her slippers and robe and then pulled a warm wrap about her shoulders to ward off the chill. Kneeling on the floor by the fireplace, her lamp at her side, she pressed a small knob in the carvings where the stone hearth met the panelled wall. With scarcely a sound, the panel slid forward, and she swung it open just far enough to allow herself to slip through. Turning the flame on her lamp as low as it might burn without guttering, she took a resolute breath and disappeared into the chilly space beyond.

This wing of Longbourn was the oldest part of the manor house by centuries. Family legend said that it dated back to the thirteenth century, to the days of Henry III, and if this story were incorrect, the ancient and weathered stones were silent on the truth. Only this one tower remained of the original structure, and it was now incorporated into the newer house, itself two hundred years old, but updated with all the modern conveniences. Elizabeth's mother had been aghast when her second daughter had moved out of the nursery and begged to move to the room in the ancient tower.

"It is draughty and cold!" Mrs. Bennet had countered. "You will catch your death of a chill, and then you will be sorry!"

But Elizabeth, in the wonders of early adolescence, spoke eloquently of the appeal of the rounded room, of the sturdiness of the thick walls, of the new windows and panels that would surely keep the draughts at bay. With her father's tacit approval, the argument was won. What had really appealed to her, though, was the secret doorway, which she had discovered upon a search for her embroidery, which the maids had last seen in the cat's mouth. Her search took her up to the old tower, and then into every corner, where the knob had almost presented itself to her hungry eyes.

No stranger to the wonders of Mrs. Radcliffe and her horrid novels of spectres and secret passages and the like, Elizabeth could not resist this hidden door. The knob that released the latch was a beacon in the darkness to a lass intent on finding adventure, and she was amazed to discover that, following carefully worded questions, her father seemed not to know of it at all. Perhaps he had not read Mrs. Radcliffe when he was young! She had passed through it many times, sometimes in a game she played with herself, sometimes merely to find a place of solitude away from her mother's plaints and her sisters' shouts.

The door led to a narrow staircase that lay between the inner and outer walls of the tower, leading down to a similar panel in the little-used parlour that lay below, and up to an unused room above. Or—rather—to a room that was supposed to be unused! Perhaps the stairs had once been a servants' stairwell, or a means of escape during times of strife, be it war or persecution. It was not the only entrance to that upstairs room, for that was a large and heavy door that led off the hallway that spanned the length of the house on that storey.

Just as her room in this ancient part of the house was at the far end of the building from the rooms of her parents and sisters, so was the upstairs space distant from the servants' rooms. It ought, by all rights, to be completely abandoned, but for a few crates that no one thought worthy of exploring. Who, then, was creeping across that cold floor? Curiosity warred with trepidation, and Elizabeth felt her palms grow damp. Nonsense, she told herself. It must just be some servants at work! But not at three o'clock in the morning, surely! Pulling her shawl snug across her shoulders, she began to climb the stairs, one silent step after another.

At the top, the narrow stairwell flattened to a small landing, which led to a secret panel similar to that in her own chamber. This one, however, was older and had not been repaired when the lower storeys had been improved some fifty or sixty years past, and the wood was cracked and shrunken. Pressing her face against the panel, she could see into the room through a chink where the panel met the wall. Her view was not complete, but it showed her much of the centre of the chamber. Covering her lamp so the light would not be seen, she put her eye to the crack and peered through.

She should have seen nothing. The room should have been in complete darkness. How strange, then, and yet how expected it was, that the space was filled with light. This was not the sudden and fitful burst of lightning upon an empty space, but the steady and warm glow of a lamp, shedding its golden light throughout the cavernous space. The draperies were drawn and the sound of the storm scarcely permeated into her concealed closet, but the room was not silent. Men were talking, barely whispering, and moving objects from place to place. This must have caused the noise that had awakened her. A large table was already set up in the centre of the space, and she could see the end of a cot at the edge of her field of vision. And there, by the window, was the side of the heavy desk that had lain dusty for too many years. She tried to shift to see further to the side of her narrow tunnel, but her robe caught on a nail and she nearly made a noise as she heard the fabric tear. She held her breath, but the whispering men seemed not to notice anything amiss.

Now she could hear distinct voices. There were two men—or two who were speaking, at any rate. To her alarm, the language was French.

"Comment puis-je vous remercier?" the first voice whispered. *How can I ever thank you?* Elizabeth had studied French, as was expected of young ladies despite the hostilities with France, and the man spoke clearly and precisely. She had little trouble understanding the conversation.

"You understand that you risk your own life by aiding me thus," he continued. "You need not attach your cause to mine. I shall not fault you should you decide to change your mind."

"*Cela ne sera pas nécessaire*," came the whispered reply. The speaker was English, his French excellent but not unaccented. The voice... surely it could not be! But no, that was impossible. She listened more keenly as the man spoke on. "I know who I am, what we are. Your aims are mine. We are brothers in this endeavour. *Fraternité*." He laughed once, a short and bitter sound that echoed in the large space. "You may remain here until your men return, and I shall come with food and books as often as possible. But I hope it will not be more than a week, for the longer you remain, the more likely you are to be discovered. Nevertheless, I shall undertake the task you asked of me, no matter what."

"If you are caught..." the first man began, but the second cut him short.

"If I am caught, I understand the consequences. I am prepared to take that risk. The benefits should I succeed make the danger worthwhile."

"Merci, mon cousin Thomas Benoit."

"Call me Bennet here, Etienne. Even in private."

Now Elizabeth clapped a hand across her mouth to stifle a cry. Her father—her beloved English father—was harbouring and abetting a Frenchman. The enemy!

The Bennet Affair: A Pride and Prejudice Variation is available in print or as an eBook at your favourite online bookseller. https://books2read.com/thebennetaffair

Other books by Riana Everly:

Teaching Eliza: Pride and Prejudice meets Pygmalion

A tale of love, manners, and the quest for perfect vowels.

Professor Fitzwilliam Darcy, expert in phonetics and linguistics, wishes for nothing more than to spend some time in peace at his friend's country estate, far from the parade of young ladies wishing for his hand, and further still from his aunt's schemes to have him marry his cousin. How annoying it is when a young lady from the neighbourhood, with her atrocious Hertfordshire accent and country manners, comes seeking his help to learn how to behave and speak as do the finest ladies of high society.

Elizabeth Bennet has disliked the professor since overhearing his flippant comments about her provincial accent, but recognizes in him her one opportunity to survive a prospective season in London. Despite her ill feelings for the man, she asks him to take her on as a student, but is unprepared for the price he demands in exchange.

"With her clever mash-up of two classics, Riana Everly has fashioned a fresh, creative storyline with an inventive take on our favorite characters, delightful dialogue and laugh out loud humor. Teaching Eliza is certain to become a reader favorite. It's a must read!" – Sophia Meredith (author of the acclaimed *On Oakham Mount* and *Miss Darcy's Companion*)

https://books2read.com/teachingeliza

The Assistant: Before Pride and Prejudice

A tale of love, secrets, and adventure across the ocean

When textile merchant Edward Gardiner rescues an injured youth, he has no notion that this simple act of kindness will change his life. The boy is bright and has a gift for numbers that soon makes him a valued assistant and part of the Gardiners' business, but he also has secrets and a set of unusual acquaintances. When he introduces Edward to his sparkling and unconventional friend, Miss Grant, Edward finds himself falling in love.

But who is this enigmatic woman who so quickly finds her way to Edward's heart? Do the deep secrets she refuses to reveal have anything to do with the appearance of a sinister stranger, or with the rumours of a missing heir to a northern estate? As danger mounts, Edward must find the answers in order to save the woman who has bewitched him ... but the answers themselves may destroy all his hopes.

Set against the background of Jane Austen's London, this Pride and Prejudice prequel casts us into the world of Elizabeth Bennet's beloved Aunt and Uncle Gardiner. Their unlikely tale takes the reader from the woods of Derbyshire, to the ballrooms of London, to the shores of Nova Scotia. With so much at stake, can they find their Happily Ever After?

https://books2read.com/theassistant

Through a Different Lens: A Pride and Prejudice Variation

A tale of second glances and second chances

Elizabeth Bennet has disliked the aloof and arrogant Mr. Darcy since he insulted her at a village dance several months before. But an unexpected conversation and a startling turn of phrase suddenly causes her to reassess everything she thought she knew about the infuriating and humourless gentleman.

Elizabeth knows something of people who think differently. Her young cousin in London has always been different from his siblings and peers, and Lizzy sees something of this boy's unusual traits in the stern gentleman from Derbyshire whose presence has plagued her for so long. She approaches him in friendship and the two begin a tentative association. But is Lizzy's new understanding of Mr. Darcy accurate? Or was she right the first time? And will the unwelcome appearance of a nemesis from the past destroy any hopes they might have of happiness?

Warning: This variation of Jane Austen's classic Pride and Prejudice depicts our hero as having a neurological difference. If you need your hero to be perfect, this might not be the book for you. But if you like adorable children, annoying birds, and wonderful dogs, and are open to a character who struggles to make his way in a world he does not quite comprehend, with a heroine who can see the man behind his challenges, and who celebrates his strengths while supporting his weaknesses, then read on! You, too, can learn what wonders can be found when we see the familiar through a different lens.

https://books2read.com/throughadifferentlens/

Love mysteries? Don't miss the *Miss Mary Investigates* series, starring Mary Bennet and her friend, investigator Alexander Lyons.

Miss Mary Investigates

Death of a Clergyman: A Pride and Prejudice Mystery

Death in Highbury: An Emma Mystery

Death of a Dandy: A Mansfield Park Mystery (coming soon)